Four Graves West

*Other Five Star Titles
by Steve Frazee:*

Hidden Gold
Ghost Mine
Voices in the Hill
Nights of Terror
Tower of Rocks

Four Graves West

A Western Duo

Steve Frazee

Five Star • Waterville, Maine

First Edition
First Printing: July 2005

Published in 2005 in conjunction
Golden West Literary Agency.

Set in 11 pt. Plantin by Elena Picard.

Printed in the United States on permanent paper.

Library of Congress Cataloging-in-Publication Data

Frazee, Steve, 1909–
    Four graves west : a western duo / by Steve Frazee.
      p. cm.
    ISBN 1-59414-126-6 (hc : alk. paper)
    1. Western stories. I. Frazee, Steve, 1909– Mormon
forge. II. Title.
PS3556.R358F68 2005
  813′.54—dc22   2005005613

Four Graves West

Table of Contents

Mormon Forge

I

His name was Patrick Stong. He was, in this year of 1881, sheriff of Antelope County, an ugly, shambling man who rode well enough but without any gracefulness. Through a night that was building rain he pushed his red roan gelding, Owlhorns, as fast as he dared up the long green country that sloped behind him to the lonesome lights of Mormon Forge. He skirted stands of aspens that whispered that the rain was coming soon. He kept peering at the dark. Somewhere ahead of him lay a long string of rocks like the shattered tail of a prehistoric monster. When he came against the rocks, he would know how close he was to the prospector's cabin on Shavano Creek.

He thought: *She was a reckless fool, Tucky McCady.* Her steeldust mare was in Youngblood's livery stable in Mormon Forge with a bullet rip across its rump and another wound where lead had splashed bone from its nose. By now the McCadys would be riding, their Scottish tempers black across their faces, their rifles bobbing in the scabbards, for Stong had sent a man pounding to the M Ranch after he had picked up the mare. The McCadys would think the same as Stong—that Kentucky McCady had not come home because of a Sartrain bullet.

Stong was afraid of that and he carried another personal fear, that he was not man enough to be sheriff of all Ante-

11

lope County, which in the old days had been so large that five counties had to be carved from it when the name Colorado emerged from the vague expanse of Kansas Territory. Antelope County had been for five years now part of the state of Colorado, but legalities 200 miles away, across three mountain ranges, cast only light shadows here in Baca Valley and the surrounding range. Pat Stong was the third sheriff. No one before him had tried to keep law beyond the confines of Mormon Forge, and some not even there. By tradition he was no more than marshal of the town. No one but Stong knew that he was not content with tradition.

Solid on the deep sod ran the hoof beats of the gelding as he probed in to find the guiding line of rocks. In him lay the troubling knowledge that keeping reasonable order among drifters, gamblers, and the fancy women of the town was vastly different from enforcing law on the great range of the county. Lightning smoldered south of him on the wedges of Las Platas Mountains. Thunder sent a shudder across the land, and then a wave of cold rolled from the high slopes. The rain had skipped the valley this afternoon but it would not miss tonight. Stong cursed the prospect in the same breath with Tucky McCady.

The vanguard of the icy sheet driven from the mountains struck him while he was swinging around an aspen thicket where bedded cattle were getting to their feet. A flash of lightning showed white faces staring at him from the edge of the trees. Sartrain cattle, chunky, straight-backed brutes that old Bedford Sartrain had switched to three years ago. They stared at the lone rider on a steaming horse, and then they crashed away. Stong pulled his hat low. He turned up the collar of his jumper. He cursed Tucky McCady.

Another flash limned the first great rocks below the cliffs. Stong veered west then; he was about two miles from the cabin. When he got there, what could he do? He could not track until morning and by then there probably would not be any tracks to follow. He doubted that Tucky would be there now. When the rain was gone, he could take a pine knot torch and try, at least, to establish the direction of her going. In the meantime, the McCadys would be riding.

The rain made a seething sound in the long grass. In fifteen minutes it would be gone. The land would be soaked, the stars would be out again, and Stong would still be blundering about on business that no sheriff before him had ever attempted. He rode hunched in the saddle, his drenched clothes flat against him. The night asked him gloomy questions he could not answer. If he went to Cross Ranch, the Sartrain stronghold, they would tell him nothing except that he was far afield from where he belonged, and then the McCadys would say that he had gone to warn the Sartrains. The determination to be sheriff of all Antelope County was an honest thought and a heavy burden.

The rifle shot somewhere behind him caught him loose and unprepared. Owlhorns lunged ahead and tried to run. Stong took the gelding in a tight circle, listening, peering into the night where the line of cliffs behind the rocks lay in utter darkness. A crackling slash of lightning showed the cliffs. Water was streaming from them. They looked like tremendous bales of moldy cotton stacked high at the base of black timber. The light was on them for one weird moment, running into the edges of the dripping trees, catching the beat of the rain against mottled rock, and then everything was gone. But Stong's vision of what he had seen held on like an afterglow. There was a figure up there, a shape crouched with a rifle on one of the highest ledges.

From that spot the rifle sliced flame a second time. The man was shooting downward, toward the talus slope. Stong heard a woman's cry, not of pain or fear or defiance, but a mixture of all three qualities, an eerie, spine-tingling sound that came thinly through the slanting rain. Thunder burst over Las Platas and rocked across the valley. Stong trotted Owlhorns along the rocks, and then swung down beside a huge boulder where water was bouncing. He wiped his sleeve across his face. Except for the rain the night was silent now.

"Stop that shooting!" His voice was loud where he stood, but he knew that it had run almost to nothing, out through the rain, to the cliffs. He identified himself and shouted the order again. When the sky flashed, the cliffs were bare.

"Kentucky!"

He heard her answer from somewhere near the base of the cliffs where the sheer walls were broken by a blowout of white quartz.

"Kentucky!"

"Limba?" She had come closer to him.

"Pat Stong."

"Oh, hell!"

"I feel the same!" Stong was savage. "Who's up there on the cliff?"

"Kinkaid Sartrain!" Tucky replied.

"Kinkaid!" Stong yelled. "Come down from there! Kinkaid, do you hear me?"

His only answer was the pitting of the rain against his clothes. Thunder split the night, and then lightning bristled with a snapping sound and revealed nothing on the ledges. Stong's next angry shout was lost in the crash of thunder. He had seen Kentucky, staggering down the talus slope. He heard stones sliding and then he heard her fall and curse like a true McCady.

He went up through the rocks. When the next streak of fire forked in the sky, he got a fair look at her. Her red hair was stringing around her face. Her eyes were wide. One sleeve of her blouse was torn away, showing the white of her shoulder above a clumsy wrapping on her upper arm. The high push of her breasts was strong against her muddy blouse.

"Why don't you go after him, Stong?" Her voice was an insult.

An instant later Stong heard her fall. She gave a small cry of pain and was silent. Stong's boots sank deeply into the soft talus underneath the spill of rocks as he stumbled toward her. He called. She did not answer. He found her at last, and picked her up. For several moments he was aware of the softness of her body as she clung to him.

Loose stones shot his feet in front of him. He came down hard, and stayed there with Tucky still in his arms. He listened to the night behind him and the night out there on the grass. The whole McCady tribe might now be close enough to have heard the shots. They would come in, wild-eyed, with their hair on end, and Sheriff Stong, who believed his duties ran to the boundaries of the entire county, would have hell on his hands when Tucky said that Kinkaid Sartrain had shot her.

He felt the bandage on her arm. She drew her breath in sharply and said: "Leave my arm alone!"

"Bullet?"

"None of your business!"

It was a bullet then. Damnation to the McCadys and the Sartrains and particularly to this woman, the only female McCady in three generations, and a woman who had ripped the lid off a feud that might have slumbered until Stong was more sure of himself.

Stong fought his way to his feet and carried Tucky down to the edge of the grass where a slanting rock broke the rain. He laid her down. The storm was thinning away now, quartering to the east as if driven in terror before the thunder.

"Who shot you, Tucky?"

"Nobody. Where's your horse?"

"I'll have a look at that arm."

She sat up. "You won't touch me."

He knelt beside her and took a match from his tobacco pouch. He struck it on the underslope of the rock. The knees of her pants were gone, showing bloody flesh smeared with talc from the hill. There was a bruise on her cheek and her nose was swollen and had bled.

"I'll have a look at the arm."

The high defiance of the McCadys flashed back at him. Her eyes were green, the planes of her face firm and full. She licked water off her lips and tried to stare him down during the brief light of the match. No matter how bedraggled she was, she was furiously alive, a woman in full bloom, an angry woman, and a woman who had always excited Stong.

He was glad when the light burned out. "I asked you." He put his hand on her arm gently. She tried to jerk away. When he clamped down, just above her elbow, she gasped and said: "All right."

His fingers were huge, square-tipped, one part of him that was not awkward. They worked deftly in the dark, and, when the lightning came again, he saw the wound. A bullet rip, neither superficial nor pretty. He had seen men turn gray and let fear overcome them from lesser hurts. But she was a McCady, with the wild, boundless stamina of all her tribe.

16

He bound her arm again. Ducking out from under the rock, he listened for the sound of horses. Just the afterwash of the storm that had spun away was falling now. There were breaks in the sky where the stars shone cleanly. The land had a fresh, new odor. The flashes of lightning were far between, and the thunder was only a mutter.

Stong heard nothing from the direction of Mormon Forge. Not yet.

"Kinkaid Sartrain, you said?" He was thinking clearly now. It could not have been a Sartrain; they would not shoot a woman, not even a McCady woman.

"I don't remember saying that."

Stong swung around, staring toward the sound of her voice. "You said Kinkaid."

"Did I?"

"You did."

"I must have been excited," Tucky said. "I saw no one. What business of yours would it be anyway?"

The McCady attitude, and the Sartrain attitude. *You mind the tame citizens of Mormon Forge, Sheriff Stong. That's why we elect sheriffs. All matters between the McCadys and the Sartrains will be settled in the usual manner. It is their ancient right. Who else founded and settled Antelope County?*

"You came from Shavano Creek along these rocks," Stong said. "From up there on the cliff somebody with a rifle put a furrow across the hind end of your steeldust. That wouldn't have spilled you, not the way you ride. But there was another shot. It went through your arm first, and then tore a chunk of bone out of your horse's nose right at the tip of the blaze. That's when you got dumped. Then what happened?"

"How do you know I came from Shavano Creek?"

"A guess."

17

"You're a liar! You spied on me!"

"I did then."

"You miserable, two-bit sneak! Wait till my father and Limba hear. . . ." She stopped suddenly.

"You'll tell them that you spent the afternoon with Goliad Sartrain at the old cabin?" Here was the weapon with which Stong thought he could bargain; she had put it into his hands herself, but the thought of using it had caused an unpleasant taste already.

"How long did you spy on us?"

"Only a few minutes. It was enough. Your personal business is not mine, Kentucky."

"Then why were you there at all?"

"What affects the peace of this county is my business. You have been riding too regularly deep into Sartrain range. Now you've wrecked the peace, and I don't know what to do about it. Was or wasn't it Kinkaid?"

"None of your business!" Her fury was coming from the fact that Stong had seen her and Goliad at the cabin. "My family will handle. . . ."

"Your family be damned. They'll handle nothing," Stong said heavily.

She was shocked into silence for a moment, and then her voice came coldly: "You're going to get the worst beating you ever had, Pat Stong. You can talk that way to the girls in Lulu Courtney's place, but when you start insulting me. . . ."

"You insulted yourself when you stayed all afternoon with a man who doesn't have guts enough to ride over on McCady range to meet you. That's your business. My job is enforcing law in this county. Who shot you?"

She did not speak for a long time, and then her voice was weak and shaky. "Take me home."

He bent over her and lit another match. Her face was white, her mouth open. She was crumpled against the rock. He removed his jacket and tried to shake water from it before he folded it. When he eased her to a prone position, the tension of her muscles told him she was not unconscious. He felt the bandage on her arm, tightening it a trifle. This was a hell of a thing, trying to force information from a wounded woman, but it had to be. He had to have a basis for dealing fast and hard with the McCadys when they came.

"Did you see the man who shot you, Tucky?"

She did not answer. He struck another match. Her eyes were open. The pain and sickness of her hurt were evident, but she was still in command of herself.

"Did you see . . . ?"

"You're the ugliest brute I ever saw."

Stong dropped the match. It hurt; it always would. He knew his face was formed in lumps and blocks, with only the expression of his yellow-flecked eyes to relieve a brutish cast. His sisters had been frank enough when he was little. He could grin when men called him ugly, but no woman had ever spoken so bluntly to him about his looks.

"What were you doing at the foot of the cliffs, Tucky?"

"Take me home," she said, "you ugly, stubborn brute."

He strode angrily into the dark. He fell over a rock and cursed viciously. He broke limbs from a dead tree at the foot of the cliffs, and stumbled back with an armload of them. From the pitchy heart of the pine he sliced shavings. Soon he had a fire going. He built it up strong until it was throwing heat against the rock where the woman lay.

"They'll see that fire," she said.

"I expect them to."

"What about the man on the cliff?"

19

"He's gone," Stong said.

"How do you know?"

"He was a sneak to start with."

"So are you, or you wouldn't be here now."

"What were you doing at the foot of the cliff?" Stong asked.

Her wounded arm was doubled across her stomach. Firelight rose and fell on the high cheek bones of her pale face. "I was trying to work past him and get into the heavy timber."

Stong blinked at the boldness of her idea. "When did you get hit?"

"Just before sunset."

It had been about forty minutes after sunset when he saw her horse running down the drift fence east of town, still tossing its head to throw off the pain in its head.

"How'd you stave him off for so long?"

"I dared him to come down into pistol range."

"Where's your pistol now?"

"I didn't have one."

That was courage that Stong could appreciate. She must have huddled behind a rock after her horse left her, and she had bluffed the fellow until he was afraid to close. If she had run into the open, going downslope, he could have shot her. Even in the early dark a figure on the grasslands would have been visible, and then the man could have ridden her down. So she had waited and tried to get past him into the safety of the timber. It could not have been a Sartrain, because no Sartrain could have been bluffed out.

"Then you didn't see anyone," Stong said. "You mentioned Kinkaid because you hate him worst of all."

"I didn't see anyone. Take me home."

Far down on the slope, Stong heard the beat of a horse.

"Some of your family will be here soon. What's our story, Tucky?"

She flared up. "*Our* story! You're not in this."

"I am if for no other reason than I saw you with Goliad this afternoon." No matter how he had to bargain, he was going to try to keep the Sartrains and the McCadys apart. "Some of Tom Patterson's shorthorns have strayed up Shavano Creek. Did you happen to see them today, and ride a little farther than you figured on, so you could tell Tom about them later?"

"I stopped by the Patterson place at noon," Tucky said.

"All right, we'll say that about the strays."

"And you don't know who shot you?"

"Did you see me at the cabin this afternoon?"

"No," Stong said.

"I don't know who shot me then, which happens to be the truth."

Goliad Sartrain. Of all the men in the country she could have chosen, Goliad was the least man of all. This was the woman he had watched at dances, with all the young bloods at her feet, the woman he had seen riding in and out of Mormon Forge in a buggy with old Limba McCady. Half of Stong had resented her, half of him had admired her, and all of him had been stirred by her. She had spent the afternoon with Goliad Sartrain.

Stong cursed under his breath as he turned to face the hoof beats coming through the night.

"Sing out, you!" he yelled angrily.

"Limba McCady!"

"Come on in."

A flick of lightning gleamed on the wet leaves of an aspen thicket downslope. Crashing through it on his steeldust stallion, Shiloh, rode the leader of the McCady

21

clan, bridle reins in his teeth, a rifle in his hands. His rush carried him to the edge of firelight before he swung down.

There were seventy-five years upon Limba McCady but he bore them with disdain. His thick iron-gray hair lay in tufts against his head. His was the fierce brown face of a raider peering across a lonely moor at shaggy cattle. He had worn buckskin when he rode with Bedford Sartrain into the valley the summer after the War Between the States. He still wore a buckskin jacket, in church or wherever else he went. It hung now from the wide span of his shoulders, dark and limp from the rain.

He looked at the woman under the rock. He shot Stong a hard, direct gaze from under shaggy brows, and it was a command to speak up quickly.

It was Tucky who finally broke the silence. "Somebody shot me in the arm, Gramps Limba."

"Which one of the Sartrains?"

Tucky said: "It was a man I've never seen before."

"Which one of the Sartrains, Tucky?"

"She said she never saw the man before." Stong pointed toward the cliffs. "He stood up there."

The tufts of Limba's brows threw heavy shadows on his forehead as he stared at Stong. "How'd *you* get here?" Stong knew it clearly meant: *What business is it of yours?*

"I picked up the steeldust. I sent Pete Snell to the M Ranch to tell you about it," Stong said evenly. He had always been awed by Limba McCady and there was some of that now, but none in Stong's voice. He stood there and faced the old man with his hands hanging from his long arms like blades of shovels. "Where's the rest?"

"They're headed in the right direction," Limba said.

Stong walked away from the fire. The stallion snorted at

him uneasily. Far out on the wet land Stong heard the pound of hoofs. The McCadys were riding like hell, and they were not coming this way; they were driving toward the Cross Ranch.

"Call them off," Stong said. "No Sartrain was in this."

Limba was squatted by the rock, examining Tucky's arm. He ignored Stong. "Can you ride, Tucky?"

"He's right, Gramps. It wasn't the Sartrains."

"Never mind," Limba said. "Can you ride?"

"Yes."

Limba listened a moment to the sounds of the horses sweeping toward the southwest. "Stong can take you into town. He should have done so before this."

"The McCadys can take her into town, all of them." Stong walked back into the firelight. He picked up Limba's rifle and fired it three times.

The old man whirled around and went toward Stong. Limba's face was all heavy bones, his eyes wicked, his mouth a tight, brutal line. "You need a lesson, Stong. I've been wondering about you for some time."

Stong shifted the rifle downward. "Will you have one of those fine cavalryman's legs wrecked, Limba McCady?"

Limba took another long stride.

"No!" Tucky cried. "He'll do it, Limba!"

The old man stopped. His heavy face swung back to his granddaughter. "Maybe you know more of this man than you should, Tucky. What's been going on over here?"

"Nothing. He . . . he's like his father, that's all."

Limba nodded slowly, staring at Stong. "I failed to see before that he is like Matthew. We made a mistake to put him into office, but not much of a mistake."

"Both you and the Sartrains," Stong said. "Your days of playing war across this county are done."

Limba smiled. "Like Matthew, indeed," he murmured. "But it isn't enough."

The hoof beats had changed direction. Now the McCadys were thundering upslope. No one, not even Sartrains, would send horses through the night at such a pace. Limba waited, smiling, letting Stong think fully on what would happen when sons and grandsons arrived to see him holding Limba's own rifle on the McCady patriarch.

"If you're not a complete fool, Limba, you'll take Tucky's words and mine that no Sartrain harmed her."

Limba growled low in his chest. "The both of you stand together on the lie, don't you? Has she been meeting you in the woods?"

"Let one of your sons say that."

The oblique reference to Limba's age brought him another step toward Stong. The same force that had stopped him once stopped him again; he knew that Stong was not bluffing. In the slow lift of Limba's head, in the narrowing of his eyes, there was arrogance, and there was also a salute to raw courage.

"You can put the rifle down, Stong."

The McCadys were crashing through the aspens now. Stong put the rifle on the ground. "There'll be no riding to the Cross, unless it's myself."

Limba weighed him silently.

The McCadys broke through the thicket. They did not hail the fire. Men had died in Baca Valley for such discourtesy but this group rode tonight in force, in anger, and with McCady arrogance.

Ruthven, Kentucky's father, was running when he hit the ground. He plunged down beside the rock. "Are you all right, Tucky?"

"I'm all right," she answered wearily. "Take me home.

24

Wind Eater stumbled and I. . . .”

"Stumbled! Two bullets scraped that mare!” Ruthven took off his jacket and put it over his daughter. He asked Fitz John McCady, his oldest son, for his jacket, and then began to tear it from him while Fitz John was getting it unbuttoned. "Get her some water!”

Young Roblado McCady, another of Ruthven's sons, said: "There ain't no water closer than Shavano. . . .”

"Get it from the hollow of a rock, you idiot!” Ruthven flung himself beside his daughter again. "Who shot at you?”

"I don't know,” she answered weakly.

Ruthven leaped up and strode to the fire, thrusting men out of his way. "Limba. . . .” He seemed to see Stong for the first time. "What are *you* doing here, Stong?” Ruthven's face was blunt and heavy, his eyes green. He had all the hot high-handedness of any McCady, but he lacked the rock-like stability of old Limba.

"I followed the mare's tracks until dark,” Stong said. One of these days they might think to thank him for sending the message, but they figured that was as far as his actions should have gone. He should have stayed in Mormon Forge, taking care of the petty business of the town.

Ruthven grunted, looking at his father. "Stong can take her in to Doc Harlan, Limba. We'll need every man tonight.”

"What for?” Stong asked.

Ruthven ignored the question. "Let's go.”

"Not to the Cross.” Stong shook his head.

Limba's face was thoughtful. "Both Tucky and Stong say the Sartrains had nothing to do with it.”

"Oh, hell!” Ruthven jerked his shoulders impatiently. "How would Stong know? This is Sartrain land. . . .”

"You're not going to the Cross,” Stong said.

25

A half dozen McCadys began to talk at once, hurling their anger at Stong. Limba's stallion chose the moment to attack a gelding that had wandered too close. The night was filled with bugling savagery and the sounds of plunging horses. Limba cursed mightily. Men leaped to grab their mounts.

"Are you trying to give us orders?" Ruthven asked.

Stong said: "Ask Tucky if she knows who shot her."

"I don't need to," Ruthven said. "I can guess."

"No you can't," Stong said. "You're not guessing a fight in this county while I'm sheriff."

"Why, damn you, Stong!" Ruthven yelled. "We put you into office. Now you're trying to outgrow your britches. What we do on the range is none of your business."

"I have business wherever the county runs. I'll run the office, Ruthven. No McCady is going to Cross Ranch tonight."

Limba was still thoughtful. Ruthven was angry, and the rest were merely mildly surprised.

Roblado McCady, long-backed and tall, a square-jawed man with white teeth and rusty red hair, laughed in Stong's face. "Taking Derringers away from tinhorns in the Otero has gone to his head, boys."

Stong knew he could not ruin himself by taking individual challenges. If he did, he would soon be deep in trouble with one of the clan and that would greatly simplify the mass decision they all had to make. He looked at old Limba, hoping for support, but Limba gave him an intense, brooding look, and let the weight rest on him.

Into the silence Tucky said: "It was no Sartrain on the cliff." Her voice was very weak.

"You McCadys have a wounded woman here, and you stand and talk of fighting, without knowing what you're about, instead of getting her to town at once." Stong walked through them, brushing roughly against Ruthven because Roblado would not stand aside. "I say you're not going to the Cross. You'd better tell them so, Limba."

Stong knelt beside Tucky. "They'll take you to help, Kentucky, after they've spent another hour blowing their foul tempers all over the country. They'll. . . ." He peered closely at the woman. He felt her face. It was as cold as the rock under which she lay. "She's fainted, and no wonder."

Now they would start to the Cross or they would not start. There was no way to stop them. He heard his gelding moving in the night ahead of him, and he went to the animal and stood there, waiting. He was afraid, not knowing what his next move should be.

Ruthven had run to his daughter. "Roblado, damn you, where's the water I told you to get?"

The man holding Shiloh grew careless. The stallion broke away from him and raged into the geldings, and once more the night was bedlam. If it had been the Sartrains, it would have been worse, Stong knew. He waited tensely. The night ran icy fingers through his wet clothes. The McCadys clustered around Tucky, cursing and arguing until Limba's voice cut through the wrangling. "We'll go to town."

They did not like it. Limba roared again. They were silent then. Stong sighed but the tension stayed with him. He had declared himself and now there was no telling when he would again know the blessings of peace.

The McCadys went toward Mormon Forge, with Limba carrying Tucky, and Roblado walking as he led the stallion. They would not break away now, Stong was sure; Limba had said the word. But still Stong kept between the McCadys and Cross, pacing Owlhorns to the slowness of the group. Limba was the source of hope. If Stong could work through him, the peace might be saved. But if the old man ever made up his mind in favor of war, he would be the worst of all.

II

A few miles from town one of the McCadys galloped ahead to tell the doctor. Stong held up, coming in behind the rest at the main gate of the drift fence. The McCadys had not bothered to close the gate, so Stong got down and did the chore.

Running east and west for twelve miles, the fence, in a way, was the unofficial boundary line between McCady and Sartrain range. Smaller ranches, including the Patterson place and old man Matthew Stong's Three Bars, lay north near the headwaters of the Mormon River. The town was on the south bank of the river, lying on a line almost directly between the Cross and the M, existing, the Sartrains and McCadys thought, for their particular convenience.

At once Stong did not like the feel of Mormon Forge this night. There were too many people on the walks, too many lights, and a waiting silence over everything. The citizens had seen the McCadys ride in with Tucky, and Stong could picture how they had arrived—grim, chopping along the street, speaking to no one, ignoring curiosity.

Busby Youngblood's bald head gleamed in the lantern light when Stong led Owlhorns into the stable. Squat and powerful, red-faced, Youngblood was a close friend of nobody. He had fought with Berdan's sharpshooters during the war, but he never waved the bloody shirt. There seemed to be a sneer always in his cold gray eyes. He had six girls, and none of them appeared afraid of him, and his wife had the bright face of a happy woman, all of which made some people wonder why Busby Youngblood was so reserved in his dealings with men.

He looked at Stong and said: "Let me take care of the horse one time. I know how."

The offer startled Stong. "Thanks, Busby."

Youngblood took one more step away from his habitual coldness. "Somebody's been waiting for you in your office since the news got around." He pulled the saddle off Owlhorns.

For a moment Stong was of a mind to ask a great favor of Youngblood. He was a man who already commanded respect, if not understanding, for his independence. The saddle horse of any drifter received as good care in this stable as any McCady steeldust or the finest buckskin the Sartrains owned. As a deputy . . . ? No, it wouldn't do to ask him. He had six kids, he was satisfied with his business and his life—and, besides, he would likely tell Stong to go to hell.

As Stong cut away from the Otero saloon, angling toward his office across the street next to Andy Kopperwit's barbershop, he heard a lounger mutter: "The law is still in one piece, I see."

Someone laughed. "You didn't think he was going to tell the McCadys anything, did you?"

Stong saw the light coming through the doorway that led to his living quarters behind the sheriff's office, but he did not go inside. He walked down the street, shambling, weighing what he saw and heard.

Todd Brewslow's general mercantile held a half dozen of the more substantial citizens of the town. They were wont to gather evenings at a poker table in the back end of the place, having a careful drink or two, playing conservative poker, and settling the political affairs of Mormon Forge. They were there tonight but they were not playing poker.

The Boston Café, Frank Budlong's place, was full of McCadys. It was said that they ate a side of beef at every war council, and that was what it looked like in the Boston now.

A man among a group at a hitch rail said: "Who else would have done it but a Sartrain? She was over on their land, wasn't she? Did you see the looks of them when they came in with old Limba? If you think Stong. . . ."

The man grunted as if someone had elbowed him hard. Stong went past the group slowly. Three or four of them said: "Howdy, Sheriff." Before, it had always been Pat or Stong, but now the title was a gentle mockery telling him what they thought of him.

Before he turned into the Five Nations saloon, Stong paused a moment to stare at the lights of Dr. Munro Harlan's house near the end of the street. The Five Nations was crowded, with most of the business at the bar. This was the Sartrain hang-out when the men of the Cross were in town. Stong saw none of them here tonight. He was relieved for an instant.

Willy Golden, who ran the gambling end of the place for big Sioux Peters, strolled casually toward Stong with his thumbs hooked in the slits of a yellow-brocaded vest. Golden had the clear, pink skin of a healthy child, a gentle voice, large, dark eyes. He looked like a ruined minister. He murmured: "The boys are betting that gunsmoke will soon be drifting high around the Cross. What do you think, Sheriff?"

Although few in the room had heard all the words, everyone was quiet, waiting on the answer.

Stong filled his pipe, taking plenty of time. Golden held a match for him, smiling gently at his own thoughts.

"Let me know who makes the biggest bets, Willy. They might be the men I'll deputize." Stong looked carefully around the room once more. "Any Sartrains in town tonight?"

Golden shook his head. "That's luck, isn't it?"

"It could be." Stong went out unhurriedly. He looked once more toward Doc Harlan's place, and then he went up the street. The McCadys were eating steaks, working at the job full tilt, as they did everything. Limba and Ruthven were not there. After a while the McCadys would decide that Stong knew certain facts that they did not know. They would come to his office. He knew he could expect it as sure as sunrise.

He went on, walking slowly, leaving little pools of silence behind him before the talk closed in again. Mormon Forge was licking its chops. There had not been an outbreak between the two tribes since Roblado McCady spun Kinkaid Sartrain around with a bullet that smashed his cheek bone; that was when Houston Doty, the last sheriff, had ducked into Mrs. Fleetwood's millinery store on urgent business. If Stong wanted deputies, he knew of only two men he could lean on heavily; one of them he had already ruled out. He could not be contemptuous of the citizens of Mormon Forge. They were afraid, he knew, but he himself was afraid, also.

Old Matthew, Stong's father, was sitting in front of a pot of coffee in the room behind the sheriff's office. The kinship was apparent, the same great hands and heavy feet, the same yellow-flecked eyes, the same granite faces that an angry sculptor had roughed out before he dropped his tools and went somewhere to get drunk.

Matthew poured a cup of coffee for his son. "Get out of those wet clothes, Patrick."

Stong hung his gun belt on a peg. He stripped to the belt and was grateful for the warmth of the stove. "How come you're here, Pop?"

"Pete Snell rode over after he left the M."

"A long, wet ride. You thought I needed help, huh?"

"Advice," Matthew said. He took a great gulp of coffee. "Something has rotted in the Sartrains since the old days, for them to do such a thing."

"They didn't do it."

"Who did then?"

"I'll have to find that out."

"Indeed?" Matthew poured himself another cup of coffee. "Since last fall when Doty waddled down to Lulu Courtney's cathouse to pay for his pleasure for a change, you've been sheriff, Patrick. You've done fair. Now what are you trying to do?"

"Should I look the other way while McCadys and Sartrains ride about, thinking they have hair on their chests?"

"The town is one thing. They are another."

"It's all the same county."

Matthew grunted like a gut-shot bear. "I've been afraid of your ideas. Why didn't you declare these things before you were elected?"

"I wouldn't have been elected if I had."

"You overweigh yourself, Patrick, to think that they would have done anything but laugh, but it would have been more honest to declare in advance. I would have been against you myself, if I had thought you had planned to interfere in their troubles."

Stong drank his coffee. He relit his pipe. The first cloud of blue smoke drifted in layers toward the chimney of the lamp, and then wound upward when the heat caught it. "Trouble, you say. You came here and took up land claimed by both sides and held it. You had a wife and a growing family but you rode squarely between the two tribes and took ground . . . and today you own it. Now you talk of interfering in their troubles."

Matthew was not pleased. "I was young then."

"I'm young now."

"You're being a fool, Patrick. You're putting your head in the jaws of a stone crusher. I won't let you do it."

"I'm not on the ranch any longer. I'm sheriff of this whole county, or nothing. When my own father starts to back up. . . ."

"That will be enough, Patrick."

"The hell it will! Would you be so concerned about this because you think I'll ruin your hopes of seeing some of my sisters married off to the McCadys?"

Matthew got out of his chair and kicked it behind him. His rough face was uglier because of its whiteness. "You made a filthy statement."

"I think it was true."

"Step out of here with me, Patrick. I'll smash you down."

"No, you won't. I've got troubles enough. To hell with. . . ."

Matthew made an open-handed sweep that would have spun his son out of his chair, but Stong had his feet under him and was going back, carrying the chair with him. The blow knocked the pipe out of his mouth and snapped it against the wall behind the stove.

"You'd go back to the ranch, would you, Pop, having to

tell Mom that you and I wallowed in the street before loafers, and then tell her what started it?"

Matthew was moving the table out of his way. He stopped, glowering. "Your ambition is making a fool out of you. Don't expect any sympathy from me when they crush you to pulp." He turned around, grabbing his hat and gun belt from a peg. He went out with his footsteps jarring the floor. He was the second of the two men that Stong would have trusted to help him.

I'm still right, Stong told himself. It was a dreary thought, for he knew that some principles are maintained only by violence, and that a man has to be a stubborn fool or a brave man to buck established currents.

He spoke to the wall: "Did you get an earful, Andy?"

On the other side of the partition, near the rack of shaving mugs, Andy Kopperwit was unabashed. "I heard the whole works, Pat. I think your old man is right. You want to know how I got this thing figured?"

"I know already."

"Huh?"

Stong moved the table back in place. He went into the office and sat on the desk, looking out on a town that ordinarily would have been asleep by now. Sometime later he saw his father ride down the street, headed out of town. The sight cut away the last doubt that Stong stood alone in his stubbornness. He did not feel good about it. In the desk were a pile of circulars, a bottle of whiskey, and a dozen pistols and Derringers he had taken from cheap toughs. The whiskey was his. He could take it, turn in his badge, and walk out of the whole mess tonight.

He went out on the walk and looked toward Doc Harlan's house. Only one light was burning there now. He went back to his room and waited for the McCadys.

He was not a patient man. He was about ready to put on his shirt and go looking on his own when the office door opened. Ruthven led them in. Behind him was Roblado, with his hat tipped back, with a toothpick in his teeth. There was Benoni, Tucky's uncle, the tallest of all the McCadys, who sometimes in a fit of rage was known to stun a horse by hitting it in the neck with his fist. Vir McCady was slow and quiet, the most reasonable of all the tribe. He was Limba's youngest son. In his youth he had run away with a Sartrain girl. The result had been tragic.

The four men nearly filled Stong's tiny living space.

"Where's the rest?" Stong asked.

"They're waiting," Ruthven said. "So are we. We want the straight of things. Whatever you put over on Limba isn't going to stick with us."

Stong held his anger down. "I saw her steeldust trotting out of town where the drift fence hooks out. I brought it in, sent a message, and then I backtracked the mare till dark. Then I heard two rifle shots. That's it."

"You sent us word to meet you at the forks of Shavano Creek," Ruthven said. "How come?"

"It was a place to meet, that's all. Her horse seemed to have come from that general direction."

Ruthven's face was tight with suspicion.

"You just happened to see her horse," Benoni growled. "The hook of that fence is a long way from town. A man would have to be expecting something to be watching out there."

"I didn't say I was in town."

"You're not saying much at all." Roblado bent the toothpick down until it looked like a thin white tusk against his heavy lips.

"Shut up, Roblado." Ruthven rolled a cigarette. "Just

answer our questions, Stong, and then you can go to bed. We'll handle whatever needs to be done."

"No," Stong said. "No, Ruthven, you won't handle anything. Not you or Limba or all of the McCadys. I'll take care of the first movement of the law in this matter."

"The first movement of the law!" Roblado sneered. He put his foot on the edge of Stong's cot.

"Bullheaded Irishman," Benoni said. He was the most stubborn man in the valley but now he used the word as an insult.

Dark blood was crowding away the little patience there had been on Ruthven's face. "I'm going to ask you one question, Stong, and then. . . ."

"Keep your one question. I'll do my best to find out who shot at Kentucky. After that, the due processes of the law will begin. In the meantime, you McCadys take care of your own affairs, which have nothing to do with the law in this county."

"Why, damn you!" Ruthven snarled. "I believe you mean that. Your old man may have made a bluff stick when he stole land from the Sartrains, but you. . . ."

Stong said: "Take your dirty boot off my bed, Roblado." His voice was not loud but it carried the strong whack of authority. They intended to start it anyway, so let it come to them first.

The McCadys looked at Roblado's foot resting on the gray blanket. It was as if the whole purpose of the argument had swung away from law and was now concentrated on a dusty boot. Roblado did not move his foot. Stong went toward him in one long step and grabbed him by the front of his jumper. He hauled the man to him with one hand and smashed him just below the toothpick with the other hand. Roblado's head rocked back as if his neck were broken.

Stong flung him toward the cot and swung back to meet Ruthven.

He was too late. Ruthven hit him in the face and drove him against the wall, and then came at him like a madman. Benoni threw the table aside. For an instant Vir McCady hesitated, and then he picked up a chair. The ball was open and Stong had started it; he knew they would not be satisfied until they had trampled him into the floor.

At close range he jammed his elbow into Ruthven's throat. Stong drove him back with the heel of his hand against Ruthven's cheek bone. He felt the flesh slide and twist. He braced his back against the wall and kicked Ruthven in the stomach and sent him staggering, doubled over, into Benoni. The floor shook as the two men collided and drove their boots hard to hold their feet.

"Get out of the way!" Vir was holding the chair high. "Get out of the way!"

He hurled the chair. Stong threw his elbows up. He took the impact of the twanging cross-wires on his arms but the point of a leg came through to gouge his cheek and rip his ear. Half blinded from the pain, Stong pushed the chair away from him. It tripped Benoni, who had pushed Ruthven out of the way and who was surging in. The chair legs broke at their dowel points as Benoni went down. He fell close to Stong, and Stong kicked him in the face.

By then both Ruthven and Vir were on the man against the wall, trampling Benoni in their frenzy to get at Stong and beat him into the partition. Benoni grabbed Stong by one leg, and tried to haul himself up. With his head lowered, with his elbows swinging from side to side, Stong battered at everything in front of him. Someone kicked him in the stomach. Blows skidded off the top of his head. Benoni tried to twist his leg loose. When the grunting weight was heavy on him, Stong butted with his head. He drove his shoulder up. He heard someone's jaws shut with a snap.

Ruthven plowed into him head on. The impact smashed the plaster and lathe between two studs in the partition. For a moment Stong was wedged tightly, kicking with his one free foot, stabbing the hard heel of his hand against sweating faces. On the barbershop side of the partition shaving mugs clattered to the floor. Andy Kopperwit cried out as if in pain.

Stong wrenched himself free. He got one clear, fair shot at Vir, with the man's face far enough away that Stong could swing. The blow was sweetly solid. Vir twisted sidewise with his feet tangled in the wreckage of the chair. He went down and there was a dull snap. Benoni grunted and let go of Stong's leg.

Ruthven McCady's rusty hair was spilled across his forehead. He staggered away from Stong and tore a leg loose from the overturned table. He raised it in both hands. Stong lurched along the wall and grabbed a shotgun from the rack. He raised it as a club, and for an instant the two men stared at each other wildly, hesitating.

Benoni struggled to his feet, his face blank and set. His right arm was hanging limp, broken when Vir had fallen across it. Benoni reached across his hips with his left hand, fumbling for his pistol. It had been kicked loose on the floor. He saw it and reached for it, and fell to his knees.

Ruthven shortened his grip on the club and inched toward Stong. Ruthven's pistol was still in its holster; for him the fight had slipped back to elemental savagery and pistols were still a thousand years in the future. Stong shortened his grip on the shotgun. Benoni got his hand on his pistol, trying to rise.

Old Limba McCady came into the room. He rumbled

something in Gælic. He shouldered Ruthven aside so violently that Ruthven fell against the cot, where Roblado was still lying. Limba took three great strides and kicked the pistol away from Benoni. The action also kicked Benoni's good arm from under him and dropped him flat on the floor again.

"Get out!" Limba growled. "Get out, the lot of you, and take the weaklings with you!" He glanced at Roblado and Vir, who were beginning to move and make vague sounds of returning life.

The McCadys went out slowly, not helping each other. Vir was the last. He bumped into the doorway between the wrecked room and the office, and clung there shakily for a while until he saw the curious crowd gathered on the walk outside. Then he drew himself together and went out, pushing through men who did not care to ask any direct questions. Kopperwit, who had at least been closer than anyone else to the fight, trotted the length of his shop to give the crowd all the details.

When Limba was the only McCady left, Stong put the shotgun away. He leaned against the rack, dazed, with his hurts beginning to come through. It was only when he turned toward Limba again that he became aware that one of his boots was off. He saw it on the floor by the shattered plaster but he did not want to try to lean over to pick it up.

"You beat them," Limba said. "What good will it do you?"

"It was because I told them the law in this county starts with me. I'll tell you that again, Limba."

Limba snorted. "You'll tell the Sartrains, too?"

"Are they any tougher than the McCadys that I wouldn't?" Stong wanted to throw himself on his cot and rest forever but he would not leave his feet while Limba was watching.

"You're stubborn, like your father. I've always wondered what would have happened years ago if we had moved against Matthew when he first came into the valley. Now I know." Limba watched Stong with cold intensity.

Stong licked blood off his lips. "For that I am proud."

Limba spoke most carefully. "Tucky speaks of seeing Patterson cattle on Shavano Creek, of doing a neighborly thing for Tom Patterson by riding to see how many there were. You will say the same, won't you?"

Stong did not like the tenor of the question, or the bitter gleam in Limba's eyes. Stong said: "Yes, there are Four Box shorthorns on the creek."

"You rode that way soon after Tucky was seen crossing the drift fence below the Patterson place."

"I did," Stong said.

"She met a man." Limba was deadly now. Stong was taken with the panic of a man who had never been able to lie well, and so he said nothing.

"Was it you, Stong?" The question was as lethal as a cocked pistol. "Answer me."

Stong shook his head.

"Who was it, then?"

"You couldn't find out from me, if I knew. It was you who said she met a man, not me. How do you know she met anyone?" Stong thanked God for the rain now.

Limba's words came with musing quietness. "Matthew was never a liar. You are like him in many ways. May God help you, Pat Stong, if you have lied to me tonight." He pointed at Stong, and the finger was like a pistol that would go off if a lie came back. "Do you know who she met?"

A wave of nausea and fear went through Stong. He

closed his eyes, partly from the sickness, but mostly to try to conceal his thoughts. He shook his head.

When he opened his eyes, Limba was leaving. Stong flopped on his cot. To his bleary vision the coffee grounds spilled from the crushed pot on the floor looked like gouts of blood. He tried to plan his next step.

If Limba ever found out that Tucky had been with Goliad Sartrain, hell would fly from a high limb. This time old Limba had asked no questions about the shooting. How had he guessed that Tucky had met anyone? He and Bedford Sartrain were the great-maned lions of their packs. When they roared, there was listening. Stong had once played with the thought that he could work through them, but now the chance was thin. Tucky had started it and she might make things worse, but now it was not she who Stong condemned. Goliad Sartrain, the laughing, polite one of his tribe, the straight-nosed one, who was always welcome at Lulu Courtney's place. A shuddering rage ran through Stong's bruised body until he was physically sick. He got up and staggered into the alley. Between spasms that rippled his back muscles he was aware that the town was still murmuring.

From the darkness at the back of the barbershop Andy Kopperwit said: "That's the way it hits a man. Can I help you?"

"Get me a bucket of water, Andy."

The well sheave squealed in the night. Kopperwit landed a full bucket with a *thump* on the wooden curbing. The smell of lotions from his shop was on him when he came close to Stong. Stong rinsed his mouth and spat. He drank, and then he gave the bucket back to Kopperwit. Starlight showed the round dome of the barber's derby, the outline of his angular face.

"Pour the water over me."

Kopperwit raised the bucket and let it spill. The icy shock was like a blessing. "Another one," Stong said. After the second one, Stong was shivering, but his head was clear. "You heard what Limba asked me?"

"Yes."

"I'm asking you to keep still about it."

"You don't have to ask me," Kopperwit said stiffly. "Not about a thing like that."

Kopperwit was as great a gossip as any man, but oddly enough Stong knew that what he said now was true.

"Somebody has got to pay for them mugs, Pat."

It seemed a trivial thing, and then Stong thought that justice touched everything or nothing. "Figure out how much the damage was," he said.

"I have. Eleven dollars and a half."

"I'll pay it."

"In that case it will be eight bucks. I was figuring you were going to collect from the McCadys."

"Thanks." Stong knew he was still alone, but even moral support was comforting in some degree.

Pete Snell came in while Stong was going to bed. He was a red-cheeked, toothless little man. Either naturally or from association with Busby Youngblood, for whom he worked, Snell was tight-mouthed. No one knew whether he was tough or not, but Stong suspected that he was. Snell looked around the room. "Heard it was a humdinger."

"Are the McCadys still in town?"

Snell nodded. That was what he had come to say, so now he walked out. A friend, but Stong knew he needed more support than friendship now.

III

Stong woke after sunrise, stiff and tired. He had not meant to sleep so long. The wreckage of the room and his own stubborn thoughts made an unpleasant greeting to the day. There were other places he could have eaten besides the Boston Café. He went there with a chip on his shoulder and was disappointed when he saw no McCadys. He realized then that he was thinking like a fool.

Frank Budlong, a pale man with bulging jowls, set eggs and steak and fried potatoes before Stong, and then he commented on the fine rain of the night before. Then, as if he had decided there was something not neutral in the rain last night, Budlong said that the rain last week was better.

Stong agreed. There was a dreary silence.

"Of course any rain will be good for that land west of your father's place where you figure on building up a ranch someday." Budlong considered that statement and read an implication into it that he had not meant, that Stong would be better off ranching than being sheriff. Budlong decided then to keep still.

Houston Doty came in. His stomach was big, his nose and cheeks veined with purple. Curling gray locks escaped the edges of his fawn hat. He wore a heavy gold chain across his gray vest, but there was no watch on one end of it; the timepiece had gone for drinks at Lulu Courtney's place.

Doty grinned. His teeth were short and even. "I hear you're prying up hell, Stong, and putting a chunk under it." Doty could not hide his pleasure over the present sheriff's unstable position.

"Bought any millinery lately?" Stong asked.

Doty's face grew blotchy red. He hitched up his coattails and sat down at the counter quickly. "I gave you good advice when you first took office. You're a smart young fellow, Stong. You'll find out, if you last long enough."

Stong knew it made no sense to jab wicked remarks into a man. Doty was a bloated wreck, and he had done no better or worse than anyone expected when he was elected.

When he closed the door and went past the window outside, he saw Doty blowing off to Budlong. Mrs. Harlan was watering bachelor buttons inside her white picket fence. She was a young woman, well-formed. Her blonde hair had been burned six shades of brown by the sun. Her face was tanned and her big-wristed hands were brown. It occurred to Stong that, if she were painted up a little, like the girls in Lulu's place, she would be a striking woman. He touched his hat.

She said—"Good morning, Patrick."—and her eyes took in the battered condition of his face.

Patrick. She had never been a stand-offish woman during the four years she and her husband had lived here. *Patrick.* Matthew Stong always used the name when he was angry or in dead earnest, and now Amy Harlan was doing the same.

"I'd like to talk to Tucky, Missus Harlan." An expression of quick reserve settled in the muscles around Mrs. Harlan's mouth and made Stong wonder. "Is she all right?"

"Feverish, of course. She's all right, Patrick."

"Did Limba or Ruthven say for me not to see her?"

Mrs. Harlan kept studying Stong. "No." She hesitated.

"Can I talk to her?"

"I'll ask the doctor." She turned.

Dr. Munro Harlan was coming through an arch of woodbines at the side of the house, with a strip of fried bacon in one hand and a cup of coffee in the other. He was a stocky man who rode as well as any cowboy in the valley. His hair was flaming red, with a hopeless cowlick that sent tufts swirling in three directions at the back of his head. He was blunt-faced and Indian-brown. At first the country had suspected him of being high-toned when he refused to treat sick horses. After one winter of ministering to human beings, the country had decided that he was too good a man to remain long in Baca Valley. But he was still here.

He pushed the bacon into his mouth and washed it down with a swallow of coffee, and gave his wife a smirk. "Hello, Sheriff. From what I heard, I thought you might be down to get patched up." He studied Stong's face and grinned. "But with a mug like that, who could tell . . . ?"

"Munro!" his wife said sharply.

Dr. Harlan downed the coffee. "Oh, hell, Pat and I understand each other. Has Amy been trying to lead you astray behind my back this morning, Sheriff?"

Stong blinked. He never would get used to Harlan, he supposed. The man was a New Yorker who had studied in Berlin and Vienna, and, although he fitted into the valley as easily as anyone here, his mannerisms and casual remarks were sometimes startling as gunshot.

"I wanted to talk to Tucky, if she's all right."

"Professional call or otherwise?" Harlan grinned, but his wife found no humor in the remark. Stong saw the sudden bleak look she gave her husband. "I'm full of it this morning. You'll have to pardon me. Come on in, Pat. Had breakfast?"

"I. . . ."

"That's fine. We'll have some more coffee then."

The Harlan summer kitchen was a glassed-in porch built against the L of the house. It looked out on a small patch of lawn and then far up the valley where the Mormon River gleamed. The floor was of red flagstones. The table and chairs were made of aspen wood taken from underwater in beaver ponds. Now the finished wood gleamed with red and purple streaks under varnish. In one end of the room sat a kerosene stove of Harlan's own manufacture. It worked well but it gave off such an odor that Amy Harlan allowed its use only on the porch.

Harlan poured two cups of coffee. All at once his light mood left him and his eyes probed Stong's face. "You got yourself into something. Can you get out?"

"I hope so."

"I didn't expect to see you alive today. He had murder in his soul when he went over to see you last night."

"Limba? He was mad enough, of course." They were talking at cross-purpose, Stong thought for a moment when he saw the puzzled look on Harlan's face. "How's Tucky?"

"Oh, she'll be all right. I'm wondering about you."

So was Stong.

Harlan rolled a cigarette, neatly, deftly. His fingers were short, square-tipped. They worked like fine pieces of machinery. He tossed his tobacco pouch across the table to Stong. "You're rigid in some of your moral concepts out here and remarkably lax in others. It's little different where I come from. Sometimes the end results of an affair out here are violently spectacular. When there's a man in the background with a moral code as tall and mighty as Limba

McCady's, there can be a hell of an explosion. No doubt you've considered that."

Stong nodded, thinking that Tucky and Goliad would meet again. It was not a happy thought.

"How'd you calm Limba down?"

"I denied knowing. . . ." How did Harlan know about Tucky and Goliad?

"Naturally. You had to deny everything. The old boy wasn't responsible last night." Harlan watched Stong with an odd expression, half-puzzled, half-admiring. "I took care of the wound. It's bad enough. She'd lost blood and she's going to be weak and feverish. I thought at the time that Limba was showing less interest in that aspect of her condition than one would expect. When Ruthven, Tucky's father, mind you, was out of the room, Limba insisted on another kind of examination. She was still under the anesthetic. I objected strongly. He insisted. I wish I could have lied afterward, Pat, but I didn't. Limba knows, of course, that you and I have been friends ever since I came here. I told him the truth. Tucky is no virgin. Ruthven and some of the others had already gone over to see you." Harlan's eyes were wide and steady. "When Limba left, he was in the coldest fury I ever want to see in a man. He was a clinical picture of all the hell a man can have inside him. It was too late for me to warn you."

Stong remembered Limba's face and quiet voice. He knew now what was in Harlan's mind, and he knew how close he had been to death last night. Half dazed at the time, Stong had not been able to appreciate the full significance of Limba's big question: *She met a man . . . was it you?*

"I don't waste time criticizing anyone's morals," Harlan said. "My views on that subject still shock my wife." He drank a cup of coffee in four swallows. "Tucky is a beautiful woman, Pat. As a physical specimen, too, I've never seen better. She must have recognized, as I and Amy have, what lies behind that ugly mug of yours. But Limba. . . ."

"It wasn't me," Stong said, and then he wished he had kept still.

"You said you denied. . . ."

"I did deny even meeting her. It was the truth."

Harlan leaned back in his chair. "Good God! I violate my ethics, make a speech, and sit here envying you, and all the time you, you ugly son-of-a-bitch, you're innocent!" He began to laugh.

The sound grated on Stong. He stared at Harlan. It took a lot of understanding to appreciate the man.

"Your part is reduced to looking forward to getting killed by the McCadys or the Sartrains only in the interest of law and order!" Harlan roared. The cowlick on his shiny red head bobbed. He looked like an overgrown boy. His laughter was so genuine that Stong could take no offense from it, but neither could he join it. Harlan stopped when he saw the grave look in Stong's eyes. "Pat, if there is anything I can do in this mess that appears to be brewing, count on me."

His seriousness was as honest as his laughter of a moment before.

Amy Harlan came to the wide doorway, wearing cotton gloves, carrying a sprinkler can. Her glance touched Stong coolly and went to her husband's face.

"What's so funny?"

"Just my idiotic sense of humor," Harlan said. He shook his head. "It wasn't Pat, Amy."

Stong felt the back of his neck burning. He did not look around. Mrs. Harlan came into the room. She stood beside

Stong without speaking. He had to look at her then. Her strong fingers touched the marks of Vir McCady's chair leg on his cheek and ear. "Make the braying jackass put something on that before you leave, Pat."

She went back to her gardening.

"There's nothing in the whole mess that's funny to a woman," Harlan said slowly. His eyes twinkled suddenly. "That gives us braying jackasses a chance to laugh, still knowing that half the human race is decent." He bounced up. "You wanted to talk to Tucky. Make it short. She didn't have a very restful night."

Stong followed Harlan across a large living room plastered white and furnished in hard maple. The end wall of the room that held a fireplace was laid with red rocks and the fireplace was six feet wide. Night coolness still held in the room, for the Harlan house was insulated with eighteen inches of sawdust in the walls and overhead.

The doctor turned down a hallway with windows all along the outside wall. There were two rooms at the back of the house where he usually put patients, but Tucky was in the Harlans' own bedroom.

Her eyes were feverish, her cheeks flushed. Her hair made a dark red splash against the pillow. Her hands, lying limply on top of the sheet, were long and slender. They reminded Stong of Mrs. Harlan's hands. He was aware of the noise his feet made on the floor, conscious of the wrinkles in his shirt and the lack of buttons on the cuffs that fell away from his flat, thick wrists. He spoke almost in a whisper, staring down at the woman.

"I thought maybe you'd remember something about the fellow that you didn't recall last night." When Tucky's long green eyes kept searching his face, Stong added: "The man on the cliff." He watched her expression. She did not appear to be thinking of his question, he thought, but after a moment she shook her head. "Nothing at all?" Stong asked.

Her eyes strayed to Harlan's face. "Will there be a bad scar?"

"Of course," Harlan said cheerfully. "Answer the sheriff's question."

Tucky looked at Stong again. "You were mad last night, weren't you?"

"Upset and afraid."

"Afraid of what?" she asked.

"Do you remember anything at all about the man on the cliff?" Stong asked gently.

She shook her head.

It was impossible, Stong thought, that she could have seen anyone for even an instant without some impression of him. He frowned. "You first said. . . ."

"Let it go for now," Harlan said. He put his fingers on Tucky's wrist. He took out his watch. "Of course, there will be a scar, but think of the scar you'd have if you'd been shot between the eyes." He made a face.

Tucky smiled at him faintly. Stong walked out, grabbing his hat in the summer kitchen.

Limba McCady was talking to Amy in the garden. She had the old man by one arm. He was listening gravely, bent forward so that the corded column of his neck was thrust away from the collar of his buckskin jacket. The full force of the man's drive and power was in his eyes when he glanced briefly at Stong, and then he gave his attention back to Mrs. Harlan.

"See you, Amy," Stong said.

She raised her free hand in acknowledgment, still talking quietly to Limba.

Todd Brewslow was waiting in front of his store. He was

a trim, fair-skinned man with thick hair that was parted in the center and turned back in long waves at the sides. He brushed flour from his black sleeve protectors, glancing up and down the street before he spoke to Stong.

"We've got a pretty good town here, Pat, don't you think?"

"It's all right."

"The mines in Las Platas are starting to boom. The railroad is looking this way. Farmers at the lower end of the valley have to come here to trade. Cattle are pretty good right now." Brewslow was mayor of Mormon Forge. He talked on as if he were sitting at a meeting of the city council. Stong heard him out. Brewslow always came to the point eventually. "It would be a shame to give people a wrong impression of the valley, Stong. We've had our share of trouble and roughness here, I'll admit, but things haven't been too bad, considering." Brewslow bowed and smiled when Mrs. Youngblood and three of her girls came from the store. He frowned when a swamper at the Otero saloon walked out and threw a bucket of filthy water toward the hitch rail. Mrs. Fleetwood came out of her store and let her awning down to protect the hats in her window.

"It's a good town. We wouldn't want anything done to give it a bad name," Brewslow said. "It will grow and things will adjust themselves in time. You've done a good job keeping order here, Stong. We've paid you a little extra on your county salary for doing that. I imagine the money has been appreciated, since you're planning to build up that land west of your father's place one of these days. With a little water there you could run five or six hundred head, couldn't you?"

"Uhn-huh." Stong watched two saddle bums come out of the Boston and stand idly on the walk. Down in the west side of town one of Lulu Courtney's bloodhounds was howling for someone to get up and feed it.

"What I'm getting at, Stong . . ."—Brewslow brushed at the white smears on his sleeve protectors—"is that anything you do to antagonize the McCadys, or the Sartrains, will result in giving us a reputation for lawlessness which we don't deserve. We want more people in Mormon Forge, people like the Harlans and the Budlongs, the Youngbloods . . . and they won't come here if they think it's a rough town."

"You mean I'm making it rough?"

"Yes. When you start telling the McCadys and the Sartrains what they have to do, it's only natural that they'll bring their quarrel right in town to show you how wrong you are."

"I'm wrong, Brewslow?"

"We've always had reasonable order in the town, Stong. If there has been trouble on the range sometimes, it has not affected us here. The council and I have agreed that we want the situation to remain unchanged. In other words, we don't favor you going far out of your way to create ill feeling between factions. Now that affair last night in your office is the sort of thing that looks very bad to an outsider. Perhaps the McCadys were a little brusque, perhaps even wrong. . . ."

"They were damned good and wrong! What's the matter with you, Brewslow? Don't you know that Tucky McCady was shot last night, and that I'm the sheriff of this county?"

"The county. Exactly, Stong. But when you bring trouble directly here to us. . . ."

"I didn't bring it! By God, I don't understand your kind of thinking, Brewslow. You sound like an old woman."

At once Brewslow's intelligent eyes were hot with

malice. "You're taking the wrong attitude, Stong. Technically, you know, you have no authority in Mormon Forge at all." He ducked his head and smiled pleasantly at Mrs. Gilbert Pesman, the minister's wife, when she approached his door and turned in with a basket.

"I've got business," Stong said. He walked up the street.

The sight of his room offended him. He kicked the bent coffee pot across the room, blinking when it jumped into the woodbox. He strapped on his pistol, took a carbine from the rack, and went over to Youngblood's stable.

Pete Snell was forking manure into a wagon at the back doors. " 'Morning." He went on working until Stong had saddled Owlhorns and was going out. "The McCadys rode southwest early."

"Yeah." Stong knew they must have, but he was betting that the long reach of Limba's authority was still on them. Tucky was the center of the problem, and old Limba was not going to explode until he had one fact.

Stong rode straight toward the cliffs where he had picked up Tucky last night. The McCadys had been there before him, tramping over everything. They had found, of course, what he saw now, the place where a horse had been tied to the trees above the cliffs. It had trampled around in the needle mat considerably. When the rider had left, he had stayed in the timber.

The McCadys had wasted no time on him, and neither did Stong. He rode toward the cabin on Shavano Creek. When he was still some distance from the cabin, he knew the McCadys were there, for he heard their voices raised in argument.

Ruthven said: "That's the track of Stong's red roan right there on the ridge, and nobody can talk me out of it!"

The structure was settling into the earth, leaning toward

one side, but the heavy logs had been saddle-notched long ago by some forgotten prospector and so the walls would hold for another generation. The Sartrains had repaired the roof and door. They used the place on roundups.

Silent and hostile, the McCadys watched Stong ride up and dismount. Benoni was not there. The bruises on Ruthven's swarthy skin were hard to see. Roblado bore no mark at all, for Stong had hit him squarely on the point of the jaw. It seemed to Stong that Vir and Fitz John, Ruthven's oldest son, not quite as dark-skinned as the others, watched him with less hostility than the rest. But there was no welcome in any of them.

"You were close to here yesterday," Ruthven said. "What for?"

Ruthven did not have the full truth about his daughter, Stong was sure, for the man lacked old Limba's iron strength of will and could not have held himself at all if he had known. Stong said: "I scouted up this way when I saw some Four Box steers on Sartrain land." Tom Patterson had had hard words with Bedford Sartrain about straying cattle and the fact was known.

The McCadys looked at each other. Roblado showed his white teeth. "They stick hard to the same story."

Ruthven paced around the grassy place. He kicked the cabin door open and let it stand that way. Stong stared at the straw-filled mattresses rolled and hanging by wires from the ridge log to keep rats from ruining them. He remembered Tucky and Goliad standing with their arms around each other. He had said that her personal business was not his, and he had thought he meant it.

"She came at least this far," Ruthven said. He cursed the rain. "Another horse was here, too, sometime yesterday, one besides yours, Stong."

"It's Sartrain range," Stong reminded him. "One of their trails passes here. What did you find on the cliffs?"

No one answered.

Roblado said: "It's damned funny, she rides this way two or three times in the last week. Each time Stong rides out from town a little later. . . ."

"You're a fool, Roblado," his father said. "Give her more credit than that." He looked at Stong and laughed harshly.

The McCadys got on their horses and splashed through the creek in the direction of Mormon Forge. Stong pulled the door shut. When he rode away, he had to remind himself forcibly that his only interest in the affair was that of law. He went east, getting behind the line of rocks at the edge of the plain, taking the easy way to the top of the cliffs, and then he began to track the horse that had been tied in the timber.

The rider had gone east, away from the Cross, holding to the edge of the trees until he reached a small glade that led up the hill. Finding out that much took Stong three hours. A bit of disturbed humus here, part of a hoof print there. The glade was heavily grassed. It took Stong another two hours to cover a quarter of a mile. The trail was then leading dead south. When he broke over the hill and into open country running up to the skirts of Las Platas, he encountered a stretch of rocky ground and lost the tracks entirely until late in the afternoon.

There had never been a clear, complete hoof mark all the way, but he picked up enough to make a guess at the kind of horse it was—well under 1,000 pounds, a short-gaited animal, unshod. Sartrain buckskins were all long-striding, clean-limned horses, with never a badly worn shoe, let alone no shoes at all.

When Stong followed the tracks from the edge of the rocky ground down into a small valley, they were headed straight toward the Cross. He lost them again near a small stream where cattle had watered that morning.

For a while he stood beside Owlhorns, smoking his pipe, reluctant to make the next move. He had to make it or get out of the game. He mounted and went toward the Sartrain stronghold.

IV

Grim urgency was riding Limba McCady when he sat down in a chair beside Tucky's bed. Harlan eyed him quietly.

"She's in no condition to talk, Limba."

"She talked to Stong."

"He asked her one question and left."

Tucky watched her grandfather uneasily. "It's all right, Doctor. I feel fine."

"Like hell you do," Harlan said. "Limba, can't you wait . . . ?"

"No. Will you leave us alone for a few minutes?"

Harlan tried to transmit courage to the woman with his glance, and then he went out and closed the door.

For several moments Limba sat in silence. Tucky met his look steadily. There was the same stubbornness in both of them, and they both recognized the fact.

"Who was it?" Limba asked at last.

She would not hedge or quibble with old Limba. They respected each other too much for petty evasions. She guessed at once the background that made his question so blunt and sure; the thought made her furious, and then an instant later it gave her a trapped and helpless feeling. It had been that way when Wind Eater stumbled and she went over his neck to lie huddled against a rock, afraid to move, afraid to peer around the rock to see who stood upon the cliff. It had been a minute or two later before she even realized that she had been shot. The quiet waiting had been merciless. It was like that now, with Limba staring at her. She had to move, to make denial, anything but meet his look. Just as she had known instantly that she could expect no quarter from the cliff, she knew that Limba would have the truth from her before he left the room.

"Who was it, Tucky?"

The climactic moments of her afternoon with Goliad ran through her mind. She loved him with a fierceness that was full of pride and worth any kind of sacrifice. To speak his name to Limba now would be like sighting a rifle on his heart. She rolled her head from side to side in a slow negative movement.

"Who was it?" Limba asked. There was terrible patience in his voice.

She had met Goliad the first time alone one day by accident when she was riding west of the Patterson place. She rode from the aspens into a meadow where a beaver dam was shining. The creamy buckskin threw its head around and snorted. Goliad was lying on his stomach, drinking. He leaped up suddenly, his face adrip with water, reaching toward his pistol. And then he smiled. The smile ran through her yet. His tawny hair looked golden in the sunlight. His nose was straight, his eyes eager and alive. There was none of the damned sneering arrogance of the Saltrains in him. She had seen him for years, of course, in church, passing on the street, racing into Mormon Forge with his brothers, but this was the first time she had really seen him.

He had stood there smiling at her. "Care for a drink of water, Miss McCady? There's enough for two."

She remembered that she had smiled back at him. What did two young people care about the ancient quarrels of their grandfathers, what meant names here in the golden sunshine of a world that was brand new to them?

"Who was it?" Limba asked.

She closed her eyes and shook her head, and escaped the old man for another minute.

Goliad had not come close to her when she got down. They had stood there, looking at the clean sweep of valley. They talked of trout fishing, of cattle, of a troupe of actors that had played the opera house in Mormon Forge. They laughed at the way Preacher Pesman pumped his knees up and down while singing hymns.

Limba's chair scraped as he twisted to get his pipe and pouch from the pocket of his buckskin jacket. He filled the pipe. The match made a rasping sound that jarred on Tucky's nerves. Just the edge of smoke drifted over to Tucky before it was swept toward the open windows. She waited for his question, but he did not speak.

It could not have been more than ten minutes she stood with Goliad that first day. But it was the beginning. He had mentioned two or three times a beaver dam on the Big Otero, east of the Stong ranch, where he sometimes fished all day.

"Who was it, Tucky?"

"I won't tell you!" There was refuge in thoughts of Goliad, because there was no mercy in Limba. The country had laughed, saying that the first McCady girl in three generations could twist old Limba around her thumb, and Tucky had thought so, too. The laughter was all wrong. Any steeldust bred at the M, except that devil Shiloh, anything she wanted that money would get, tantrums that would have brought blisters to her brothers if they had tried them—yes, she had wound her father and Limba around her finger to that extent but now she was against a rock column.

"Does Papa know?" she asked.

"No," Limba said. "It's enough that I know. Tell me the truth."

"I won't!" She could not tell. She had seen Kinkaid Sartrain spin around and fall to his knees that day when Roblado McCady shot him. If she told, Goliad would spin and fall, but he would not get up.

There had been some thought of that the second time she and Goliad met. Now she knew that fear had dogged their minds all the time, but it could not spoil their love. Matthew Stong might have seen them one day, but he had never spoken about it. It was after that they began to meet on Sartrain land. It was safer there, Goliad said.

"Ruthven and I are to blame in part," Limba said. "We let you run wild." He puffed his pipe. "But the only harm that could have come to you was through yourself. Who was it, Tucky?"

"Stop asking that!" She rolled over and looked at Limba. His face was like granite. She drank from the glass on the stand by the bed. The water took the hotness from her throat, and then her greedy, burning tissues soaked up the coolness and she was as feverish as ever. "I'm hurt, Gramps. I don't want to talk about it now."

Limba did not stir.

She thought of telling him that she needed Mrs. Harlan, but that would merely postpone the problem. He would come back; he would sit here forever.

Goliad smiling down at her. Goliad holding her. She remembered the noisy sounds of Shavano Creek growing louder and louder, thundering, and then the world had trembled. Goliad.

"Tell me, Tucky."

Limba's insistence bound her in a grip of iron. He was

unyielding Scottish granite. He was a patient monster who knew nothing of the passions of youth and love. *Who was it, Tucky? Tell me, Tucky. Who was it? The truth, the truth, the truth!* The words beat with the fever in her. *Goliad, Goliad, Goliad.* . . . She was afraid she would cry out the name.

"Go away, Gramps. Please go away!" She closed her eyes. If she were not so hot and confused, she could face him squarely. She was frightened. The rifle on the cliff spat at her. She had been trying to creep up the break in the cliff, to escape into the timber. Out of the night, stealing up from sensory channels that ran to unknown depths, there came the terrible knowledge that the man had heard her and was waiting for her. She made a noise. The rifle flashed. She fell on the talus slope when she tried to run. The rain pelted her. An angry voice from the friendly side of the rocks cried a challenge.

"Tell me who it was," Limba said quietly.

Even now Limba's voice seemed to come from far away. But it had not been Limba there in the rain, pushing back the terror of the night. It was Pat Stong, ugly Pat Stong, and she had been disappointed. She remembered that he had carried her gently. She remembered, too, when she had been under the rock, that the light of a match on his face had shown her something in his eyes that made her forget for a time the rest of his features.

"Who was it?" Limba asked.

His voice was like a soft hammer. It fell upon a drum in solemn strokes and sent echoes trailing away into hollowness. *Goliad, Goliad, Goliad Sartrain.* . . . She lay on hot sheets.

Pat Stong had stood by the fire, with his wet pants twisted against the muscles of his legs, his broad face grim and solid. She had felt the force of him when he spoke quietly and made Limba stop and back away. He was not afraid of Limba or of all the McCadys.

"Was it Fred Patterson, Tucky?"

Fred Patterson! Old Tom Patterson's boy. Tucky wanted to laugh. Fred Patterson had a long neck. His Adam's apple jerked and he grew red clear to his eyes whenever Tucky spoke to him. "No!" she cried. She had a bad vision of a harmless boy trapped in a circle of dark-faced McCadys. "No," she said. "Not Fred."

"I'll not speak any more names. Tell me who it was."

She twisted on the bed to look at Limba again. His short, iron-gray hair looked light against the hard brown of his face. She should have known, she told herself; she had seen him lay his will on sons and grandsons, and they had never got around him. She could not get around him, either. So now, desperate and trapped, she hated Limba. He was beating her down with the same question over and over, and in the end, if she did not get rid of him, he would have the truth about Goliad.

"Who was the man?"

She covered her eyes with the backs of her hands. "Pat Stong."

She could hear Limba's slow breathing. His pipe had gone out. He burbled tar in it, just once, and that was like an exclamation of surprise. "Stong?" he said.

"Yes!" She threw the answer desperately, thinking of nothing but Goliad's safety, remembering only that she loved him. The rest of the world could go to hell.

Limba McCady sat still for one long minute. He rose and went out, leaving the door open. Tucky let her hands slide to her sides. Her arm was a fury of pain clear to her elbow. She stared at the ceiling and it was a blur. "Goliad," she murmured, and then she was clutched by the fear that she had cried the name aloud.

Amy Harlan came into the room. She felt Tucky's forehead and her eyes narrowed. She poured a glass of water. She felt the terrible burning heat of the wounded woman's back when she raised her to drink. The glass clinked against Tucky's teeth. She swallowed in small gulps while the bright points of fever in her eyes looked at Mrs. Harlan.

"I told him, Amy. I told him it was Pat Stong."

The glass jerked in Mrs. Harlan's hand, but a fraction of a second later it was steady. "You fooled him, didn't you?" she asked in a pleasant, non-committal voice.

Tucky nodded. She pushed the glass away and fell back on the pillow, breathing rapidly.

Harlan was in the yard, looking at Limba McCady striding down the street. "He went by me like a man on a mission to African heathens. Did he upset Tucky?"

"She's out of her head with fever. He certainly didn't help her any."

Harlan started inside quickly.

"She told her grandfather it was Stong."

He turned around in the middle of a stride. "The son-of-a-gun! He fooled me completely."

"You idiot! He told the truth!"

Harlan's expression was ludicrous. "I'm glad you women are so damned sure of things." He looked after Limba, already nearing the Boston. "Pat left town a while ago. I'll have to find him and. . . ."

"No." Mrs. Harlan pointed toward the house.

"All right, all right, don't make a speech about my duty as a doctor. Sometimes I wish I were a cowboy. Get your horse, Amy. I saw Stong go south. Ride after. . . ."

"Forewarned or not, he'll have to face Limba anyway.

I'm not going on a wild-goose chase across the country. I'll go talk to Limba instead."

Harlan nodded. "But from the looks of his face when he sailed past me. . . ."

"All I can do is try."

"You'd better take a club with you. He's black Scot and he thinks the honor of the clan has been outraged. The whole country will be involved before this winds up, and all because a man and a woman chose to go to the woods for a little innocent pleasure. Look what could happen to the world if. . . ."

"Munro, her fever is frightful."

"I'm going. All right, it wasn't innocent pleasure, then . . . just pleasure." Harlan went up the three steps to the summer kitchen in one bound. "Some lucky clod-hopper," he murmured.

He looked like a red-headed imp as he went to see his patient. A few moments later he was serious as any gray-bearded doctor in the world, and considerably better than the average.

"You're in a hell of a shape, Tucky."

She smiled at him vaguely and said: "Goliad. . . ."

Limba McCady went up the street as if he were striding across a prairie where no animal life was worthy of notice. For one of the few times in his life he had made a vast mistake in believing a man's word on a vital matter.

Houston Doty came out of the Boston with a secret that lay a shine of triumph all over his bloated face. "What's the big hurry there, Limba? Did you . . . ?" The smile faded into Doty's blue-veined features as Limba steamed past without a glance. Doty's eyes went sidewise to see if anyone had seen the rebuff. Doty quivered with indignation that was not honest enough to be anger. He pushed his lips together. They trembled. He headed for the Five Nations to restore the pleasant feeling with which he had faced the day.

Coming lazily across the street from the Shavano House, Willy Golden, his white cuffs shining an inch below the sleeves of his gray broadcloth coat, took in the stony set of Limba's face and his surging walk. The old warrior was ready to behead all Sartrains this morning. Willy yawned. He glanced down the street. Amy Harlan was not puttering in her yard as usual. It was said that Kentucky McCady had a bad chest wound. A bitterness stirred in Golden. He was an impersonal admirer of beauty wherever he saw it, and Kentucky was a beautiful woman. He watched Limba approach Brewslow's store. Todd was on the walk, directing two clerks unloading a freight wagon.

Brewslow stepped away from the wagon. "Good morning, Limba. I wonder if you could spare . . . ?"

Limba passed him like a steer in the road. The look of shock and offended vanity was still on Brewslow's face when he turned around. He brushed his sleeve protectors. "Come on, come on!" he said loudly. "Let's not wait until dark to unload that wagon."

Smiling to himself, Willy Golden went into the Five Nations saloon. Bull-shouldered Sioux Peters was behind the bar during the slack morning period.

Houston Doty, Andy Kopperwit, and two drifting cowboys were the only customers at the moment. Golden went around the bar and poured himself a glass of wine. One glass before each meal, one after his afternoon nap.

Doty resumed a conversation that had been going on before Golden came in. "Stong's grabbed himself a grizzly bear. I always said. . . ."

"He might throw it," Kopperwit said. He was at the free lunch, with a mug of beer, helping himself to a pork sandwich. The two cowboys were eyeing the free lunch, too, but there was only one nickel beer on the bar before them—and Sioux Peters was eyeing them.

"We might bury Stong, too," Doty said. "He never did know how to run this town. When he took office, I gave him good advice, but would he listen?"

There was a bottle before Doty. His credit had been worthless for a long time. Now there was a gleam in his eye. Peters was on the city council and Todd Brewslow had come in and called him out last night after the fight. Willy Golden put small facts together. He thought he knew the answer. It amused him.

Golden sipped his wine and watched the cowboys. They looked like brothers, youngsters cut loose from home not long before. Last night they had tried to make something of three silver dollars in the monte game. Now they were down to a single five-cent beer.

"Help yourself to the lunch, boys," Golden said. "If you want to, that is. Give them some beer, Sioux. You trying to take your money to hell with you?"

The cowboys looked at Peters. He gave them a second glass of beer and filled the one that was almost empty. He did not like it, but, if he made an objection, Golden would toss ten dollars on the bar and walk away smiling. The cowboys eased toward the lunch. They said, almost together: "Thanks."

Doty watched them. "Too many bums, these days."

The youngsters turned red. Sioux shook his head.

Without heat, Golden thought: *The sodden bastard.* He said casually: "What time is it, Doty?"

A bluish tinge came up in Doty's face. He glared at

Golden but the gambler had turned away to watch Mrs. Harlan hurrying up the street. The ex-sheriff had another drink. "I need a shave and haircut, Andy. You eating here all day?"

"Go up to the shop if you're in a hurry. It'll take ten minutes to soak that beard of yours anyway."

Doty went out. As he passed Golden, he hesitated, wanting to say something hard and cutting. The gambler's mocking dark eyes and gentle smile warned him off. No man ever got the best of words with Willy Golden.

It must be hell, Golden thought, to live without a shred of moral courage. A man could be a physical coward and only a greater coward would be fool enough to laugh at him. He said to the cowboys: "A few days ago Matt Stong was looking for three hands to build fence."

"Stong? Any relation to your sheriff?"

"Father," Kopperwit said.

One of the cowboys asked: "Where's his place?"

Golden told them. He watched their expressions. He decided that they would ride to Three Bars and see about the job. "Hear anything about a Kentucky McCady this morning, Sioux?"

Sioux shook his head. "I guess she's alive. I heard three of the young ones were bad off with summer complaint and Ruthven's wife couldn't get to town right away."

Andy Kopperwit spoke with his mouth full. "Good pork, Sioux. Brewslow's?"

"Butchered fresh," Sioux answered.

Willy Golden put his wine glass down. "Last month," he said.

Houston Doty went up the street with his ruffled feelings mellowing under the effects of the five drinks he had taken. As soon as he got cleaned up in the barbershop, he would go down and talk Lulu into giving him his watch back. He'd taken enough insults over that watch from tinhorns like Willy Golden. Things were going to be much better now. He saw Limba McCady talking to Busby Youngblood near the watering trough in front of the stable. Mrs. Harlan was going toward them. Doty tried the front door of the barber-shop. It was locked. He went around to the back and entered through Kopperwit's living quarters.

He was stretched out in the chair with a hot towel on his face when someone entered Stong's room on the other side of the partition.

Mrs. Harlan said: "She didn't know what she was saying, Limba." Chairs were scraped and bumped in the room. "She was out of her head with fever. I know Pat Stong too well to accept that."

There was a long silence.

"Don't you understand, Limba?"

"I understand what she told me."

"No, no! She said that just to get rid of you."

"She doesn't lie," Limba said harshly.

"And neither does Pat. You drove her almost to the point of collapse, Limba. It's doubtful that she'll even remember what she said."

"I will, Missus Harlan."

"Did you ask Stong directly last night?"

"Yes."

"You believed him then, didn't you?"

"A man can lie," Limba said. "He did."

"And a woman can lie, deliberately, or when she's badgered to the point of collapse. I would do it, and any woman would do it to protect the man she loves. That's what happened."

"Tucky doesn't lie."

"It was not said as a lie. It was done in desperation. Wait, Limba. Wait until she has recovered, and then talk to her again."

"I respect you, Missus Harlan, but you and your husband are great friends of Pat Stong. She named him, so he is the man."

There was a long silence.

"Can you sit there like that, just waiting to kill him when you're not even sure of the truth?" Mrs. Harlan's voice had lost some of its calmness.

"Yes. I can wait forever."

"Then the whole country will know!"

"Let it be so."

"Don't you love Tucky? Can't you understand the emotions of your own granddaughter? Such a thing could happen to any woman." Mrs. Harlan talked on. Her words broke against a stubborn silence. "Believe me, you're wrong. You'll do something you'll regret all your life."

"I have done that before, but I'm not wrong this time."

"I intend to warn Pat."

"He won't run. Do as you please, Missus Harlan."

A few moments later Doty heard the woman leave. A little later Limba went out. When he did not pass in front of the barbershop, Doty went to the window and saw him going toward Youngblood's livery. Doty went back to the chair and a moment later Kopperwit unlocked the front door.

With his curling gray locks combed damply, his face still tingling pleasantly from bay rum, Doty hurried down to Lulu Courtney's place on the west side near Arbor's feed and grain store. Two bloodhounds bumped against his legs, crowding to the door when he knocked.

Lulu's place was a two-story, sprawling building with a small bar in the front room, and a dance hall on the second floor. The usual routine was reversed here. Customers went up to dance first, or at least to look, and then came down with partners.

The door opened and a short, heavily built woman in a kimono glared at him. "You old goat, what are you doing here at this time of day?"

Doty pushed his way inside and headed for the bar.

"Just a minute there!" The hounds were inside and racing toward the kitchen. Lulu Courtney cursed. Her eyes were snapping black, her braided hair the same color. She had a pudgy nose and a square jaw. "Damn you, Doty! You already owe me enough. . . ."

"Take it easy, Lulu. That's what I came to see you about. You'll be paid and things will be back to normal right away."

The woman hauled her pink kimono closer around her. She went over to the bar and observed that Doty was drinking the best whiskey in the house.

"What is it?" she demanded.

"Don't rush me." Doty was more at home here than anywhere else in town. He put his fawn hat on the bar and smoothed his hair. "First, I want my watch back."

"Oh, hell!"

"I've got two pieces of interesting news. Get me my watch, Lulu."

"Let's hear the news first." Lulu yawned.

"Tucky McCady has been running to the woods with Stong." Doty went into details he did not know.

"That doesn't hurt my trade one bit. I'm more interested in who shot her." Lulu took the bottle of whiskey and put it away. "What do you expect me to do . . . drop

71

my jaw on my chest and faint?"

In the kitchen, Oklahoma Sal, née Annie Lowderbaum, paused in the act of feeding the hounds that had wakened her. So Tucky McCady was only a fancy slut after all, and Oklahoma Sal reflected on certain estimates she had made of the sheriff. Some of those ugly ones. . . . She left the hounds to eat whatever they could find and hurried to Mary Randolph's room.

There were ten girls in Lulu's place, and soon they all had something to talk about.

In the ante room, Lulu said: "That makes sense. That's better. I'll get your watch." Houston Doty was marshal of Mormon Forge now. The city fathers had got it up in their necks, thinking that Stong was bringing them trouble. Sioux Peters undoubtedly had not voted with the rest of the council, but that was of no moment.

Lulu locked up the choice whiskey and set before the new marshal a bottle that was half full of drinks that had been poured back from unfinished glasses. Pat Stong had been damned unpleasant about customers who came to this place and complained afterward of shortages of money that could not be accounted for as expenses of the evening. Doty always understood how $100 could be spent on carnal pleasure, especially by a man who had been too drunk to remember all details.

Lulu went to the safe in her room to get Marshal Houston Doty's watch.

In the barroom of Lulu's place, the marshal recalled how Limba McCady had gone up the street. There was going to be hell to pay when Stong returned to town. Stong was as good as buried. He might get the best of four McCadys with his fists, but he couldn't absorb bullets any better than the puniest man in town.

Doty decided to stay right where he was. Things would be normal afterward. Why, hell, they'd even appoint him sheriff then, and he could still get extra money from the city for his work as marshal. There was just one flaw in the whole thing. Houston Doty was an intelligent man, and he was cursed with enough conscience to know what else he was. He took another drink.

V

From a ridge above West Shavano Creek, Pat Stong looked down on the great meadows east of Cross. Limba McCady and Bedford Sartrain had originally settled in the valley, close together. Then they had gone back East for their families. In the summer of 1867 they had had their tremendous quarrel. They had divided 400 square miles of country they did not own, Bedford Sartrain coming here, with his back against Las Platas.

The original cabin under the lee of a long, bare hill was now lost among clusters of buildings that ran for three-quarters of a mile. Unlike the McCadys, whose family groups had jumped all over the Antelope Hills like Burma grass, the Sartrains were still close together. The McCadys sometimes could not get along with each other. The Sartrains could not get along with anyone but themselves. If one of them began to play a banjo in the middle of the night, the whole tribe was likely to wind up dancing, singing, and drinking until daylight. Then they would go about their work as if they had slept since sundown the night before.

Pat Stong went through the gate, and, when he swung his horse around and shut the gate without dismounting, he considered for a moment the solid, final sound the bar made when it chunked into the mortise in the post. When he was within a quarter of a mile of the first house, a pack of dogs of all sizes and descriptions came boiling toward him. In the excitement a loping greyhound stuck his long snout between the hind legs of another dog and flipped him end over end and then tied into him as if the underdog were a coyote. A half-breed bulldog jumped the greyhound. A shepherd of sorts leaped in. There was a first-class dogfight in no time.

Two young Sartrains were digging out a head-gate box on the creek nearby. They came running with their shovels, and then they leaned upon the shovels and watched the fight happily. They were two of Jefferson Sartrain's kids, Stong thought. Jeff was Bedford's third or fourth son, somewhere in there. Individual dogs spun away from the fight when the going became too heavy. When it was all over, the greyhound had killed the bulldog.

One of the Sartrains said: "Whose bulldog was that, Tom?"

"It looks some like one of Uncle Kinkaid's. Maybe we'd better bury it." Tom glanced at Stong. "Howdy, Sheriff. You come along just about right for the dance." The Sartrains dragged the dog toward the creek and began to dig a hole.

Stong picked his way through the welter of buildings. Near one of the lesser cabins a slender, barelegged girl was gathering clothes from a line. Her hair was jet black. She wore a red calico dress with small yellow flowers as the figure background. She glanced casually at Stong, reached toward a snow-white petticoat on the line, and then swung back toward him.

Avlona Oleano. Her father, Jim Oleano, had broken horses for the Sartrains for years until one day two summers ago a powerful buckskin stallion had broken Oleano's neck.

She lived now with her mother and three brothers who were following their father's trade.

"Sheriff Pat!" Her smile was slow and warm, her teeth very white against her dusky skin.

Stong touched his hat. He stopped Owlhorns and slouched in the saddle, smiling. "You've grown up, Lona." Seventeen or eighteen now? It seemed but yesterday she had been a pug-nosed brat running after her tall brothers. She was pleased by his observation. "Your mother?"

"Good."

"The brothers?"

She pointed west. "On the Sandoval Grant they break horses, but only for one month." She hugged her arms to her, giving meaning to the gesture. "Tonight there is the barbeque and dancing, Sheriff Pat. Bedford will ask you to stay, yes?"

Stong grinned. "You're a flirt, Lona. But if I'm here tonight, you will dance with me, yes?"

"We will see."

Stong rode on.

Bare to the waist, old Bedford was supervising the final stages of barbequing a steer above a huge pit of charcoal near his house. Three cottonwoods stood at one edge of the open space with heavy tables built in a circle around them.

"Pat Stong, you old son-of-a-bitch!" Bedford yelled. He was a spare, tall man, with the spring-like strength and grace of a deer. His chest was brown from the sun, and this in a country where few men cared to expose more than their faces and hands. All the Sartrain features sprang from him. His high-bridged nose was thin, almost hooked. His tawny hair flowed long, covering the tops of his ears. His eyes were small, bright blue. "Man, you came on the right day! We're aiming to rassle and fight and drink and dance and eat all night. Take his horse, Jasper! Bring us a jug, Burley! Git a move on! It ain't every day we have the sheriff here. Watch that dripping grease, Brock, you hammerhead! Scorch that steer and I'll throw you in the pit!"

One of Bedford's grandsons trotted away with Owlhorns. Another brought a jug from the house. Bedford uncorked it, wiped his palm across the mouth, and passed it over to Stong. The Sartrains ran their own distillery.

Stong drank.

Bedford drank, and let out a mighty sigh. "First one in a month. I'm getting old and feeble. Come on, let's wash up before the shindig starts."

"Not your way." Stong grinned.

"Bring me a towel, one of you Sartrain whelps!" When no towel appeared out of the air, Bedford shook his head. "Seventeen or twenty grandsons around here and an old man can't get no help." He strode across the yard to where a rusty pipe spilled icy water from a spring under the hill. He grabbed a handful of soft soap from a wooden bucket and walked into the stream until water was bouncing from his chest.

There he soaped and grunted and sluiced vigorously until the ground ran gray. Stong marveled at the lean, sinewy strength of him. Bedford and Limba were about the same ages. When they were young, they must have been $700 worth of forked lightning with tails on them.

When Bedford stepped from under the water, a young Sartrain was waiting with a towel. The old man took it and tried to rub his skin off, and then he snapped his grandson in the rear with the towel and went toward the house. "Come on, come on, Stong! We'll sit a spell and you can tell me what's this I heard about old Limba's girl getting shot up and you killing a half dozen McCadys with your bare hands." Tucky was Ruthven's daughter, but Bedford usually referred to any McCady as belonging to Limba.

The hewn logs of Bedford's living room had been white-washed until they gleamed. Overhead was a wagon wheel suspended by chains, holding four gleaming brass Rivers lamps.

"Sprawl out somewhere," Bedford said, "until I change my pants."

His wife, the fourth one, came in with a cup of coffee that she placed on the broad arm of the hide-bottomed chair where Stong sat. She was a large, placid-looking woman who moved like a rock through the swirls of Sartrain energy that would have wrecked a nervous woman.

"How is she, Pat?" Mrs. Sartrain asked.

"Tucky? She's not feeling too chipper but she'll be all right."

Mrs. Sartrain shook her head. "A miserable thing. Who would have done that?"

"I don't know." Stong thought of the tracks that he had followed almost to the last ridge east of the big meadows.

"Some drifter?"

"No." Stong did not intend that his answer come out as flatly as the single word sounded.

A wary expression moved on Mrs. Sartrain's smooth features. "It wouldn't have been anyone from here. You didn't come here thinking . . . or did you?"

"Just to ask a question or two, Missus Sartrain."

She gave Stong a steady look that was at once full of warning and sympathy, and then she went unhurriedly toward a room where Bedford was yelling: "Callie! Callie! Where the hell are my new boots?"

"You probably took your bath in them."

A moment later Stong heard Bedford say: "By Ned! I did

just that! Where's the old pair, then?"

Stong knew no way to sidle up to the subject on his mind, yet he did not care to blurt out all he knew. When Bedford was again in the room, Stong answered his questions about the shooting.

"Wild young whelp of a girl! Old Limba let all his kids run loose like that."

It would not do to mention that one of Bedford's daughters and Vir McCady had run away together when they were eighteen years old. "Any drifters around here lately?"

Bedford shook his head.

"There were some tracks down there where she was shot. Not a big horse, say eight-fifty or thereabouts. It walked fat, or maybe it's a little old. No shoes."

"So?" Bedford had stiffened. "So?"

"That's my guess on the horse."

Bedford nodded. His eyes were cold. "Did the McCadys do any trailing?"

"Not that I know of. I don't think I left any clear tracks of that horse after I passed."

"Uhn-huh. Why was that?"

All the old man's toughness was plain to see now.

Stong spoke slowly. "The horse came this way, Bedford."

Outside, the noise of the Sartrains came clearly. Someone was tuning a guitar. Young voices were arguing about whose turn it was to carry benches to the tables under the trees.

"Let me get some light in here," Bedford said. He lit all four lamps overhead, and then he stood with his head cocked, looking at Stong. "What are you trying to say, boy?"

Telling the McCadys had been easier because anger had

cleared the way. "First . . . I'm the sheriff of the whole county, Bedford. The man who shot Tucky McCady is my meat. I have told Limba so. Second . . . if the man came from Cross and I find it out, I will take him back to town with me."

Bedford was grinning like a wolf. "You think he did?"

"I didn't say that. I said horse tracks came this way from the place where she was shot."

"You want me to think you're straining a gut to be fair? Is that it?"

"I am being fair. As sheriff I'll do what the law requires, McCadys, Sartrains, or farmers from the east end of the valley. Now, do you know of such a horse as I described?"

"Hell, no. We ride good horses up here, Stong, not potbellied circus ponies."

Bedford Sartrain's record was clear of lies and trickery. Yet, the horse had come this way. "Will you ask others here if they have seen such a horse?"

"Damn it, I said there was no such horse here!"

"Your word is good, but do you know every horse and dog on Sartrain land?"

Bedford balanced for a moment on the thin edge separating anger and amusement, and then he grinned. "You've grown to be like old Matthew, who took land from under the McCadys' pious noses and laughed at them. Yeah, I'll ask the boys. Now tell me how you broke Benoni's arm and smashed the other half dozen McCadys who jumped you in your office."

"There were only four. Whoever rode this way was not reliable with his news, Bedford. I didn't bust Benoni's arm. Vir did when he fell on it."

"Who hit Vir to make him fall?"

"I did."

Bedford roared. "You ugly, fighting bastard! I think I'll adopt you. Where's that jug at?"

The lanterns hung from tree limbs, from spars on poles rigged out from wagons. The musicians sat on a hayrack, assailed continually by other Sartrains scrambling up to demonstrate their musical superiority. Jefferson Sartrain called the dances. He was the only bearded one of the tribe, and his beard looked red in the firelight as he stamped his feet and clapped his hands. There were children everywhere, some of them holding their own dances, the younger ones darting, rumbling, yelling, and fighting near the edges of the hard-packed area.

Under the cottonwoods the tables were laden with food and jugs. There were wash boilers of coffee. The carvers at the pit sliced dripping steer meat for those who came and went and came again. "All we want to see of this steer is bones!" Haswell Sartrain bellowed. There were dogs everywhere around the edge of darkness, snapping, growling, and fighting as the young Sartrains fed them.

Old Bedford Sartrain did a jig, and then a buck-and-wing. He leaped three feet high and cracked his heels. Then, having proved that age meant nothing to him, he retired to the business of being a patriarch, which included proving that he could outdrink any man present.

Stong danced twice with Avlona Oleano. She made him aware of her rounded body. She made him dance a third time when he would have turned her over to Burley Sartrain. Then he caught her expression when she glanced at Goliad Sartrain, dancing with his mother.

There was willfulness and defiance on her face. It passed quickly, and she smiled at Stong. But he had seen and his thoughts began to drift relentlessly toward a dark premise.

He teased Avlona gently. "You like Goliad, Lona?"

"That one?" She laughed. "He has too many women in the town." The laughter came too quick, too high.

I must not be like the McCadys, Stong thought, *jumping at long conclusions.*

Goliad was as tall as his grandfather, and his clean, straight nose made him a better-looking man than Bedford ever had been. He escorted his mother to a bench beneath the trees. He brought her coffee, and stood beside her, smiling, careless. He watched Avlona and Stong casually. He was amused, and Avlona saw as much. Standing close to Stong, she gave him bright attention. A child, the daughter of a man the Sartrains had accepted as one of themselves. Of course she could look at Goliad and love him, and wish to make him jealous, and that might be all there was to it.

The musicians began a reel. Jefferson bellowed. Burley Sartrain, hesitant and shy, edged over toward Stong and Avlona. "Here, Burley," Stong said, "Lona belongs with someone limber and full of life like you. I'll go have a drink with Bedford before he gets it all."

Over his shoulder he saw Goliad watching. *Damn his eyes, I hope I don't find out what I'm thinking.*

He had a drink with Bedford and was surprised to find the old man drunker than he had thought. No man could beat the long years, no matter how much wire and rawhide there was in his system. A wrangle began at the hayrack, where five Sartrains who had been pushed off the rack were playing their own version of the reel while standing on the ground. Bedford went growling away to adjust matters.

Stong joined Mrs. Oleano in the outer rim of light on Bedford's porch. She was a tiny woman with a black shawl over her hair. She still thought in Spanish, which made her English slow. Stong used her own language.

"We old ones are good but to sit and watch. Your daughter, *Señora* Oleano, is with too much life for me."

Mrs. Oleano smiled faintly. "You are very young, Patrick."

He sat beside her. There was the tiniest odor of perfume about her and the sweet odor of clean clothes and skin and hair. She had been a flashing beauty, the old men of Baca Valley said, when she rode up from the south long ago with black-haired Jim Oleano.

She watched her daughter in the reel with Burley. "Such dancing is strange to me yet."

Stong said: "Avlona is a woman now."

"Yes."

He thought there was more than affirmation in the way Mrs. Oleano said the word. "Your boys will be back soon?"

"Soon."

"You wish it sooner?"

She looked at him without expression. "You ask strange questions, Patrick."

"Jim Oleano was a man tall with honor. My father says there was none greater. His sons are the same. Will there be trouble here, *Señora* Oleano, when they return?"

Her voice was almost a whisper. "You ask strange questions."

"Does Avlona ride the hills sometimes?"

"Now you are the sheriff, Patrick, and you are in a bad place for asking the questions of a sheriff."

"She does, then."

Mrs. Oleano was silent.

Goliad Sartrain came through the gloom beside the porch. "Tired already, Stong?" His voice was lazy. In many ways he was not a Sartrain at all, for they did not cover their insults with innuendo. "Did he ask you to dance with him, Aunt Felicia?"

"I no longer dance." The words were a trifle sharp.

"He should have asked, however, shouldn't you, Stong?"

"Who put the chip on your shoulder, Goliad?"

Goliad laughed. "You've pushed a couple of McCadys out of your way and now I think it's you who has a chip on his shoulder. Will you dance with me, Aunt Felicia?"

"I no longer dance," the woman said.

Goliad bowed and walked away, a tall man, swinging easily. He went to a group where Kinkaid and some of the wilder members of the tribe had given over all activity to drinking.

"Avlona likes this one?" Stong asked.

Mrs. Oleano rose. "It is cool now. I will go. Good night, Sheriff Patrick."

Young Brock got Avlona away from Burley for the next dance. Burley spotted Stong on the porch and came over to him. "You oughta dance with Haswell's wife, Pat. You're big enough to really swing her."

"Lona wore me out, Burley. I'm no dancer."

Burley sighed. "Gosh, ain't she pretty. She's just like a feather when you're dancing with her."

"Does she ride like her brothers?"

"That's a funny thing . . . she don't ride good at all. She's half afraid of a horse. Diego got her a little old pony last month, so broad you can play cards on its back, and that's the only horse she'll ride."

Stong said: "That chunky little gelding I saw down by the creek today?"

"Naw! You didn't see it. It's up in the hill pasture Goliad fixed for it, so it wouldn't get kicked to death."

Stong let the matter drop as if it were of no importance.

After a time Burley went back to the dance, but young Jasper Sartrain beat him to Avlona.

A fiddler fell off the hayrack, trying to play and dance at the same time. Someone whooped and shot out a lantern on one of the limbs. The dance went on. An hour later Bedford was in such condition that two of his sons laid him out on one of the tables. "I'm all right, you understand! I just need to scratch my legs a mite!" He fell asleep at once.

Stong was at a table eating ribs with Haswell when Kinkaid and Goliad and five other young bloods came over with a jug.

"You don't want that." Kinkaid threw the ribs toward the ever-alert dogs prowling the edge of the *fiesta* area. He plunked the jug in front of Stong. "You ain't been drinking up, Sheriff. We might get the idea you don't like our hospitality. Now that wouldn't be right, would it?"

He was drunk. He was mean, drunk or sober. Light from the glowing bed of charcoal in the pit fell on the scarred side of his face where a McCady bullet had struck.

Stong grinned. He drank. He shook the jug. "Just a little more than I want, Kinkaid, but I'll try to handle it." He drank again.

Jockney Sartrain roared and pounded him on the back. "Old Stong . . . hell, he'll run the still dry if he sets his mind to it!" He batted Kinkaid in the back of the head with the heel of his hand. "We won't get no rise out of Stong. Let's get after that friend of Jeff's. He looks like a preacher."

"By God, you're ugly, Stong," Kinkaid said.

"So I've been told."

"Look who's talking!" Jockney yelled. He batted Kinkaid again. "Come on, come on, leave him alone."

Kinkaid went away reluctantly. Goliad smiled to himself. They would be back, Stong knew. He said to Haswell:

"Where'd the Oleano boys pick up the little horse they gave to their sister?"

"Look, Stong," Haswell said quietly, "old Bedford don't know everything that goes on here, and there's stuff we don't bother to tell him. Don't be interested in that horse of Lona's at all."

"It happens that I am."

"Don't be. Have a good time, Stong. Forget the horse." Haswell got up and walked away.

His advice, Stong thought, was as good as any man could get, but Stong knew he could not take it. He got up and danced with Haswell's wife. She was a heavy woman and she let her weight ride in the swings just to see how strong he was. He was sweating when the dance was over.

He danced with Callie, Bedford's wife. When they were stepping around each other with their arms locked, she murmured: "You're asking too many questions, Pat, and Bedford isn't going to be on his feet to hold Kinkaid and a few others down."

"Is what I think about Goliad and Lona true?"

"What is it you think?"

"That it's best for old friendships that Jim Oleano is gone."

"Whatever you think is a matter for the Sartrains only."

It was an around-the-bush admission. The cross-currents of something that had started here had touched Kentucky McCady violently and was brewing hell among all the McCadys. It was Stong's business.

He was in the next set with Avlona and once again Goliad, who had danced little this night, was watching, with Kinkaid and others beside him.

"You did a very bad thing, Lona. Your mother is worried. Your brothers. . . ."

"My brothers! Are they monks? I have heard them talking of the things they do when they go away from home."

"You are a woman, Lona. You cannot do as they do."

She mocked his solemnity. "Are you the priest, Sheriff Pat? Shall I confess to you?"

The musicians twanged their instruments. The violins wailed and someone was too drunk to know what he was trying to play. At the charcoal pit Jefferson Sartrain danced alone in a tall white cook's hat, brandishing a two-foot carving knife. "Nothing but bones!" he whooped.

"You tried to kill her, Lona," Stong said. "Do you want to see the McCadys and the Sartrains at each other's throats like the hundred dogs around this place?"

"We will not dance any more. Come." Avlona took Stong's arm and led him past Bedford's house to the darkness near a corral. "I tried to kill her, yes! I thought I had when she went from her horse. She is a wildcat. She had a pistol and she screamed for me to come close to her so she could shoot me. I walked on the cliff in the rain. She was trying to sneak up on me when you came. I am not sorry that I tried to kill her!"

"Not so loud." Now that Stong knew what he had come to find out, the problem was worse than ever. "Goliad?"

"Yes! He is mine, not hers!"

"Does Bedford know about you and Goliad?"

"Bedford! It is not his business. He is old now. We laugh at him. When Goliad and I are married, it will be some of his business, a little is all."

Stong looked into the dark above Avlona's head.

She laughed softly. "You will not do anything to me, will you? I am not like the bad women of the town. My father was Jim Oleano and soon I will be a Sartrain."

"You have stepped on your father's grave and you have brought trouble to your brothers and dishonor to your mother. You are a child, Avlona, a silly child."

"If you put me in jail, everyone would say why, and then it would be known about my Goliad and the red-haired bitch, and the McCadys would make a great quarrel."

It was so. It was a hell of a mess and Stong was trapped by it. He stared through the shifting shadows at the dancers.

Goliad spoke from the dark close by. "You want to see a horse, Stong? You asked Burley about a horse, I hear." A half dozen tall Sartrain figures crowded up out of the gloom. "You go back to the dance, Lona," Goliad said. "The sheriff wants to see a horse."

"No! No!" Avlona cried. "Patrick is all right. He will say nothing. He. . . ."

Someone jerked her away from Stong. Kinkaid said: "You sneaking bog-trotter, drinking our whiskey and trying to knife us in the back! You god-damn' lousy Irisher! You. . . ."

Stong's only clear and pleasant memory of the fight came when he estimated Kinkaid's position exactly and hit him in the mouth as hard as 200 pounds of weight could deliver. He knew by the cracking sound that he had given Kinkaid something to match his cheek bone.

He tried to get his back against the corral. He never made it. They came into him from all sides and against his legs. He knew that he got two of them fairly, one with the heel of his hand and another with his elbow, and he was sure that he dented one or two more. But they took him down like greyhounds on a wolf.

The music went on. The dancers clapped and whooped. Stong surged to his feet once, like a buck with dogs hanging to him. He got someone by the neck and tried to swing the man but there was no room. A hard forearm came across his neck from behind. Goliad said: "You son-of-a-bitch, we'll kill you!"

Stong tried to crack the back of his head into Goliad's face but the man was pressed in too hard. Fingers clawed at Stong's eyes. He tore the hand from his face and tried to break the wrist. Someone kneed him in the groin. Fists cracked into his chest. Off to the side, two Sartrains were hammering each other by mistake. When they found that out, they came crashing into Stong, doubly enraged.

"Kill him!" Goliad said.

They very nearly did. They ground him down and were trying to stamp and kick the life from him when Avlona came back with Jefferson and Haswell and two more of Bedford's sons. The last Stong thought before a boot against his temple laid him out was that he had not laid a hand on Goliad. If he could have had one fair swing at Goliad. . . .

He woke up in a bed somewhere. Callie Sartrain was looking down at him, and over her shoulder, Bedford, bleary-eyed and weaving. "He's all right. Where's my bed at, Callie? I'm a mite tuckered."

"You're two jugs past drunk," his wife said. "Find your bed wherever you can."

Stong knew that someone washed his face and gave him gentle treatment. Someone asked him a question in Spanish and he answered, and then, partly from the beating and partly from the whiskey in him, he went out again.

He woke up with a murderous light in his eyes. After a time he discovered it was sunlight coming through the window. He was so bruised and sore he doubted that he could move.

Soft Spanish came at him. The slight movement to turn his head so he could look across his shoulder at Mrs. Oleano made him think his neck was broken.

"Bueno," he said, answering the question. His tongue was swollen. There were lumps inside his cheeks. He moved his arms slowly under the covers, feeling where the pain was worst. He realized he was naked. He tried to swallow down the sudden panic the thought gave him. His effort died against a great bruised area in his throat. By lying utterly still, he achieved a sense of soundness. The least movement made him think he was coming apart.

"Yes, you are very good," Mrs. Oleano said. "Kinkaid is very good, too. There are no teeth in front. And one has many broken . . ."—she tapped her ribs—"here. Another. . . ." She put her finger against her tiny nose and pushed it flat. She shook her head.

"Goliad?"

Mrs. Oleano's eyes darkened. "That one is all right."

Stong licked his puffy lips. "You know . . . about Avlona?"

"I am a mother, Patrick. I have known from the first." She hesitated. "What will you do?"

"Nothing." He had blotted out the tracks of Lona's horse. The McCadys, having had a cooling-off period, would not go wild now without some evidence. Limba's main concern had shifted toward the man Tucky had met at the cabin. Stong now must extend the protection of his silence to two women. The straight, hard course of law, as he had stated it, had run into difficulties. The worst of things: the more he discovered, the less his accomplishment.

"Does Bedford know of Goliad and Avlona?" he asked.

"I think not. But others here know, and my boys will find out." Mrs. Oleano leaned forward. Her eyes flashed. In quick, spitting Spanish she told him what she thought of Goliad Sartrain. Some of the words were pure Castilian. Stong had to guess at their meaning but he caught enough to understand plenty.

"Put him in jail, Patrick. One time he will try to escape, at night perhaps." Mrs. Oleano shrugged with Spanish simplicity. "It is done. No Goliad." She watched his face. "You are not afraid, I know."

"Don't you want him to marry Avlona?"

"Marry? He would never, not even if Bedford said it must be done. I would not have him for my son. Put him in your jail, Patrick. You will say he tried to escape. . . ."

Stong tried to shake his head. It almost fell off and pain sprayed into his neck and skull. "I can't. . . ."

Bedford was stamping toward the door. He was singing. He came into the room, rubbing his bare chest with a towel. "Get in there under the pipe, Stong! It'll clear your head up and do you good."

Stong groaned. "Oh, Jesus!"

"What started it last night?"

Mrs. Oleano said quickly: "He danced too much with Avlona."

"Those jealous-hearted whelps! They done that to another fellow once." Bedford threw the towel into a corner. "I'll tell you, Felicia, we've got to get that girl married off one of these fine days. Who does she like around the place, anyway? Burley? Jasper?"

Mrs. Oleano's expression had faded inward. *"No lo sé."*

"Speak American," Bedford muttered. "My head is sort of thick this morning. Now, let me see. . . ."

It was true, Stong realized. Bedford did not know all that

was going on. He was old. Cross was a tremendous place, a small community in itself, and, as Haswell had said, there were many things that no one bothered to carry to Bedford. In the old days, when he brought his family here, he had made all major decisions and his word was law. The energy and fire were still in him. He could make individuals jump, but the solid, sprawling weight of growth and change was against him.

Bedford grinned. "If nature hadn't already beaten them to it, I'd say the boys wrecked your face." He slapped his chest. "Damned whelps! If it had been a McCady, there would have been some sense to it. Well, get up, get up! It's way past time for breakfast."

When Stong rode away, Avlona smiled at him and waved. He shook his head dolefully, remembering good old days when he had thought a free-for-all fight in the streets of Mormon Forge or a ruckus at Lulu's place were important matters.

Before he had ridden two miles in the hot sun he was sick. His right knee had been wrenched. He had been kicked in the stomach. His groin was shooting pains. He got down and lay under a tree.

He was there when Pete Snell found him. Snell dismounted slowly. He pushed his lips out from his toothless mouth. He picked up a piece of flint, examined it carefully, dropped it. "Youngblood sent me."

Stong sat up. He rubbed the back of his neck. "What for?"

"I see the McCadys a few miles back." Snell pulled a leaf from an aspen and put it between his lips. "Spied on them a little. They said you tramped out some tracks."

"Where'd they go?"

Snell spat out the leaf. "Back to town."

Now they would say that Stong was trying to cover up something. He blinked wearily. That was exactly what he was doing. That Tucky, she sure had got things twisted into a fine tangle, and there she was, lying in a nice soft bed with a piddling bullet wound—well, piddling when Doc Harlan got through with it.

"Why'd Busby send you, Pete?"

"A story got around. I think Missus Harlan talked to him before that, though."

"What story?"

Snell pulled another leaf from the tree. "About you and Kentucky."

"What!"

"Yeah." Snell nodded. He sucked on the leaf.

"It's a lie, Pete."

Snell said nothing.

Stong rose. His injured knee almost gave way. He could not stand straight because of the agony in his stomach. He leaned against a tree.

"You all right, Pat?"

"I'll make it."

They got on their horses. Stong wished he were under the tree again. He doubted that he could ride to Mormon Forge.

"Busby said to tell you Limba's waiting to kill you," Snell said casually.

"Fine!" Stong was savage. "Fine! I hope he does a fast, clean job of it!"

Pete Snell said: "Don't think he won't try."

VI

Quiet and ugly, Matthew Stong sat at the domino table near the window of the Five Nations. From there he could see the road leading south toward the Cross, and he had a good view of the front of the Otero. Limba, Ruthven, and Roblado were in there, three generations of McCadys. The rest had gone back to their ranches in the Antelope Hills.

There were aspects about the situation that puzzled Matthew. He was not sure that Ruthven and his son knew the rumor about Pat and Tucky. Limba knew, there was no doubt. Matthew had not seen him so coldly furious since Texans had tried to graze a trail herd of 2,000 cattle on his land several years ago. The town was talking behind its hand, laughing obscenely, buzzing with anticipation. It still was possible that Ruthven and Roblado did not know about it. Roblado had spoken civilly enough to Matthew when they met in the Boston. He was courting Jennifer, Matthew's oldest girl. Fitz John was mooning around Marian, the next oldest, and all four of them were supposed to go to a dance at the Old Forge schoolhouse Saturday night. *That boy Pat and Tucky,* Matthew thought, *they've really made a mess of things.*

There were side issues that troubled him. He had seen Tucky and Goliad Sartrain together on the Big Otero several weeks ago. What was she, just a fly-up-the-crick, jumping from Goliad to Pat? Customarily the man was always wrong, and, if any of Matthew's girls had been involved in anything like this, he would have held to the normal view without hesitation. But now his son was involved and that was different. Matthew could justify the difference because Tucky had been with more than one man, which made her a strumpet. That had not been Matthew's view previously of Kentucky McCady but now he had to accept it. He had slid by the consideration that Pat could be innocent.

Now there were men—certainly one at least—waiting to kill Pat Stong. He was Matthew's son; therefore, Matthew's quarrel with Pat, the effect that violence would have on the young McCadys' courtship of the Stong girls, and all other minor points, must be ignored. For good reasons or otherwise, no one was going to shoot Pat Stong while his old man was around, and Matthew was going to be around. With a wicked expression on his coarse features, with his pistol freshly cleaned and loaded, Matthew waited.

Sioux Peters was nervous. He was no stranger to the raw forms of violence, but he was not a lover of them, either. He said: "Did you hire the two kids Golden sent out to your place, Matt?"

"Yeah."

"They all right?"

"Yeah."

Peters let it go at that. He cursed Brewslow's idea of making Doty marshal. What good was that? Where was Doty now, with trouble building four ways from the middle? Even as he stood behind his bar, growling to himself about the marshal, he saw Doty pass the door. Peters went out on the walk to watch him. Slowly, like a man keeping an eye peeled for the slightest rupture of peace and order, Doty went up to the end of the street. He crossed to Youngblood's livery and was there a few moments.

He came down the east side of the street, with his fawn hat tipped back on his gray curls. When he passed the Otero, he glanced inside, and then he looked quickly across the street at the Five Nations. The marshal held to his slow pace for another twenty feet, and then he began to walk faster until he cut toward the west side and disappeared.

Roblado came from the Otero. He angled across the street with his pistol moving gently with his walk. He nodded at Peters, went in, and stood uncertainly beside the table where Matthew sat. Peters went back to the bar.

" 'Morning, Mister Stong."

The kid was wary, stiff, and full of McCady pride, but he had made no bones about coming across the street. Matthew said: "Sit down, Roblado." In the back of the room the poker players craned to look.

"We might have rubbed Pat the wrong way last night," Roblado said.

It was quite an admission from a McCady. Roblado must be damned well in love with Jennifer and afraid of what trouble would do to their relationship. Matthew looked him over slowly. A clean-looking, square-jawed boy, with all the honesty of the McCadys—and all the hard-headedness, too.

"He had a point about keeping law, all right," Roblado said, "if it applies to the Sartrains, too."

"It will . . . if he makes it stick."

Roblado glanced at the poker players. He lowered his voice even more. "From where Tucky was shot, we trailed a horse, Mister Stong. It went south, and then it turned west and went toward the Cross."

"Yeah?"

"It seemed that Pat had trampled over those tracks a little more than he should have. He was ahead of us."

"I don't understand that," Matthew said.

"Neither does my father. He's boiling, but Limba doesn't seem too put out about it."

That was the worst news of all, confirming that Limba was interested in only one aspect of the affair. Matthew shook his head. "I don't understand about the tracks, Roblado. When Pat comes back. . . ."

They looked at each other bleakly, both thinking the same thing. "Even my father has tried to talk him out of it, Mister Stong. We don't know what's got into him."

Matthew spoke bluntly. "What's the situation between you and Jennifer?"

Roblado met his eyes squarely. "We love each other, Mister Stong. We want to get married this fall."

Matthew grunted. His wife had told him the same thing and now he had it from Roblado. "Go home. Get out of this whole thing."

Roblado shook his head. He was miserable. "I can't. There's still a chance we can do something with Limba."

There was no chance. Matthew Stong knew it. And when trouble started, Roblado would be bound to support Limba just as Matthew was bound to support his son.

"The next best advice I can give then is to stay out of the trouble."

Roblado rose. He stood, stiff-backed and straight. He had shaved that morning. Matthew saw the bruise on his jaw where Pat had hit him. "Limba is an old man, Mister Stong."

He was also the coldest pistol man Matthew had ever seen, not fast but deadly. Even Bedford Sartrain, the fastest man in the valley in his younger days, had never wanted a shoot-out with Limba McCady. Nor did Matthew Stong, who was probably more dangerous than either of them.

"Stay out of it," Matthew said, the yellow-flecked eyes in his ugly face looking up steadily at Roblado.

Roblado went out and walked across the street toward the Otero.

Busby Youngblood came in. He nodded at Matthew and gave him a brief glance from cold gray eyes as he walked on to the bar. He drank one small beer slowly, his back to the bar, his red face turned toward the poker table. Willy Golden, who knew that Youngblood seldom took any kind of drink in the middle of the day, made a bet with himself on Youngblood's next move.

It came. On his way out Youngblood stopped where Matthew sat. "Can I get that hay this week?"

Matthew nodded. "Send Snell out any time you want."

The poker players heard that much and then the conversation at the front table drifted to other matters, and later the words were only sounds.

"Nothing yet," Youngblood said. "Snell was to make an excuse and come in ahead of him after he gave him the message."

Matthew nodded. "He's still trying to read sign out there." It would not do to figure that Pat had fallen into trouble with the Sartrains; there was enough trouble waiting here. "I'll try to get in between them."

"Want help?"

"Can't afford it." Matthew grinned briefly.

It occurred to Youngblood that this waiting was roundabout. Nobody was going to get between Limba and his target without having to shoot. Matthew's mind was made up and Limba's mind was set, so why dilly-dally about the cause, or wait for Pat Stong? Settle the thing now and have it done. Youngblood rose. "I'll send Snell for the hay day after tomorrow." He went out.

Kentucky McCady, who had caused it all, lay in a restless, burning sleep in a cool room. Her mother sat beside her in a rocking chair, a tall, wind-tanned woman with black braids wrapped around her head. She was mending socks, rocking gently as she worked. Harlan had said the fever should begin to diminish this evening.

Suddenly Tucky said—"Goliad? Goliad?"—so naturally that for a moment her mother thought the fever must have broken, but when she put her fingers on her daughter's forehead, the terrible heat was still there. Tucky reached up and clasped the hand, and then she began to talk.

Long before her voice sank back into the red mists that surrounded her, Tucky had babbled on until her mother was pale and thoughtful. Shortly afterward Amy Harlan came in quietly. Mrs. McCady put her mending aside. "Will you stay a while, Amy? I have an errand." She spoke so calmly that Mrs. Harlan guessed nothing of her mind.

Harlan was sitting in the shade reading a book.

"How is she resting?" he asked.

Tucky's mother said: "She seems to be about the same." She started toward the gate, and then she hesitated. "Did you happen to see my husband ride out of town?"

"No."

"Then he'll be around the Otero."

Mrs. McCady was at the gate when Harlan said: "Wait a minute." He studied her face as he walked toward her. "Did Tucky say something in her fever?"

The woman did not answer but her suddenly wary expression told Harlan that he was right. "Come over here and sit down, Missus McCady."

"I must find my husband."

"No. That's the worst thing you could do. You've seen how Limba is acting, haven't you?" Harlan shook his head. "Come over here and sit down, Missus McCady."

He told her the whole story. "Aside from her condition, I don't know why she lied about Pat Stong."

"I can understand that," Mrs. McCady said softly. "If, as you say, Pat Stong is innocent, then it's more important than ever that I tell Ruthven. If he is waiting. . . ."

"He hasn't even heard the story. Limba hasn't told him, I'm sure."

Mrs. McCady nodded. "I saw Matthew Stong ride into town early this morning. There will be a murderous fight, Doctor Harlan. I'm going to tell my husband the truth."

"And then it will be the McCadys against the Sartrains, not three or four men involved but two whole. . . ."

"Would you sacrifice an innocent man to hide what will be known eventually anyway?"

"Pat Stong may not return before Tucky is rational." Harlan hoped so. He had talked to Youngblood that morning and he knew that Snell had gone to find Stong. "Then she can deny to Limba what she told him to protect Goliad. The very thing that Stong wants to stop is a full-scale war between the two families. Let's give him all the help we can."

"You'll get him killed instead, Doctor Harlan. I know Limba when his temper is up. No. Both Limba and Ruthven had better have the truth now."

"And how can you convince them that it is the truth? My wife already talked to Limba. He would not believe her. Force the truth on Limba and your husband, and there will be dead men in this valley now and dead men later on.

You'll be stirring up more hell than the whole affair is worth."

She was silent.

"Your daughter did something quite natural. It happens every day, Missus McCady. Why should the whole country be torn to pieces because of a natural act? There's a chance that things can be smoothed out some way. Let's take the chance. I'll go out right now and look for Pat and try to keep him away from town until Tucky is rational."

Mrs. McCady stood up. Her face was still pale. She walked back into the house.

In the Otero saloon, Ruthven and Roblado sat at a table watching Limba uneasily. He had placed a chair close to the window, sitting there with his feet on the sill. His face was stony. He had not talked to them all morning. They knew that Matthew Stong was waiting in the Five Nations, and that Pat might ride into town any minute. None of this was to the liking of Ruthven and Roblado. The sheriff's actions had been high-handed, and there was a possibility that he might have tramped over some horse tracks they had tried to follow, but still they had no urgent reason to kill him.

Ruthven said to his son: "You'd better go on home."

Roblado shook his head.

Ruthven got up and went over to his father. "Look, Limba, is there something about this we don't know?"

Limba did not look at him. "Go home, Ruthven. I was settling worse than this when you were a wet-eared pup."

Pale with anger, Ruthven went back and sat down again with his own son who would not obey him.

Munro Harlan rode by on a wiry grulla. He was wearing a big-brimmed hat, his bag was lashed under a slicker behind the saddle; he might be going somewhere to see a patient. Old Limba weighed the thought carefully.

Pete Snell built a fire in the stove of the cabin on Shavano Creek. He noticed that the ashes were almost up to the firebox. When he pulled the ash pan out, he found it rusted away six inches from the face, a scoop instead of a proper long pan. He found a broken-handled shovel and went to work.

"I'll go in after dark and get Doc Harlan," he said.

"I'll be all right tomorrow." Stong was lying in a bunk with his knees doubled back. There was sweat on his face.

Snell regarded him sourly. Stong had fallen to his hands and knees when he tried to dismount. He hadn't been able to straighten up and he had needed help to get into the bunk. Snell took the first shovel full of ashes out. The smoke was curling down from the rusty pipe. The air was heavy. It was going to rain like hell before long.

He was inside raiding the heavy chuck box for coffee when the shout came. Snell jerked around, reaching toward his gun as he went toward the door. He grunted.

Harlan came in. He sniffed. "Pete, you've got a rat smell in here. Where's . . . ?" He saw Stong then. "What're you doing in bed, Pat?"

"He got the hell tromped out of him," Snell said.

Ten minutes later Harlan agreed. "Your kidneys are probably traumatized, Pat. What did they hit you with in the groin . . . a fence pole? You're not going to be worth a nickel for a few days. Straighten your legs out." He watched Stong's face as Stong obeyed. "Vomit any?"

Stong shook his head. "How's Tucky?"

"Fine, fine." Harlan took a hypodermic syringe from his bag. "Have you a headache?"

"Yeah."

Harlan put the needle away. "After dark, Pete or me can ride into town and get some medicine."

"I don't like this hiding out," Stong said. "Limba will think. . . ."

"Let him think it." Harlan laughed. "Whether you want to or not, Stong, you can't even get out of that bunk, let alone ride to Mormon Forge to get shot."

Stong made slow, painful movements with his legs. He stared at the poles of the bunk above him and was silent. The rain swept in, striking the dirt roof softly. Snell hauled the door shut and built up the fire. The coffee pot began to thump. Harlan prowled around until he found an old magazine stuffed between the cracks as chinking.

Snell drank a cup of coffee. He unwired one of the mattresses hanging from the ridge log, threw it into the bunk above Stong, and climbed up, almost lost in the gloom. Harlan lit the lamp. It made a puddle of light around the table, leaving the corners of the room shadowy. He sat, drinking coffee and turning the leaves of the rat-chewed magazine.

In a half hour the rain was gone. Harlan looked at his watch. "Another hour and a half until dark."

There was no warning. The door was kicked open and Limba McCady ducked in with a pistol in his hand.

"You'd wreck a man's nervous system," Harlan said.

Limba's hard old eyes took in the room. His face gleamed wetly in the lamplight. "Get out of that bunk, Stong."

"He can't," Harlan said. "Why don't you shoot him right where he is?"

Stong got up on one elbow. "You're 'way off the track, Limba. You. . . ."

"Get up, Stong."

"He's been hurt," Harlan said.

"Get up!" Limba walked, stiff-legged, toward the bunk. He put his pistol away. "Get out of there, Stong."

"Don't be an idiot, Limba!" Harlan grabbed the old man by the arm. Limba tried to throw him off. Instead, Harlan jerked Limba off balance. "You listen to me."

Limba swung his shoulders hard then. Stronger than the average man, Harlan was jerked one way, and then the other. His grip slipped from the wet buckskin of Limba's coat and he staggered into the woodbox.

"I'll help you out of there." Limba reached for Stong.

Pete Snell leaned down from the upper bunk. He said: "McCady."

For an instant it seemed that Limba had not heard or was not going to stop if he had heard, and then he raised his head slowly, his hands still curled toward Stong. He looked almost at face level into Snell's pistol.

"Back away," Snell whispered. The words were like a cold hiss.

Limba backed up slowly until his legs were against the table. Even then it seemed that he might ignore the threat and lunge in at Stong.

"You're wrong," Snell said in the same hoarse whisper. "You're wrong, Limba."

"You certainly are," Harlan said.

Limba's brooding look took them in one by one, the man leaning on his elbow in the lower bunk, the solid, red-cheeked face behind the pistol, blunt-jawed Munro Harlan staring from the end of the room. No perceptible change touched Limba's features. His head swung like a grizzly's as he looked them all over, and then he turned and walked out.

Snell leaped out of the bunk. He slipped out the door.

Ten minutes later he returned, his pants legs wet from the soaked grass.

"He was alone," he said. "He left." His face was bitter.

"He knows he's wrong," Harlan said, "but he's not going to admit it until he finds out who. . . ."

"Don't tell me about it," Snell said, half angrily. "I didn't figure to get in this deep in the first place." He grabbed his hat from a peg. "If you want that medicine, I'll get it now."

Harlan wrote a note and gave it to him. Snell left without another word, an embittered little man who appeared to be acting against his better judgment.

Stong inched himself backward until he was half sitting in the bunk. "Let me have some of that coffee." After a while he asked: "Where did the story come from?"

"Tucky herself."

"What do you mean?"

"She told Limba it was you. She did it because she wanted to protect Goliad." Harlan grinned. "You'll have to understand, Pat. Maybe she thought it was better not to start a blood-letting between the McCadys and the Sartrains."

"Cut it out, Doc."

"Well. . . ." Harland shrugged. He looked steadily at Stong. "*Was* it you, as well as Goliad?"

"No. What's the matter with you?"

Harlan sighed. "I have an evil mind. By the way, Pat, your father was sitting in the Five Nations when I left town. He'd been there all day, looking like the wrath of God, ready to get in the middle of anything that came up when you rode into town."

"Help me out of here."

"All right."

Stong's face was gray and sweating when he got his feet on the floor. He could not straighten up.

"Shall I saddle Owlhorns?" Harlan asked.

Stong gripped the edge of the bunk, remembering the agony of the last mile to the cabin. He tried to get back into the bunk. Harlan did not help him until he was forced to ask for assistance.

"No matter what you think you are, Pat, you're no tougher than Nature made you. In two or three days maybe you can walk all right, but you're not going to like riding."

Late that night Pete Snell returned with the medicine Harlan had sent him for. "The town's disappointed." He put a gunny sack of food on the table.

"How's Tucky?" Harlan asked.

"Fever's gone, your wife said. Her mother wouldn't let Limba or Ruthven in the room. They went home. Matthew went home."

"A reprieve, Pat," Harlan said. "What's the town saying, Pete?"

Snell looked sour. "That Stong was afraid of the McCadys. That the story was true."

Harlan laughed. "Sure! That's the natural reaction."

VII

Sitting on his porch at Cross, Bedford Sartrain could feel the pulsing of the great industry around him. That's what it was, an industry. The day was gone when you threw thin-rumped cattle on the range, let them run wild, and took the profit of a hit-and-miss increase. Bedford was satisfied. He had founded something big. He still had his health, and he was law around the place when it came to the important things such as switching from shorthorns to blocky red-and-whites. Maybe he was getting on in years, but he could still put on a show to make them think he was young.

Haswell and Jockney rode up to tell him they were going back to Deep Meadows for a few days to see how things were shaping up on 300 head placed there two weeks before.

"Keep an eye out for lion sign," Bedford advised. "Three-fourths of the stuff we lose that you fellows blame on bears was really lion-killed. The bear will leave his sign around a carcass that was a lion's work, and then you get all riled up about bears. . . ."

The lecture did not vary much from previous times. Haswell and Jockney listened, nodding.

"I wish the Oleano boys was back," Bedford said. "When it comes to breaking horses or tracking mountain lions. . . ."

His sons listened respectfully. Now and then they glanced toward the Oleano cabin. They rode away. It did occur to Bedford that his grandsons were not much for riding past to get his advice.

He watched Goliad ride toward one of the corrals. He veered toward the Oleano cabin and his buckskin was moving slowly when Avlona came out. That girl, it would be a good idea to see that she got married up one of these days. There must be a half dozen young Sartrains moon-eyed about her.

Goliad and Avlona talked idly for a few minutes, and then Goliad rode on. Later, Bedford saw the buckskin cutting up the hill west of the house. Not long afterward Avlona came out again and strolled around Jefferson's house. Her mother called to her sharply from the doorway. The girl went on. Mrs. Oleano glanced toward the house where Bedford sat. She stayed in the doorway until her daughter was out of sight. Girls. They were a damned sight harder to raise than boys. None of Jim Oleano's boys had ever got away with turning their backs and walking off when he called them, and none of Bedford Sartrain's kids had ever got away with it, either.

Bedford dozed. It was a kind of resting that left him aware of the noises around him, and, if there was need, he could be wide awake in a moment, with no one knowing that he had been dozing. He opened one eye when a wagon with some planks on it went through the yard. Two of his grandsons, Burley and Tom, were on it.

"Where's that lumber going?" Bedford asked.

"New head gates," Burley answered, and would have driven on.

"Come here!"

Burley stopped the wagon. He gave the lines to Tom and

came over to the porch. "When I ask you a question," Bedford said, "don't be answering me on the fly."

"Yes, sir."

Although he never admitted it, Bedford sometimes had difficulty keeping his grandsons straight, but he knew Burley well enough. The boy was one of his favorites.

"What are you sulking about?"

"Nothing."

There was something eating the kid, and he was not the sulky kind. "Sore about having to build head gates instead of riding?"

"That don't bother me any, Grandpa." Burley glanced toward the Oleano cabin.

"How are you and Lona getting along, Burley?"

Burley was more sullen in an instant. "All right."

"She's pretty, huh?"

"I guess so." Burley looked at the ground.

This was not the free and easy exchange of confidences that Bedford fancied he enjoyed with all the Sartrains. The fact irritated him. "What started that fight the other night when the sheriff was here, Burley?"

"I don't know."

"The hell you don't! Why didn't you get out there and dance with her, instead of sulking like you are now?"

Burley shrugged. He glanced toward the hill where Goliad had ridden.

"Go build the head gates," Bedford said.

He lit a cigar and sat there looking far across Sartrain land. After a while he went over to the Oleano cabin.

Mrs. Oleano was sitting at a table with her head in her hands. She looked small and crumpled and very old, and the last fact reflected strongly on Bedford. They spoke in Spanish of trivial things, and then Bedford said: "It's about time Avlona picked a suitor, don't you think, Felicia?"

"Such things must not be hurried." Mrs. Oleano's dark eyes were unreadable.

"When you're young, there isn't any time. Did you ask your father and mother when you rode away with Jim?"

"That was long ago." The woman's voice carried the timbre of days far gone.

Bedford puffed his cigar. "Where's Avlona now?"

"At Jefferson's house to make the dress. At Haswell's house, perhaps. She visits much."

Bedford started out.

"No! Tonight we will talk to her, Bedford."

"Now. When there's something to do, do it."

Bedford spent an hour going along the hill to various Sartrain houses. His temper shortened when time after time he was told that Avlona had gone somewhere else just shortly before his coming. Finally a granddaughter whose first name he was not sure of told him that Avlona had gone to get her horse.

"Her horse? I never see her riding."

The girl pointed up the hill. "She keeps it in the little pasture where Cousin Goliad made the fence."

By the Lord, old Bedford thought, *the kids around here know things I don't know.* He strode away and saddled up Sundown, the buckskin stallion that had killed Jim Oleano. They went up the hill as one, Bedford's tawny hair streaming, the creamy tail of the stallion flying. He found the pasture in an aspen park where his second wife had once kept milch cows.

He rode around to the bar gate and looked at the tracks of two horses. His small eyes squinted down when he back-tracked the shod horse a short distance. Why, hell, that was Goliad's horse; the marks of the unshod animal tallied out

110

with the description of tracks that Pat Stong had asked about.

Bedford rode out on the merged trail of the two horses along the top of the bare hill above the houses until he spotted Jefferson, directing a hay crew in the north meadows.

Jefferson looked once at the old man's face, and then turned his horse away from the stack where hay was going up in slings.

"Why ain't I been told what's going on around here?" Bedford demanded.

"What is it now?"

"That hide-out pasture up there in the quakers! Lona and Goliad. Why don't I know about these things?"

"Well, we. . . ."

"We! Who's we? Are you trying to say the whole layout knows about Goliad and Lona? He's your boy, Jeff. Can't you control him? How far has it gone?"

"Too far," Jefferson said. "It ain't good."

Bedford cursed bitterly. "You let the haying go to hell for now, Jeff. You get that mess straightened out right away. There's going to be a marrying around here."

Jefferson tilted his head. "It ain't that easy."

"Oh, yes, it is!"

Sundown made a lunge at Jefferson's gelding. Bedford hauled the stallion back and beat him in the neck with his fist. Jefferson swung his mount aside and got down, yelling at one of his sons near the stacker team. The boy came and led the gelding away.

"What do you mean, it ain't that easy?" Bedford demanded. "I say it is."

"Don't think I haven't been after Goliad myself. I talked to Felicia, too. She don't want Goliad for a son-in-law."

"She'll have him," Bedford said grimly. "You'll see to it, or else I will. Jim Oleano's girl. Jim was as near a brother as I ever had. I don't think much of your judgment to let this thing happen."

"To let it happen! Do you think I'm . . . ?"

"You and Felicia fix it up, Jeff." Bedford started to wheel the stallion. "I'll give you two days."

"Wait a minute, Pa. There's other things in this, too. You remember Pat Stong asked you about a horse. You mentioned it the night of the dance."

"Yeah. Lona's horse that the bunch of you kept hidden from me."

Jefferson wiped a film of dust and sweat on his forehead. "Lona shot Kentucky McCady."

Bedford got off his horse. He walked close to his son as if he were going to strike him. "A fine bunch I've raised around here, sneaking and lying and telling me nothing!"

"There wasn't any point in telling you. We didn't want to worry you."

"Worry me! I worried Cross into what it is today, and now I've got a mealy-mouthed bunch of sons and grandsons afraid to tell me the truth." Bedford's hawkish face was white. "It makes me wonder what I've worked for all my life."

Jefferson said: "Kentucky McCady and Goliad have been meeting each other. Avlona found it out, and so she tried to kill Kentucky."

"She should have killed Goliad! This whole family has double-crossed Jim Oleano, a man who rode with me and saved my life." Bedford was bitter now. "Bring Goliad to my place tonight. I'll lay down the law, and then it's up to you to see that it's carried out."

He leaped on Sundown and rode away.

★ ★ ★ ★ ★

They waited for Goliad under the brass lamps in Bedford's living room. Jefferson's face was bleak; this was not something to be cleared up in one of Bedford's stormy conferences. He didn't know Goliad at all.

Ten minutes later Goliad came in. His smooth good nature was an affront to Bedford, the handsome face, the straight nose, the easy manner. Bedford glowered. Something in the Sartrain blood line had gone wrong here. He said: "You're going to marry Avlona."

Goliad appeared mildly surprised. "That's sort of sudden, I'd say."

"Nobody's asking you how sudden it is. Day after tomorrow."

Goliad shrugged. "She won't listen to that, I'm afraid. We had a quarrel today."

"That don't matter," Bedford said.

"Tell *her* it doesn't matter." Goliad smiled. "Tell Aunt Felicia, too. She hasn't got any use for me, Gramps."

"We'll take care of that part," Bedford said.

"All right."

Bedford was suspicious. He had prepared himself for a typical Sartrain slam-bang argument with shouts and curses. He was at his best in a brawl of words. It was the Sartrain way of blowing off steam, and in the end everything generally leveled off into agreement. But Bedford felt now that he had lunged hard at a barrier and found it imaginary. It occurred to him that no one had brought him a serious Sartrain argument for a long time. He did not like the easy manner with which Goliad faced him, or the wary, cautious expression on Jefferson's face.

"You admit everything, then?" Bedford said.

"I haven't been accused of anything yet," Goliad answered.

Slippery with his words, he was not much of a Sartrain. He was a flannel-mouthed lawyer. The longer Bedford looked at his grandson, the greater was his rage and frustration—Goliad represented something alien in the Sartrain line. Awareness of all this coming so late brought also the realization that there must be a great many other details of the family that had escaped Bedford's attention in the last few years.

"You've been chasing through the woods with old Limba McCady's girl, too, haven't you?" he demanded.

"I don't deny it."

Damn such a blatant whelp.

"Women like me, Gramps," Goliad said.

Bedford ground his teeth. "You didn't care what kind of trouble you caused between us and the McCadys?"

"We're not afraid of them, are we?"

The implication of this twisted around in Bedford. Here was a pup who didn't know what it meant to carry lead in his carcass. He didn't know what the old days had been like. He didn't know that every fight the Sartrains and the McCadys had ever had was something to look back upon without guilt because there had never been any sneaking or loss of honor in the trouble, and he was also hinting that Bedford was old and afraid.

The fury in old Bedford rose to a white heat. "Get him out of here, Jeff! Get the filthy pup out of my sight!"

Goliad left unhurriedly.

Jefferson sat staring at the floor. He had long known things about his son that Bedford was just realizing.

"Let's go talk to Felicia," Bedford said.

Mrs. Oleano listened quietly. "I do not want him. He is not good for my daughter. I do not want him."

114

"He's my grandson," Bedford said. "He. . . ."

"And Avlona is Jim Oleano's daughter and he was your great friend, Bedford."

The quiet statement lay like an accusation on Bedford. It gave him a feeling of failure he had never experienced before. "I'm only trying to make things right, Felicia."

"Will it be all right to have for my daughter one who runs to all the women of the country?"

Bedford went over to the girl. "You quarreled, you and Goliad, but it will be good later, no?"

"Speak English," Avlona said.

That was another blow, a sensing of the great gap between the old days and now. "I'll talk Spanish and you'll answer me!"

Avlona's dark, liquid eyes met the old man's angry stare without a trace of fear. She spat: "Keep your Goliad! I would not have him. He is no good, a liar, a cheat, with no honor! Give him to Kentucky McCady." She whirled into her room and slammed the door in Bedford's face.

Bedford went back to Mrs. Oleano. "Felicia, you've got to make that girl listen."

Mrs. Oleano stared at the lamp. "Do the young listen? Does Goliad listen to you or his father?"

Bedford and Jefferson sat down. For a half hour they talked to Mrs. Oleano. She listened and she shook her head gently. Pressed against the door of her room, Avlona listened, too. She wanted to giggle at the solemnity of the old ones trying to settle her affairs. What did the old know of love? Among other things, they did not know that Goliad had said that someday things might come to this, and then she was to pretend she did not want him. Later, they would have their marriage properly, with the priest, with all the Sartrains there to see Jim Oleano's daughter married.

So Avlona listened, holding back her laughter at the bab-
bling of the ancient ones who had long ago forgotten what
great love was. After a time they would go away, and then
she would meet Goliad again.

It was so. After a time Bedford and Jefferson went away.

Standing in the starlight, Bedford said: "I'll see that it's
done."

"I don't know how, when the girl ain't willing." That
was a surprise to Jefferson; he had expected trouble from
Goliad, not Avlona.

Bedford tramped off toward his house. He was tired. He
felt beaten down by the knowledge that all around him for a
long time there had been a growing away from patriarch
law. But he was still formidable. And then, when he turned
on his steps to look at the buildings running on both sides
of him, filled with people who were young, he knew that he
had lost forever his tight rein on Cross. Times had changed.
He had been a fool not to see the changes as they came.

His wife was waiting in the living room.

"Did you know about Goliad and Avlona?" Bedford asked.

Callie Sartrain nodded.

"Why the hell didn't you tell me?"

"I knew about Goliad and Kentucky McCady, too, ever
since Brock saw them together."

Bedford paced the floor. "That ain't so bad."

"Why not?" his wife asked sharply.

"Lona is Jim Oleano's kid, and me and Jim were. . . ."

"And so were you and Limba McCady once the best of
friends. What's foul in one place is foul in another."

"He can't marry them both!"

"He won't marry either one of them, if I know him."

"We'll see about that!" The threat was hollow, even to
Bedford. Now there would be hell with the McCadys, and

he had to admit that the prospect no longer gave him pleasure. No matter how hard and deadly relations had been before, there had never been any foulness as a reason for fighting. Now Bedford felt that he was personally at fault because of Goliad.

Callie Sartrain said: "Tom Patterson sent his boy by tonight while you were at Felicia's. He said that all their strays on Shavano Creek had been driven back."

Bedford grunted, hearing but not caring.

"He also said there is a story around about Kentucky and Pat Stong. I'll admit I dug that out of him. He was red to his ears before he got away."

"Pat Stong?" Bedford stopped pacing. "No one over there knows about Goliad?"

"Apparently not."

Why sure! There would have been hell to pay before this if old Limba knew. Bedford grinned, but his humor did not last long. He and Limba had lived by the same code. Sartrains and McCadys could shoot each other and they had, but they did not compromise honor by any filthy tricks. What Goliad had done was a reflection on Bedford, proof to anyone that Bedford could not handle him at Cross, let alone on the entire range.

Old Bedford went to pacing. He would swear that problems had been easier in the days when he was struggling to make Cross what it was today. When he and Limba rode into Baca Valley the first time. . . .

He sat down slowly, stretching his legs, feeling the tiredness in them, feeling the age in them. He was not a man to moon over things long gone but now memories of his first months in the valley came back pleasantly. He wondered— and the thought came as a mild shock—if his and Limba's quarrel long ago had not been senseless.

VIII

Pat Stong rode into Mormon Forge slowly. His face was gaunt and bore four days of beard. The flesh around one eye was yellowish and the eye was still bloodshot from a Sartrain thumb that had tried to gouge it out. He saw loafers on the street turn quickly into doorways to tell others that the sheriff was back. He saw Houston Doty come out of the Five Nations and stand on the walk, his badge shining in the sun.

Busby Youngblood watched Stong dismount, noting the effort, saying nothing.

"Anybody in town?" Stong asked.

"Goliad." Youngblood's mouth snapped shut. He led Owlhorns away.

Stong stood straight and walked carefully on his way to his office. He felt the eyes of the town on him and knew what men were saying. He had ducked out of a pistol fight. Sure, he might have been beat up a little, but that was no reason for hiding out. And then, they would be talking about him and Tucky.

The odor of fresh bread and roasting meat came to him when he stepped inside the office. Amy Harlan and Mrs. Youngblood were in his room. The place was clean.

"Munro said you'd be in today," Mrs. Harlan said.

Mrs. Youngblood smiled. She was a trim, brown-haired

woman whose face always had a clean, smiling look about it. "We're glad to see you back, Pat."

"Thanks for straightening things."

"Oh, we didn't do that. Your sisters were here. We just brought you something to eat." Mrs. Youngblood took her apron off and folded it. "I've got to skip back to the girls now, Amy. See that he eats a square meal." She left.

Still moving deliberately, Stong washed up, and sat down to the meal Amy Harlan put before him. She sat on the edge of his cot and watched him. She was poised and quiet. Stong decided she did not need paint, after all, to be a beautiful woman.

Andy Kopperwit spoke through the broken place in the partition. "Glad you're back in one piece, Pat. I'm going to eat now, so don't be afraid of talking." He went out and locked the front door behind him.

"How's Tucky?" Stong asked.

"She's on her feet." Mrs. Harlan hesitated. "She's going to stay with us for a week or two, I think."

She wouldn't find it pleasant at home, naturally. Stong reached to the stove for more coffee. "How was Limba when he left?"

"In a cold fury. Tucky told him she had lied about you. Whether he fully believed her or not is hard to say, but he was confused enough to go home. It's impossible for Limba to guess the truth because he'll never even consider that she would look at a Sartrain. The whole affair is still hanging." Mrs. Harlan shook her head. "You should be grateful that Tucky tried to clear you."

"I'd be more grateful if she hadn't lied to start."

"You must understand her reasons."

"I can understand easier that Limba McCady would have busted me in two if it hadn't been for Pete Snell."

Mrs. Harlan came over to the table. "Have you ever been in love?"

"No."

"It would help if you had. The people of this town, with a few exceptions, consider only that Tucky stayed with a man. They don't know or they wouldn't care how much she loves him. Don't be like the little people of Mormon Forge, Pat."

She had stayed with Goliad. He was in town now. For several reasons it would be a pleasure to kill Goliad Sartrain.

"When you found Tucky after she had been shot, you made her tell a lie to keep the truth from the McCadys. Let's say it was partly to protect her but also because you have a great ambition to maintain peace. To do that you must go on lying until something more honest can be worked out of the situation. You can't let yourself do what I think you'd like to do to Goliad."

Stong knew that very well. At first he had grasped at anything to keep the two families apart. He knew who had shot Tucky and he intended to do nothing about the fact. All his hopes were resting on an insecure foundation that could collapse and expose him as a liar and a braggart.

"There are your sisters to consider, too," Mrs. Harlan said. "In spite of everything they were at the dance with Roblado and Fitz John McCady Saturday night."

"Yeah." Stong was unhappy. If he could just move to the side of the road and let things whirl by as they pleased, it would be simple. But beyond duty, there was a stubborn determination to do just what he had told the McCadys and the Sartrains he intended to do.

"Come down and see us, Pat." Mrs. Harlan picked up a white dishtowel that had covered a loaf of bread. She went out.

She was scarcely gone when Marshal Doty came in. His eyes were clear, his face less bloated than when Stong had last seen him. His drinking habits were not so strong in him when he was feeding on the exercise of authority. He looked around the room and smiled.

"I wish I was such a popular man with the ladies."

Stong looked at him steadily until Doty's color rose.

"Now I didn't mean anything in particular by that, Sheriff. I . . . I guess you know I'm marshal now."

"I heard that."

"There's folks here who figured you might bring us more trouble than we're entitled to."

"Sure. What did you come to say, Doty?"

The marshal played with his badge, not looking directly at Stong. "Goliad Sartrain is in town. I don't know why, but he's said some hard things about you, Stong. I don't want trouble here. You don't have no right to start trouble in Mormon Forge any more."

"Did you tell Goliad that?"

"Yes, I did."

"All right. I'll not start trouble with him."

Doty did not like the answer. He opened and closed his mouth. He saw that he was going to get no better reply, so he turned and walked out.

There was a twisted streak of meanness in Goliad Sartrain. He was enjoying himself. He had promoted the fight at Cross when he found out why Stong was there. Now he was looking for trouble that Stong could not afford.

After a while Stong went down the street to find Goliad. He had a good idea of where he would be. He was right. Lulu Courtney was behind her bar. Goliad and Mary Randolph and Oklahoma Sal were in front of it. They were not drunk because Lulu allowed no one to get drunk in her place before the evening.

Oklahoma Sal nudged the girl beside her. They both turned to look speculatively at Stong. Goliad was aware of his presence but he did not turn around.

"I want to see you, Goliad."

"Here I am."

"Outside."

Goliad turned then. Underlying his smooth expression was a hotness of anger that startled Stong. He walked out past Stong, and they went to the side of Jake Arbor's hay barn.

"Get it off your chest, Goliad."

"You keep away from Tucky." There was no mask of politeness on Goliad's face now. All the strength and weakness of his character lay raw and violent across his features.

"If you believe that story, you're as dumb as the rest," Stong said.

"Stay away from her."

The man did believe. It was only natural. He was playing fast and loose himself, and he was so selfish he could not judge the conduct of others except by his own standards. It was incredible that Tucky McCady could be in love with him.

"Don't believe gossip, Goliad. Go talk to Tucky."

Goliad's lips twisted. "I have."

"You didn't believe her?"

"Stay away from her."

He was rotten to the core. Only a bullet could make a man of him. "I see no reason to," Stong said. "I might tell her about Lona."

Goliad laughed. "No, you won't. You're the big, noble sheriff who's going to run the whole county, keep the

Sartrains and the McCadys apart. You can't afford to tell anybody anything. You've got a streak up your back. Where were you when Limba McCady was waiting for you? Sick?" Goliad cursed. "You were hiding out in the same cabin where you spied on me and Tucky. You and her had probably been there before, no matter what the two of you say. Now you stay away from her, Stong, or I'll finish what we started at Cross. You can get by with your fists, but when it comes to real guts with a pistol, you're not there. You. . . ."

"Shut up," Stong said. Goliad was running around wild, deliberately building up a fight. "I intend to keep the Sartrains and the McCadys apart, if I can. Now I'll tell you something, Goliad . . . *you* stay away from Tucky."

For an instant surprise made Goliad's features slack, and that was what Stong wanted, to break into his anger, to slow him down, and then to get away from him before a fight developed that could ruin everything.

"Oh, I see." Goliad smiled. "Tell Roblado and Fitz John McCady to stay away from your sisters while you're at it."

The implication robbed Stong of all the calmness he had brought to the meeting. He struck Goliad across the mouth and knocked him against the brown boards of the barn wall. Goliad hung there a moment in shock. Stong started to strike him again, and then he turned and walked away.

"Stong!"

Stong walked on. He knew how thinly balanced it was now. If he turned, he would get a bullet in the chest. If he kept on, he might get it in the back. He had to go on, a shambling, rough-featured man laying his life against the slim chance of still holding peace as he had bragged he would.

"Stong!"

Stong did not hurry, although he wanted to dive to the

ground and draw his pistol as he rolled. His back crawled. He was afraid. He kept walking.

In front of Lulu's place he almost ran into Willy Golden. The gambler gave Stong a quiet look, and then he stepped out of the way. "I thought he was going to do it," Golden murmured, and then Stong knew he was clear for the moment.

He did not turn until later. Goliad was still standing by the barn, his hat on the ground, his pistol in his hand. Willy Golden relit his cigar, and resumed his stroll. When he met Goliad, now coming toward Lulu's place, some expression on the gambler's ruined face must have mocked the man, for Goliad spoke sharply and swung around, standing with a coiled viciousness in his pose.

Willy Golden went on, giving Goliad his back, insulated from fear by the creeping rot of boredom.

Marshal Doty was coming down the street. "Damn it, Stong!" His lips quivered. "You promised me not to start anything."

"I didn't start it."

"You went looking for him." It was almost a wail.

Todd Brewslow was standing with a group of men in front of his store. "What are you trying to do, Stong . . . ruin us?"

There was no way to explain to Brewslow. Stong shook his head at him, and walked on. The man had his point and Stong could understand it. The whole trouble was the deeper he got into the affairs of people the more interwoven they became, obscuring the clear pronouncements of law with the drapery of a dozen individual problems. To date Stong knew he had settled nothing, not even his initial boast that he would bring to justice the person who had shot Tucky. The Sartrains would be laughing about that, the McCadys snarling and brooding. None of it was circumstance, he thought savagely; it was all the result of deliberate acts by Goliad Sartrain and Tucky McCady.

IX

The Old Forge schoolhouse was five miles west of town at the junction of the Big Otero and the Mormon. It was here that fifty families of the Church of Jesus Christ of Latter-Day Saints had stopped to tighten tires on shrinking wagon wheels during their trek to Deseret. When Limba McCady and Bedford Sartrain came into the valley, some of the stone forge stands were still there, and it was from them that the town and the schoolhouse took their names.

There had been dancing and singing when the Mormons took their nightly breaks in the struggle against vastness. Tonight there was merriment again. Andy Kopperwit played the fiddle and Frank Budlong, pale and sweating as if he were still over a stove in the Boston, played the guitar. Cold-eyed as ever, bald, squat Busby Youngblood was at the door to check pistols.

Pat Stong arrived late, with no intention of going inside. He left Owlhorns at the corner of the corral behind the schoolhouse. Tom Patterson and some of the older ranchers were there, talking of range matters. Stong had a word with them, and then strolled among the buggies.

He climbed into a buggy and sat looking through the window. He saw Tom and Jasper and Burley Sartrain. Burley was dancing with Avlona Oleano, Roblado and Fitz John McCady were dancing with Stong's sisters. It was not unusual for a group of young McCadys and Sartrains to get along under a sort of truce at these affairs, but Stong was troubled. Any minor explosion now might expand considerably. He had to know how many of each family there were inside.

He was getting out of the buggy when Benoni McCady, his arm in a sling, came from the direction of the corral.

"What's the matter, Stong? Afraid to show your face inside?"

"What do you mean by that?"

Benoni went on up the steps without answering. He was a high, square-shouldered shape as the light of the open doorway cut around him.

Stong went inside, putting his back to the wall. Busby Youngblood came over and stood beside him, looking at his pistol.

"I'll be only a minute." Stong had already looked the room over. There did not seem to be any troublemakers present.

"Better check it, anyway," Youngblood said.

Stong gave him the pistol belt. Women were coming and going from the teacher's living quarters where babies were piled in fat bundles on mattresses brought along for the occasion. Avlona waved gaily. At the far end of the room, Tucky and Mrs. Harlan were sitting together. Tucky's face was pale, her hair dark red. She watched Stong casually for a few moments, and then said something to Amy Harlan.

The dance ended. Frank Budlong wiped his face with a blue bandanna. There was a shifting on the floor. Jennifer and Marian Stong came over to their brother, their long dresses swishing. Fitz John and Roblado would have followed, but Benoni said something to them and drew them toward a corner.

"Old sobersides Pat," Jennifer said. "Where's your girl?" Both she and Marian were tall, even-featured, with none of their father's heaviness about them.

"He just came out to keep the boys from fighting around the buggies," Marian said.

They examined his face critically. "You'll be all right if you keep out of fist fights," Jennifer said. "You'll be handsome someday."

They smiled at him, their talk was light, but he sensed an undercurrent of worry in their manner, and he saw Marian glance toward Tucky. "You brats get back to your beaux." He turned them around and gave them a gentle shove.

Avlona came over, dragging Burley Sartrain by the hand. "You will dance with me, Sheriff Pat?"

"Not tonight, Lona. The last time nearly ruined me." He winked at Burley. "How's Bedford?"

"Pretty good." Burley was embarrassed.

Stong felt sympathy for him. Avlona was with him only because she was trying to make Goliad jealous.

Jake Arbor announced a waltz. Bob Haviland, the blacksmith, with a head of sandy hair big enough to fill a bushel basket, went booming across the floor to dance with Amy Harlan. Tucky sat alone. No doubt it had been that way all night, Stong thought.

Stong worked his way along the edge of the floor. Men dancing with their wives spoke to him, but some of the wives did not. He stood before Tucky and said: "Let's have a go at it."

"Is that the way you generally ask?"

Her eyes were long and green and angry. He saw a tiny muscle pulsing in her throat. She was as beautiful as he had always thought. The defiance in her expression was the only change. Suddenly his hatred of Goliad was on a personal level.

"I don't need your sympathy, Sheriff."

"Maybe I need yours. Come on. You owe me something, Tucky. You very nearly got me killed." He grinned.

She was light in his arms. She watched his face as they danced. Someone jabbed an elbow into his back, and, when he turned his head, he saw Avlona, dancing with Burley. Her eyes were dark and spiteful.

"I didn't mean to get you killed, Pat. It was a terrible thing that I lied about you."

Stong nodded. "Sure. But you'd do it again . . . for him, wouldn't you?"

"Not unless I had to."

"What happens when Ruthven and Limba find out about him?"

"I can't help what happens now."

For a time, dancing here with Tucky, he was able to reject part of the duty he felt. She was a beautiful woman whom he had always admired. He couldn't condemn her, and, out of the understanding the Harlans had forced upon him, he could not condemn Avlona either, but there was no forgiveness in him for Goliad Sartrain.

The music ended. He took Tucky back to her chair. Benoni was there with Amy Harlan. His face was bitter hot. "I want to talk to you, Stong."

"In a minute." Stong smiled at Mrs. Harlan. "Where's the old man tonight?"

"He'll be here later. He was called out to the Patterson place." Mrs. Harlan's eyes were worried as she watched Benoni going toward the door. He stopped against the wall and stood there, looking back across the room.

Tucky clutched Stong's arm. "Don't go talk to him.

Don't go out there. He's heard something."

"Of course," Stong said. "That rumor about you and me couldn't blow past McCady ears forever. And Benoni has a small grudge against me besides." He turned away. Benoni made a slight nod toward the door.

As Stong crossed the room, he observed that Roblado and Fitz John were gone, but there was no surging of men toward the door. The McCadys, for once, were being casual. They had made their set-up outside without attracting attention.

Busby Youngblood thrust Stong's gun belt at him. "Sorry to see you going home so soon."

"Did they take their pistols?"

"No." Youngblood's voice was a murmur, his red face grim. "What's the use of being beat up all the time?" He held the belt and pistol out.

Stong buckled on the belt. Youngblood gave him his hat.

"Over here," Benoni McCady said. He was waiting with Roblado and Fitz John where the desks from the schoolroom had been carried to the side yard. Stong had a good look at the three dark, angry faces as he walked away from the steps. He pulled his pistol.

"All right, boys, you've heard something. Benoni, you hauled Fitz John and Roblado out here to make a beef of it. It isn't going to be." Stong held the pistol on them. "You'd better talk to Limba before you try jumping me."

He had taken the initiative away from them, and now they were surprised and doubly angry. Benoni said: "So you want it the rough way? Then that's how it will be the next time we see you."

Stong swung sidewise when he heard quick footsteps behind him. Then Tucky was at his side. "You fools!" she said. "Uncle Benoni, this is none of your business!"

"The two of you in there flaunting yourselves before the whole country!" Benoni said savagely. "You're worse than he is, Tucky. You. . . ."

"Keep your voice down," Stong said.

It was too late. Someone going toward the steps had seen and heard. In a moment men were jamming the doorway to get into the yard. Inside the building someone yelled: "Fight!"

"Take me home, Pat," Tucky said.

The request caught Stong by surprise.

"Oh, no, he won't!" Benoni said.

"I believe I will." Stong backed away with Tucky at his side. The McCadys followed and the crowd spread wide to watch.

Todd Brewslow came clumping down the steps. "What's going on here?" He saw what it was. "Stong again!"

The McCadys veered away and rushed toward the building to get their pistols. For a time they were blocked by people still pouring out, and then, when the way was clear, Busby Youngblood, a pistol in his hand, was standing in the doorway. "Nobody checks back his pistol to start trouble."

Benoni cursed him.

"I won't take much of that," Youngblood said. He meant it. "No pistols checked out till things simmer down."

Stong and Tucky rode away together under starlight. The musicians were playing. A few people straggled inside but the evening was broken now and the country had more fuel for conversation. First, Goliad. He was ready to kill Stong on sight, and now Benoni had made threats that he must back. Things were not working out at all, and Stong had black doubts that they ever would.

"Did Limba believe it wasn't me?" he asked.

"He must have. You're still alive."

"But now the rest of your family knows what he wouldn't tell them. Why didn't he tell them, Tucky?"

"Pride." Her voice was small. "I've broken my grandfather's heart."

"Yeah? Well, he'll have to get over it. When do you and Goliad figure to get married?"

"I don't know."

"Had he ever asked you to marry him?"

"What business is that of yours?"

"Quite a bit. I'm being pounded by both sides. I'm not keeping the peace. I'm only making things worse every time I make a move." Stong reined Owlhorns closer to Tucky's steeldust. "Did Goliad ever ask you to marry him?"

"Yes! A dozen times."

"You think you love him?"

"I know I do!"

"Well, then, marry him and get this situation off my neck," Stong said bitterly. "Once you're married, all you'll have to do is live down the lie about me. Goliad believes that, incidentally."

"I know." Her voice was suddenly small. "You don't like the Sartrains, do you? You think. . . ."

"I don't like Goliad."

"Why not?"

"He's no good!"

"How do you mean?"

"I mean he's a sneaky, lying, tricky. . . ."

"You! You say that about Goliad! You were spying on me and Goliad! You got into a fight over Avlona Oleano. She was jealous tonight when she saw me dancing with you. You've got a lot of nerve to call Goliad. . . ."

"Marry him! Find out what he is."

"I will!"

They rode on, both too angry to talk.

After a while Tucky asked: "Why did you cover up the tracks of the man who shot me?"

Stong did not answer at once, and then he said: "To keep peace."

"Is that all you think about?"

"It's plenty for me."

"Then you do know who tried to kill me?"

"Yes!"

"Was it Kinkaid, after all? Why isn't he in jail?"

"It wasn't Kinkaid. It wasn't any Sartrain man. I mean, it wasn't anyone at Cross."

"Oh?" The timbre of her voice, her silence told Stong how she had caught at his slip. "Are you hinting that it was a woman?" she asked.

"I'm hinting nothing." Stong knew their mutual pact of secrecy would hold good up to a point, but the point might be Avlona. There was nothing noble in Stong's reticence concerning Avlona and Goliad. It was a grinding curse in him that he could not tell Tucky. She might not believe him, but, if she did, he was afraid that the temper of a two-timed woman would blow so high Goliad would stand exposed before the McCadys. Stong could not take the chance.

"I'm hinting nothing," he said.

"You're the sheriff who bragged before my family about upholding the law in this country, and now you're protecting the woman who shot me."

"I didn't say it was a woman."

"It was, though. It was Avlona. I saw the way she ran to you tonight, and I saw her eyes when you danced with me. And now she believes the story about us."

"You were shot before that ever started."

"If you spied on me and Goliad once, you probably did so several times. Avlona must have seen you and me riding in the same direction on Sartrain land. She misunderstood. Being jealous over you, she shot me. No wonder you're protecting her."

It was incredible. Only a woman could get things so twisted. "You think Lona and I have been running out together?"

"Yes," Tucky said. "I'm sure of it."

Stong groaned. "Oh, my God."

"Of course, you'd want to protect her, just as I want to keep my family from finding out about Goliad until we're married. She's a hellcat, Pat, but since it's that way between you two, you and I have our reasons for keeping quiet."

Stong reached out and stopped the steeldust. "You're crazy, Tucky. If Lona saw me riding after you, which I did only twice, wouldn't she be more likely to see Goliad?"

"Not necessarily. He was always very careful."

"So was I. You didn't see me trailing you."

"No, I didn't," Tucky said. "But if I were in love with you and you were going to another woman, I would have seen you, never you worry. You and Avlona. . . ."

"You're out of your head."

"She did shoot me, didn't she, Pat?"

"Of course not."

"She did, too. I saw her there on the cliff."

"The night I found you, you said Kinkaid had shot you, and later you admitted you didn't know who it was. Now you're saying. . . ."

"It was Avlona. I saw her. She was wearing a man's hat. She was crouched down. I thought there was something strange about that one glimpse I had, but I was too excited and scared to think. Now I'm sure."

"Your memory sure came back mighty sudden," Stong said. "Don't you think it's odd that Avlona would be so close to the place where you and Goliad met?"

He saw her pale face looking at him in the starlight. She shook her head. "Where were you going to meet her that day, Pat?"

"I wasn't going to meet her anywhere." Stong knew his words were breaking futilely against the wall of her faith in an utterly worthless man. He was almost to the point of telling her about Goliad and Avlona, but still he was afraid to do so.

Her voice was musing. "Goliad was at the cabin for an hour before I got there. She didn't see him, I'm sure, but from high in the hills she saw my mare, and later, your red roan. She knew the way I would go on my way home, so she went to the cliffs and waited."

"You're as wrong as you can be," Stong said.

"Then why would she shoot me? The only other reason could have been Goliad." Tucky laughed. "And do you think I would believe he would even look twice at her?"

"No," Stong said shortly. He released her horse. They rode the rest of the way to Mormon Forge without speaking. Beside the Harlan house Stong took the reins of Tucky's horse when she dismounted. There was a light somewhere in the back of the house. She said good night stiffly.

Stong was halfway to Youngblood's livery before he realized why he was attracting so much attention. Tucky's steeldust. It was another clincher in the rumor about him and her. Pete Snell walked down the line of stalls with a lantern. He yawned, and then his mouth shut tightly when he saw the horse Stong had led in.

Stong said: "Pete, I managed to get you at odds with

135

Limba McCady and now tonight I got Youngblood snarled up with Benoni and Ruthven's kids."

"Can't be helped, I guess."

"You and Busby have never mixed around much."

Snell pulled off the saddle. "Your old man could tell you why, Pat. Busby and me came here wanted men. We may still be wanted. We got our side of the story, but I ain't going into that. We've lived so we wouldn't attract no undue attention. Getting into the mess here ain't to our liking, but it happened." It was a long speech. Snell shut his mouth suddenly and went on with his work.

Standing beside Owlhorns at the water trough outside, Stong tried to think it over clearly. Everyone was getting sucked into the affairs of Antelope County. Youngblood and Snell were wanted. They were his friends and he was a sheriff. A few months ago, when law and justice seemed clear-cut and simple, he would have felt it his duty to inquire into the history of Pete Snell and Busby Youngblood. Now he did not want to know.

Goliad again. It was becoming increasingly easier to forget Tucky's original part. Stong swung up on Owlhorns. He started toward the M. Before he could do anything, he must get the McCadys off his neck. He must make very sure that they knew he was not the man they needed to kill, and still he could not tell them who the man was.

136

X

Tucky dropped into the first chair she found in the dark
Harlan living room. Her arm was hurting. A fear was beginning to writhe in her because of what Pat Stong had hinted
indirectly. Avlona and Goliad? Her own strong, swirling
emotions had always carried her past any doubts of
Goliad—his hesitation about getting married, his evasions
about plans for the future, but now the knots of doubt were
hardening.

Footsteps sounded in the hallway. Dr. Harlan said:
"Amy? Is that you?"

"It's me."

"Where's Amy?" Harlan entered the room and fumbled
with a lamp. "The dance isn't over yet, is it?"

"I came in early with Pat Stong. Amy is still there,
waiting for you."

"You'll get Stong killed yet." Harlan struck a match. "I
had another call to make when I left the Patterson place. It
took me so far south I just swung on home. I'm no dancer,
anyway. How was the shindig?"

"All right."

The lamp spread light across the room. Harlan stood beside it, shaking the match. "Yes, I see it wasn't so good."

"Not the dance particularly," Tucky said. "Benoni and
two of my brothers made fools of themselves, but, after-

ward, when Pat and I were coming home. . . ."

Harlan waited. "It sounds interesting. He turned into a cad, eh? Well, after all, considering what you told about him. . . ."

"It was nothing like that."

Harlan stopped smiling. "Of course, of course. I was merely joshing, Tucky. What's the matter?"

"I can't tell you." All at once she was crying.

Harlan flipped the match toward the fireplace. He waited until Tucky gained control of herself, and then he walked across the room to her. "You're going to face a tough run from now on. It won't hurt to cry occasionally, unless you make a habit of it. Come on. You get to bed and tell Amy about it when she comes in."

"I won't tell anyone."

"Wrong attitude, Tucky."

She wiped her eyes, and stood up. She was close to Munro Harlan. He was looking down at her with a smile, and then the smile faded and a curious light raised in his eyes. He reached out and drew her to him. He kissed her hard and long, feeling the first startled resistance in her melt away after a moment.

When he stepped back a trifle, holding her by the shoulders, his expression was as startled as Tucky's. Munro Harlan was a man who moved on impulse frequently. She stared at him in frank wonder, and then her eyes were quickly troubled and she walked past him, going to her room. He wandered over to a table and picked up a pipe. When he observed the trembling of his fingers, he put the pipe down at once.

I'll be damned, he thought. *You'd think I was fourteen years old.*

He heard the front gate swing and listened to Amy's long

stride on the graveled walk. For a fleeting instant he thought it was odd that she had come in that way. Generally she slapped her horse toward the livery stable and came to the house by the side yard where there was no gate. And then his mind was honestly involved once more with the reason for his act a minute before. As his wife came through the doorway from the summer kitchen, Munro Harlan decided that he had kissed Tucky because he damned well wanted to.

Mrs. Harlan was pulling at her buckskin riding gloves, giving them deliberate and frowning attention. While she stood there, the closet door in Tucky's room was opened and closed.

"Do you want some coffee, Munro? I do."

Harlan studied his wife's face as she went across the room briskly. "Yes, sure," he said. "Did someone take your horse to Youngblood's? I didn't hear you ride in."

"I headed him for the barn as usual."

It was childish, this clumsy sparring for information, and it was alien to Harlan's nature. He wondered why he was doing it. When he picked up the pipe again, his fingers were steady. He filled it slowly, staring at the wall, listening to the sounds in the kitchen.

Of course, Amy had seen him and Tucky. She had been coming across the side yard lawn, and then she had walked to the front gate and swung it to warn them. The fact that she had not faced the matter directly worried Harlan more than his own hesitation. He stood there with the unlighted pipe in his mouth.

Starlight caught the rim of white fences at M as Stong rode up from the river. It was late but there were lights in the main house and horses standing in the yard. This was the fountainhead of the McCady empire. Ruthven's family lived here and Limba, whose wife was dead, was still here, and Vir McCady, who had once defied his own family and the Sartrains by running away with Alice Sartrain.

As Stong came closer, he recognized one of the horses in the yard, a big-boned, hammer-headed steeldust. Benoni's horse. As violent as the man himself, Stong had hoped to have a talk alone with Limba. He hesitated, looking at the house. It would be easier to face a man with a pistol than to walk in on the McCadys now.

He stayed in the yard and hailed the house. It was Benoni who flung the door open. "Who's out there?"

"Stong."

Benoni put his hand on his pistol. Ruthven crowded in beside him, and they both started across the porch.

"You fools!" old Limba bellowed. "Bring him in here. Are you a bunch of savages trying to think with your fists?"

"You've got your guts!" Benoni growled as Stong walked past him into the house. "I warned you once."

The McCadys built big. The room was thirty-five feet long, the plastered ceiling twelve feet high. The furniture was heavy. There were fireplaces at both ends of the room, and a tall man could have lain in either one and had room to spare.

Limba was standing by a dark oak table in his undershirt. His silver belt buckle lay flat on his trim waist. He spread his feet and glared at Stong. Vir McCady was sitting at the far end of the room beside a fireplace. Benoni and Ruthven flanked the visitor, watching him darkly. No one spoke.

Stong walked to the nearest fireplace and stood with his back to the embers. Benoni and Ruthven turned to face him. Only Benoni was armed. It was apparent that Ruthven had been roused from bed, for his shirt was unbuttoned and his red hair on end.

Stong spoke directly to Benoni. "So you heard a lie at the dance and you didn't bother to ask me or Tucky before you tried to start a fight. That lie, Benoni, has been all over the country. Naturally the McCadys would be the last to hear it."

"Go on," Ruthven said.

"I will. The only sense I've seen in this matter yet is that you came to Limba with the story." Stong was playing for the old man's support and praying that Limba had not told them everything he knew. "Ruthven, ask your daughter about that lie, not me. Have your wife ask her."

"Don't tell me what to do," Ruthven said.

From the far end of the room Vir said quietly: "I think he's telling the truth, Ruthven."

"Nobody asked you for an opinion," Ruthven said. There were McCadys who had never forgiven Vir his defection from tribal policy with Alice Sartrain.

"She sat at the dance and no one would go near her," Benoni said savagely. "And then you came in and flaunted. . . ."

"I danced with her," Stong said. "I'll do it again, with her permission, anytime I see her sitting alone." He looked at Limba. "Where did the lie start? That's what I'd like to know."

Limba glared at him. Limba could not answer in honesty and Stong knew it.

Benoni said: "Rumor like that just don't start from nothing. You're the man, Stong. You're. . . ."

"Shut up, Benoni," Limba said. "The man came here in good faith. He's never been a liar. I don't think he is now."

Stong let his breath out slowly. Limba's opinion might free him of one great weight. But the central problem was still unchanged, and Ruthven began thrusting at it immediately.

"I don't say I believe you, Stong . . . not yet." Ruthven's face was dark, his eyes narrow. "I saw you covered up horse tracks from the place where Tucky was shot. I want you to answer that."

"I may have tramped on them by accident."

"No tracker does that."

"Talk up, damn you!" Benoni said. "You and your big blabber about the first movement of the law."

Limba's eyes were accusing. He, too, was waiting for the answer. They had dropped, reluctantly, one accusation and now all the force of the first one was added to this other one.

"I covered the tracks, yes," Stong said. "They headed for Cross. That was my business, not McCady business. I was afraid you'd go straight to the Sartrains and start a fight. The night before you had started to do so without any evidence at all. The tracks didn't go to Cross. They turned south into the mountains east of Cross. At dusk I lost them. They were still headed south. I went to Cross and found no horse there that could be the one. Bedford Sartrain had never seen such a horse as I described. I'll take his word any day." This mixing of truth and falsehood was much simpler than straight lying. "You people have had time to cool off. You're fools if you think any Sartrain shot Tucky."

The room was silent, the dark faces unchanged, and then the McCadys looked at each other slowly. Stong could not be sure of Limba's expression, and he knew that he could not stand questioning from the old man.

"You had no right to mess up those tracks," Benoni

growled. It was like the sullen muttering of a storm that had passed.

"It was a mistake, yes," Stong said. "But I have the right to do anything in this county that I think will keep men from killing each other." He walked out then, leaving before Limba could remember questions that he had asked before.

Someone followed him down the steps. It was Vir McCady. He walked Stong to Owlhorns. "You told the truth about Tucky, Stong, but the matter of those tracks was something else." There was no hostility in Vir's voice. Caught by the excitement of a fight, Vir had tried to crack Stong's head with a chair, but he was still the most reasonable of all the McCadys. Some men said he was weak because something had broken in him long ago when he and Alice Sartrain rode away to be married. In the half light of the yard he looked like a typical McCady, blunt and obstinate. The difference lay in the manner of his speech. "This feud has been a curse on the valley, Stong."

Vir had reason to think so. He and Alice Sartrain had been in Sandoval, looking for a preacher when a stray bullet from a saloon fight crashed through a window and killed the girl. Even Bedford, who was riding to overtake his daughter, had been stunned by the terrible quietness of Vir McCady when he found him. For weeks thereafter Vir was a silent man, not speaking to his own family. The whole country said what was obvious: that, if the Sartrains and the McCadys lived like normal human beings, Vir and Alice would have been married in the church at Mormon Forge.

"I figure things from your conduct that the others may have missed," Vir said. "I think maybe Tucky has got mixed up with a Sartrain."

Stong got on his horse. "It wouldn't be my business to guess about that."

"You say so, but I believe that's exactly why you're so concerned, Stong. Not personally, of course, but because you see the law blowing up in your face if the facts become known." Vir's voice was slow and solemn. "Tucky has a right to anyone she wants."

"I agree there. Tell Limba that."

"Limba knows my thoughts from long ago. The way I see it, this whole country isn't worth keeping a man and woman apart if they want each other." Vir's voice went on slowly but his tone became hard and bitter. "If you're trying to interfere in her affairs, Stong, I'm your enemy."

"Now I've been accused of everything."

"I haven't accused you. I've only warned you. Tucky will have trouble enough with her own family, without you or anyone else throwing weight against her."

"There's Sartrains that I respect as much as any McCady," Stong said carefully. "And there's others that need killing. A woman could make a mistake, Vir."

"She would have that right. Don't interfere with it." Vir's warning was edged and sure and cold, to be taken more seriously than any of the wild vaporings of angry McCadys who could cool down to a semblance of reason later.

Vir would not change, Stong knew. He had been tormented through silent years by something that had happened long ago, and now he did not want it to happen to his niece. What he had lost he would not see lost again.

"I've talked to Tucky," Vir said. "She wouldn't tell me anything. Will you?"

"No." Stong rode away.

XI

The dodger was ten years old. The inking was so dark that Stong knew why he had looked at it when he first took office and then put it back in his desk with numerous others that meant nothing. He had thought that he did not want to know about Youngblood and Snell, but he had gone through the stack of dodgers anyway. They were listed here as the Young brothers, King and Snell. They were wanted by the state of Texas for the murder of four men in Terrell County, and that was where Matthew Stong had lived before he came north. Stong put the circular in his pocket and went to the livery stable. Snell was hitching a team to a wagon, and Youngblood was talking to him.

Stong gave the dodger to Youngblood, who barely glanced at it before his cold gray eyes trained on Stong.

"It's you two?"

Youngblood nodded. Snell came over beside him. They did not look like brothers; they probably never had, Stong thought. "It says murder," Stong said.

"You'd do something about it?" Youngblood asked.

"Yes."

"All right," Youngblood said. "I'll tell you. We were both with Berdan's sharpshooters in the war. You've heard that the Rebs caught hell after the war in Texas. Snell and me don't feel sorry about that at all. We had a little ranch down there near the border. We were Union men. We caught hell right and left from the Rebs. It don't mention on this paper that we lost two brothers. It just says we murdered four men. That happened, Stong, when a bunch of wild-eyed Texans came out to our place to finish off the Youngs. Politics was a strange thing down there at times. In the capital, things were Union, but that didn't hold where we were. It came out murder. They sent Union troops, by God, to pick us up. Ask your father how we got away. He was a Southerner. In fact, he was the sheriff down there at the time."

Youngblood gave the dodger back to Stong.

"Did you think I knew about you?" Stong asked.

Youngblood said: "We knew you didn't."

So what help they had given him had been honest. Stong struck a match on the hind wheel of the wagon. He lit the circular, and let it drop. He walked away. He had settled one thing that had risen from the troubles of Antelope County and it gave him satisfaction to have it clearly done.

He had not gone five steps when he saw Goliad and Kinkaid Sartrain riding into town. He waited. They came directly to the livery stable. Goliad's glance was casual. Kinkaid's brutally scarred face was toward Stong much longer. He was still waiting when they came outside.

"Anything on your minds, boys?"

Goliad smiled, but there was a tight pulsing under his expression. "You're overrating your importance, Stong."

He and Kinkaid went down the street. When they were twenty feet away, Kinkaid laughed loudly, and Goliad glanced back at Stong.

Pete Snell's voice was hoarse. "Where we come from, they. . . ."

Youngblood said: "Get the hay, Snell." He gave Stong a

brief glance and went inside the stable.

Stong watched the Sartrains go to the Five Nations. After his last meeting with Goliad the man had been ready to kill him on sight. Nothing was changed except Goliad's approach, and Kinkaid was with him now. Kinkaid was not too smart. Goliad could handle him easily. If Roblado McCady, whose bullet had left Kinkaid's face misshapen, showed up now. . . .

Legally the town was no longer Stong's affair, but he could not accept that. He went back to his office and sat down. It was only five minutes before Doty came in.

"Goliad and Kinkaid. . . ."

"I saw them," Stong said.

"You promised the last time you wouldn't start trouble, Stong. I. . . ."

"Goliad insulted my sisters."

"He did?" Doty's purplish lips compressed. "By God, that's different then." But a moment later the starch went out of him once more. "Is he after you?"

"Sure. I slapped him into a wall and turned my back on him. You know that. I won't start trouble with him, Doty."

"He said the same thing," the marshal complained.

Doty was working as hard as he could to maintain peace, Stong knew. If a man's sand ran out on him at a critical time, you couldn't always condemn him. "You have my promise," Stong said. And then he added wickedly: "Has anyone been robbed at Lulu's lately?"

Doty licked his lips. "A man who gets drunk in her place is a fool, Stong. That includes me." He laid his weakness in the open. "I'd like to hold my job. I don't drink so much then." He took a deep breath and went out, hurrying down the street.

Stong was still in his office when Bedford Sartrain went

past in a buggy with his wife and Avlona Oleano. Stong went out on the walk to watch.

At the Shavano House Bedford helped his wife and Avlona down. They went inside. Bedford cramped the wheels hard, turned, and came back up the street to Youngblood's. He was dressed in black. The clothing made him look older than Stong remembered from their last meeting.

He came across the street a few minutes later, glancing into the barbershop where Kopperwit was shaving Willy Golden. "See you in a minute, Stong."

They went inside, and Stong closed the door to his living quarters. Bedford dropped his hat on the desk and ran his wrist along the film of sweat and dust on his forehead. "Hot day," he said. "I didn't used to notice it."

Something about him seemed to have shrunk. There were wrinkles on his face that must have been there before, but Stong had not noticed them as he did now, and the high, sharp bones of his features were showing strongly.

"What did you and Goliad get into it about?" he asked suddenly.

"He thought I'd been running with Tucky McCady."

Bedford nodded. It was apparent that he did not care whether the current rumor was true or not, or perhaps he had not heard it. "He'll be looking for a fight."

"Him and Kinkaid."

The old man glared. "Goliad can take care of himself."

"Still, he brought Kinkaid along." Stong shook his head. "I can't afford a fight with Goliad, and you can't, either, Bedford."

"What do you mean?"

"Avlona."

"How'd you find that out?"

"She told me," Stong said.

"Strangers at Cross found out what I didn't know until a few days ago," Bedford said bitterly.

"You feel that you owe Jim Oleano's daughter as much as if she were your own girl, don't you, Bedford?"

"Why, hell, yes."

"Then you don't know how Limba McCady feels, but he doesn't know about Goliad . . . not yet. Suppose he walked in here now and asked you what you were going to do about Goliad, what would you tell him?"

"To keep his girl from riding wild all over the country! That's what. . . ."

"Avlona stayed home, Bedford. Would you tell Jim Oleano's boys what you would tell Limba?"

"That's different!" Bedford eyed Stong wickedly. "Another thing, it ain't one bit of your business."

"It is." Stong inclined his head toward the barbershop, a warning to keep the talk quiet. "Avlona shot Tucky. If I'm forced to it, I'll see that she stands trial for that. It won't be the McCadys alone then that the whole country will babble about if that happens."

"You'll play hell ever touching her," Bedford growled.

They were looking at each other steadily when Pete Snell and Busby Youngblood walked in. It was the first time Stong had ever seen Youngblood armed; he was wearing a cedar-handled Colt. The wood was slick and dark. Youngblood's face was cold.

He said: "We figured we'd just as well go whole hog, now that we're started. Let us know, Stong, what you're likely to need."

"I don't look for any trouble today," Stong said.

"That's fine." Youngblood started out.

"Just a minute," Bedford said. "Suppose the McCadys

were down there, instead . . . ?"

"All the same," Youngblood said. He and his brother
went on out.

"They've already held pistols on the McCadys," Stong
said. "There's others like them here, who don't want to see
another blow-up between the Sartrains and the McCadys."
He wondered if he could name five, and, out of the five,
one who would give Bedford warning in advance like
Youngblood.

"What are you after, Stong?" Bedford asked darkly.

"Peace."

"How you going to have it when that damned old fool
Limba finds out about his girl skyhooting around with
Goliad? Do you think I'm going to let him tell me . . . ?"

"It might help some if Goliad and Avlona were married.
I guess you could see to that, couldn't you?"

"I. . . ." Bedford's jaw set in a hard line. "Don't tell me
how to run my family, Stong."

"I'm not." Marriage between Goliad and Avlona
wouldn't cool the tempers of the McCadys one degree.
"I'm telling you I want no trouble with Goliad and Kinkaid.
I'd appreciate it if you'd keep them off me, Bedford."

The old man growled something that might have been
yes or no or go to hell. He went outside, squinting in the
sun, and then he walked toward the Five Nations.

Stong sighed. Pistol work would not settle anything. He
did not know what would.

XII

After sundown, when the long waves of coolness rolled from the mountains, Mormon Forge was still breathing tensely. The fight had not come but it was here and ready. Vir McCady was now in town, visiting his niece at Dr. Harlan's house.

Busby Youngblood was wearing a pistol. Toothless Pete Snell was a shadow at his side. Busby had held a pistol on McCadys at the Old Forge schoolhouse in defense of Pat Stong. How could the McCadys overlook that? They had sent Vir, the mildest of them all, to scout around and see how many other friends Stong had.

More than likely they were ready for a showdown with the sheriff. The McCadys had delayed overly long about that already. Now they faced complications. Matt Stong was in town, grim as a skull, and with him were the Jackson brothers, two strangers who he had recently hired. At first they had appeared to be no more than drifting cowboys, looking for work, but fast running speculation had made them wanted gunmen.

Sioux Peters said Matthew was sore about them tagging him into town, but that was no doubt a stall. Matthew knew what he was doing, all right, and the Jackson brothers were no doubt the heller sons or grandsons of someone he had known in Texas long ago.

151

Then there were the Sartrains. Kinkaid was half drunk and had tried to start trouble with Andy Kopperwit. Goliad was not drunk. He had to watch himself, for he had sworn the last time he was in town that he would get Pat Stong. The sheriff was lying low. There were those who said he was hiding out, just as he had hidden out when Limba McCady was looking for him. Others said he was just waiting.

Old Bedford was here, too. He had talked privately to Goliad and Kinkaid, and then he had spent most of the afternoon with his wife and Avlona Oleano in the Shavano House. The clerk said there had been one long argument between Bedford and the girl all afternoon, but unfortunately the clerk had been unable to get the details.

The sides were not lined up clearly just yet, and the issues were confused, but everyone thought he knew the answers. Pretty soon Vir McCady would drift out of town, and then one of the Sartrains would leave—and both would be going for reinforcements.

On the whole, Mormon Forge was not unhappy over the prospects. Look what pistol fights had done for places like Tombstone and Dodge City. Among those who did not like the situation was Marshal Houston Doty. He was at Lulu Courtney's bar but he was not three sheets in the wind, not yet.

Lulu smiled to herself when she said: "You could run Goliad out of town. That's where the main trouble seems to be."

Doty glared at her. When she shrugged, with a half smile still mocking him, he said: "You know, I'm getting a little fed up with the way you're robbing people here. I might get rough about that, Lulu. I just might." Curiously enough, he was serious.

"Take another drink, you old goat."

Doty turned away suddenly. There was little he would do, he knew, because he was not man enough, but still he would not stand here drinking. He went out to make a slow tour of the town, to give himself, at least, the feeling that he was not entirely without courage.

Sitting in the dark on a wagon box near Youngblood's livery stable, Pat Stong watched Doty go in and out of the places where the sharp points of trouble were; he thought that Marshal Doty was doing the best he could. Some men with greater physical courage would have done much less.

In the Five Nations Willy Golden made the rounds of the gambling tables and was bored when he saw that the house was winning about as usual. He strolled over to the free lunch where the Jackson brothers were stuffing themselves. This time they could pay for their beer, and behind that lay an assurance and pride which was the only change in them. It was, Golden thought, a significant enough change, although hardly enough to make them the dangerous pistolmen that a great many people now thought they were.

Goliad and Kinkaid Sartrain were at the bar. Kinkaid said: "Just how crooked are your games here, Golden?" His tone, rather than the question, made a waiting silence at the bar.

Golden smiled, reaching slowly toward the inside pocket of his gray coat. "How much did you lose?" He drew out a wallet.

"I happened to win," Kinkaid said. He was at once marked with the sullenness of a man who finds himself turned aside by gentle words. "But the question. . . ."

"Shut up, Kinkaid," Goliad said.

"I just want to know. . . ."

"Shut up!" Goliad's voice was sharp-edged but not loud. He grinned at the gambler. "He knows your games are no more crooked than anywhere else."

"Thank you." Golden put his money away. Of the two, Goliad was the worthless one. You couldn't play cards with a man without learning a great deal about him. The layers of Goliad's character were shifting and uncertain. When Kinkaid was drunk, he was mean, but he was directly honest, although blessed with fewer brains than the average Sartrain. Goliad would use him, see him killed, and never have a bad moment about it.

Stupidity manipulated by trickery, Golden thought; there might be the whole history of mankind. Willy Golden went about his own business. He was not unaware when one of Rube Archuleta's boys came in and spoke to Goliad a few minutes later. The gambler saw quick exasperation on Goliad's face. Goliad spoke to his brother, giving him orders, and then he went out.

Matthew Stong appeared not to notice his leaving. The Jackson brothers were worried. One of them drifted over to Matt's table and stood there uncertainly. The other stayed near Kinkaid.

XIII

Goliad strode past Arbor's freight yard, going toward the river. Pat Stong had more friends than he had thought. Old Bedford wasn't acting right, either. He had told Goliad flatly not to start trouble. Bedford was old. He had lost his steam.

Avlona was waiting in Rubrio Archuleta's house on the south bank of the Mormon. Rubrio worked for Fritz John McCady but that meant nothing, for the loyalties of Spanish people among themselves made for wondrous silence on many matters. Still wearing her silly patch of a bonnet, Avlona was telling a story to four little Archuletas. The sight made Goliad uneasy. Avlona made him wait until she broke off and hustled the children into another room, and then she closed the door and came running to him.

Goliad embraced her automatically. Her perfume was too strong. He did not like the odors of the house. "What do you want?"

She pulled back from him, studying his face. Her expression then was not young and simple. "You came," she said. "It will be well that you always do."

"Oh, hell! What do you want?"

"I do not like you here so close to Tucky."

"I came on business."

"Yes! She is the business!"

"I don't want one of your damned spitfire quarrels! I've got enough grief on my hands as it is."

"Sheriff Pat, yes. He will kill you, Goliad. He will kill you fast if you start trouble over Tucky."

There was a sure ring of truth in her words; Goliad had been thinking along similar lines himself. "Why did Bedford and his wife bring you in?"

"Because they knew I was going to follow you."

"Why did you send for me, Lona?"

"I am afraid. Bedford is growing very stern and angry because I say I don't want to marry you. I think it is time we tell him no more lies. You are trying to fool me, also, as well as him? If you are not, we will tell him tonight that we are ready to be married."

Marriage. Bedford had dinned the word until Goliad was sick of it. He remembered Avlona as he had seen her a few minutes ago, with brown-faced kids surrounding her. He said: "Let's not rush things."

"Rush? Maybe we are too long now. I do not like it, Goliad, that you come to see this woman."

"I didn't come to see her. Now shut up about it." Goliad turned away. "I've got to get back."

"To her?"

In the back of the house children were protesting about going to bed. Mrs. Archuleta's voice was raised sharply. It was a foreshadowing of things to come if a man was damned fool enough to get married. Goliad said: "I've got business."

"Business with her!" Avlona cursed him in Spanish. "I will tell Bedford then that I wish to marry you! I will not lie to him any more."

Goliad smiled slowly. He held the smile and stood looking down at the girl until she tried to hit him in the face with her fist, the way she had fought with her brothers. He caught her wrist and pulled her to him. She beat at him for a while, and then she grabbed him around the neck and struggled no more.

When he let her down, a fragment of her anger returned. "You are not going to her?"

"No. Come on, I'll take you back to the hotel. You can sit at your window and watch the front of the Five Nations if you want to. That's where I'll be."

When they were on the porch, with the light from the doorway streaming on them, Avlona said—"Again."—and put her arms around Goliad's neck.

There was a rider coming across the ford above the bridge. Goliad listened to the sliding of hoofs on the heavy gravel of the river. He heard the horse churn up the bank and strike the sod. "Again!" Avlona said fiercely, and Goliad had to kiss her. The rider turned toward the first buildings. Goliad abruptly went to the Five Nations.

Kinkaid had tried to start a fight with one of the Jackson brothers, and the youngster, being scared, was overeager to accommodate. Sioux Peters had broken up things even while Matthew was coming from the front table.

Goliad took his brother by the arm. "You need something to eat." He hustled Kinkaid out the back door, and then he cursed him. "You fool! There's a half dozen backing Stong. Those two kids work for his old man. When you start trouble where it won't do any good, that means you're drunk." He took Kinkaid down to the Boston and shoved him in the back door. "You eat a full meal and wait here till I come back."

Amy Harlan answered Goliad's knock. She had never liked him and now he saw her feeling was even stronger, and that pleased him. He wondered how long it would take her to change her attitude if he set his mind to the task. Women—no matter where they came from—they were all about the same.

"I'd like to see Tucky, if I may, Missus Harlan."

"Come in." Mrs. Harlan took Goliad's hat, and led him into the living room where Tucky was sitting, cross-legged, on a braided rug before the fireplace. She rose quickly, smoothing her skirt.

From the kitchen Dr. Harlan called: "Amy, if that's another baby, tell him his wife can't have it until day after tomorrow!"

"It's Goliad Sartrain," Mrs. Harlan said. Her calm scrutiny was more disturbing than her dislike. "My husband just came in from a call and now he has to go at once to the east end of the valley." She started toward the kitchen.

Harlan stuck his head around the door. "Hi, there, Goliad. If you ever have any kids, see that they're not born in the middle of the night, will you?"

"Excuse us, please." Amy Harlan pushed her husband back into the kitchen and closed the door.

Tucky was pale. Illness or the marks of it always troubled Goliad, but, of course, Tucky would be all right before long. At that, her paleness was a pleasant contrast to Lona's dusky skin and dark eyes.

"How are you feeling, Tucky?"

"Fine."

"I couldn't come to see you more than that one time. You understand how it is."

"Yes."

Goliad hesitated. "What's the matter?"

"Nothing."

He went to her and put both hands on her shoulders gently. He kissed her, and all at once the surging fire of everything between them came alive.

"It's been hell," Goliad said, "you were sick and hurt and me seeing you only that one time." The sounds in the adjacent room bothered him. "Let's go outside."

They stood by the honey locusts at the corner of the yard. The starlight was like knife points twinkling and the lights of the town were warm.

"When can we meet again?" Goliad asked.

"I don't know. With everything upset the way it is. . . ."

"Pat Stong, you mean? Has he been here again?" A blackness came into Goliad's voice. "Tucky. . . ."

"You don't still believe that story?"

"Where there's smoke, there's fire. I'm going to kill him, Tucky. I started the other day but he turned his back on me."

"Don't you trust me?"

"I can trust you better when he's dead."

"You've got to believe me!"

For an instant Tucky's sincerity almost forced belief on Goliad, but there was too much weight on the other side and the greatest pressure of all was his own lack of will to believe and a readiness to hate Pat Stong.

"Goliad, when are we going to be married?"

Tucky's voice had changed. The question irritated Goliad but he let his words come easily. "You know it's impossible for a while. Your grandfather. . . ."

"Limba has nothing to do with it. We'll leave the valley. We can go to Sandoval or Glenwood and then. . . ."

"Sure! When I have enough money to start right."

"I can get the money," Tucky said quietly. "I can get it tomorrow, all we'll need to make a start somewhere."

Goliad considered the prospect briefly. He shared in the

Sartrain holdings. His life was pleasant, his responsibilities very light.

"We can meet here tomorrow night," Tucky said. "Go home so you can avoid a quarrel with Pat Stong. . . ."

"Stong, huh? You don't want him hurt. Just what is the deal between him and your family? He and Limba were ready to kill each other not so long ago and now you and all the other McCadys seem worried about his health."

"For heaven's sake, Goliad. . . ."

"He's in everybody's affairs." Goliad stared up the street.

"I can get the money tomorrow," Tucky said. "Shall I?"

"If we run away, people will say I was afraid to marry you and stay here. I'm not afraid to face all the talk. I'm. . . ."

"So far you haven't faced anything, Goliad. So far Pat Stong and I have been the marks for filthy talk. I feel guilty because I dragged him. . . ."

"Stong! Stong! Are you going to throw him in my face forever?"

Tucky was silent for a long time, and Goliad made the mistake of thinking he had beaten down her insistence, and then she asked: "If it's only money, Goliad, I can get it. What else holds you back?"

"Your money. That's a fine thing. People would say I couldn't even support a wife."

"We'll go where people won't know, if you're really so concerned about what they think."

"You're rushing things." Pinned tight, Goliad resorted to a very simple strategy that always worked. He took Tucky in his arms.

She broke away from him with sudden violence. "You haven't even given me an honest word since you've been here, and you reek of the perfume of Avlona Oleano! I didn't believe it, Goliad, but now I do. Pat Stong hinted at it. . . ."

"I imagine he did! That must have been a pretty subject of conversation while you and him were laying. . . ."

She slapped him. He reacted as he would have in Lulu's place. He knocked her down with the flat of his hand, and started to kick her with the side of his foot. He was shocked at himself then, and reached to help her up. For a moment he thought she was injured, the way she lay on her side, her pale face staring up at him.

"Tucky! My God, I'm sorry!"

She got up slowly, by herself. "I guess I've been the route now. They say the McCadys always learn the hard way, but some of them do learn."

"I'm sorry, Tucky. I. . . ."

"I imagine you are." She laughed suddenly, and walked toward the house.

"Tucky!"

The laughter was Goliad's answer. He could have withstood anger and threats or tears and pleas but his vanity could not stand laughter, for it told him that he had lost her forever. The loss itself was nothing; the blow against his pride was tremendous.

She stopped laughing and he waited for sobs that would have helped restore his confidence, but she said calmly: "Your level is Lulu's place. Go back there, Goliad."

"You're no better than any painted woman there," he said viciously.

"You're probably right." She laughed at him again.

Goliad kicked the gate open, and strode away. At the moment he was savage enough to tackle Stong in a straight-out fight, but the shifting depths of his nature tempered that thought by the time he found Kinkaid still eating in the Boston Café.

Coffee and food had taken the belligerent edge from Kinkaid's drunkenness. He rubbed his mangled cheek and said: "It ain't so good. Bedford has been in here, looking me over. He wanted to know where you were. Those Jackson brothers, Youngblood and Snell and old Matt Stong are all lined up against us, Goliad."

They had been all the time. Kinkaid, the fool, was just realizing it.

"I really ain't got nothing against Pat Stong," Kinkaid said. "Of course, I'll back up any play you make, and so will Bedford. We got to do that, but it's up to you to make the play."

"You think I'm afraid to?"

"No," Kinkaid said quickly, but his glance slid away from his brother's face. "I know you ain't, but all that fuss just over a woman. Hell, Goliad, the way you chase around. . . ."

"Shut up!"

Kinkaid shrugged. He went back to eating his steak. "I'm with you. You know that, but I don't see no use of a pistol fight just for fun."

"Was it fun with you and Roblado McCady?"

Kinkaid put down his fork. His eyes grew pale. "I won't take that kind of talk."

"I'm trying to tell you this isn't just trouble between me and Stong. He's got the whole McCady bunch into it. Why do you think Vir was here today? Tucky told him about me and her. He's gone back to the M to bring the whole tribe down on us. Stong's backing it because I took Tucky away from him in the first place."

"That's different." Kinkaid rubbed his cheek.

"They'd like nothing better than to come in here and wipe out you and me and Bedford, with the sheriff and the other scum standing behind the whole deal."

Kinkaid started to rise. "Let's tell Bedford."

"Sit down! What will he do? He's lost his fire. He'll say let's get back to the Cross. He'll make us the laughingstock of the country for running from the McCadys."

"He has been sort of logy lately." Kinkaid shook his head. "That miserable Roblado McCady. . . ."

Goliad went to the kitchen, poured himself a cup of coffee, and returned to the table. He leaned back in his chair. Tucky had laughed in his face. Now he hated all McCadys. Stong had ruined everything, and Goliad was pledged to kill him, but Goliad was afraid. The knowledge added to his savagery.

Gunsmoke between the McCadys and the Sartrains would blow away a lot of Goliad's worries. If they met in town, Stong, the damned fool, would try to step between them and he would be the first to go down. For an instant Goliad was appalled at the thought of cold-bloodedly bringing about a fight between the two families but he overcame this by telling himself it was inevitable anyway. In anger, because he had jilted her, Tucky might tell the truth; in addition, Avlona was primed to blow up and scatter facts. Goliad would then be the first target of the McCadys. Consequences that he had given small thought to before now rode him hard. As he sat there, his moral scruples disintegrated and the breaking-down took the last of his courage. Hatred and cunning rose starkly above the ruins.

"Go home, Kinkaid. Tell them the McCadys are pushing in on me and Bedford. Tell them Limba has found out about me and Tucky."

"Has he?"

"Of course! Tucky told Vir, and he's gone home to bring the whole tribe down on us."

"The hell! We'd better get Bedford and. . . ."

"Forget Bedford. I'll watch out for him."

Kinkaid shook his head. "I ain't leaving him here to get shot up. We can come back, all of us."

"Bedford won't run. You know that. Anyway, the McCadys won't be here before morning. Get back to Cross right away, Kinkaid. Tell Pa. He'll take care of things."

Kinkaid had to wait at the door while Andy Kopperwit and Willy Golden came in. They sat down at the counter.

Goliad knew the next move was going to be tricky. He had to bring the McCadys into town with blood in their eyes. He considered sending a note to Ruthven or Limba, exposing himself. That wouldn't be so good. The messenger would be questioned; then, too, some of the McCadys might come boiling in before the Sartrains arrived. With his thinking geared along those lines he received a bad start when Vir McCady came through the doorway. Good Lord, was the whole tribe here already? He hadn't left town. Goliad watched him uneasily when Vir sat down with Golden and Kopperwit. Several times Vir glanced his way, a calm, speculative look upon his face.

Goliad went to the kitchen for more coffee. He considered going out the back door. Goliad's pride asserted itself. He took his coffee back to the table. Why, Vir wasn't even armed, and he must be the only McCady in town, and he had no reputation as a fighter. By the time Golden and Kopperwit finished their coffee and left, Goliad had evolved a plan so bold and sure he was pleased with himself.

On his way out he stopped beside Vir and said: "I'd like to talk to you, McCady."

Vir did not look around. "Room One-Oh-Two at the

hotel," he said. "I'll be over right away."

Quick suspicion rose in Goliad. It was too easy. There was something devious here. He went out on the walk, and looked around. The saloons were going strong. He had a feeling of being surrounded by enemies. After a few moments he went over to the Shavano House.

Avlona was sitting alone in the lobby. Her face was distorted when she came toward him. "Liar! You went to see her. I had José Archuleta watch you."

"I had to. I had to tell her we were through. Keep your voice down, you little idiot."

"You told her this?"

"Yes, I did. It's all over."

"Then you will come to me tonight?"

"With Bedford and Callie here? Don't be silly."

"They will not know. If you are lying to me. . . ."

Someone was coming down the stairs. It was Bedford. His face was grim when he saw his grandson and Avlona. "Where's Kinkaid?"

"He went home," Goliad said.

"Why didn't you?"

"I didn't want to, Gramps."

"Don't Gramps me, damn you." Bedford scowled. "Lona, you get up to bed. You're staying with Callie tonight, understand me? I'll use your room. Go on! Get up there!"

There was a force of anger in the old man that made the girl obey. She went up the steps reluctantly. Bedford glared at Goliad, and then he went outside. Goliad went down the hall to 102. There was an edge of light under the door.

All his nameless suspicions returned. He stood close to the door facing, listening to the quiet room, peopling it with deadly things that sprang from the trickery of his own imagination. He drew his pistol, and flung the door open.

There was no one in the room. The lamp on the table was turned low. Vir's gun belt was hanging on a bedpost. He punched the cartridges from the pistol on the bedpost and sat down on the bed.

It was not long before Vir McCady, chewing a toothpick, came down the hall with a heavy tread. He did not hesitate when he opened the door and entered. His calm acceptance of the meeting made Goliad even more wary. There must be a deeply laid McCady plot in all this, even if he had started the thing himself.

"I suspected it was you," Vir said. He crossed the room and fought the window up.

"Suspected what?"

Vir turned from the window. "Maybe you'd better tell me what you wanted first."

"Tucky and me have been seeing each other." Goliad gripped his pistol.

Vir nodded. "That's what I meant."

"You know that already?" Goliad was coiled tightly. He had a terrible feeling that this was a trap, that there were dark-faced McCadys listening outside the window. Vir's slow, easy manner was covering something.

"I guessed it," Vir said. He looked at his visitor thoughtfully. "What's the matter?"

The shade sucked against the window casing as hot air rushed out of the room. It made a scraping sound. Goliad drew his pistol and leaped against the wall. "One move out there and Vir gets it! Do you hear me?"

"There's nobody out there, Sartrain. What . . . ?"

"Don't move!" Goliad backed to the doorway, fumbling behind him for the knob.

"Wait a minute!" Vir said.

Goliad backed out and jerked the door shut. His heart was bumping. His hand on the pistol was sweaty. The gloom of the hall was comforting, and all at once he allowed that maybe he had lost his head. At any rate his purpose was accomplished. A McCady had the truth now, and that must have been why Vir had come to town in the first place—to find out from Tucky. Now he knew. He had put on a good show in there, but in a minute Vir would be riding like hell to the M to bring the McCadys into Mormon Forge.

"That is a McCady room!" Avlona was peering down the hall. "Why do you go to a McCady room if you and Tucky are through? You are a liar, Goliad."

One thing after another. Goliad cursed under his breath. He backed down the hall with his pistol still in his hand, and then he whirled on Avlona. "You saw how I had to come out of there!"

"Why were you there to start? You liar! You. . . ."

Goliad flung the girl aside, and crossed the lobby in long strides. If he had met Pat Stong outside just then, the rage in him would have carried him into a fight. He walked toward Lulu's place. He had worked out a good plan. He had been wary. When hell broke loose in Mormon Forge tomorrow, old Bedford would have more important things on his mind than Avlona. It could be that Bedford would get shot. He was old enough to die anyway.

The dance was on upstairs in Lulu's place and the old girl herself was alone at the bar. She sized Goliad up and saw that he had been shaken by fear. She had always suspected he was a man without any guts. Now she was sure of it.

"I want a room, Lulu, and I don't want anyone to know I'm here."

"Sure, Goliad. The evening's still young, though."

"No. I want just a room and that's all."

Fear had taken everything out of him, Lulu thought. That's the way it was with those who weren't real men. She said: "You haven't got into a scrape, have you?"

"Damn you, Lulu! I want a room. I've left enough money in this place. . . ."

"Come on." Lulu led him to a small room next to her own on the main floor. A door led from it into the alley. As unstable as Goliad was, he might slip away in the night and Lulu hoped he would. Lulu had grief of her own, including a sudden moral rising in Marshal Houston Doty.

Goliad went to bed completely twisted with bitterness. Too many people were finding out what he was. Even that old hag Lulu had read him like a book. All blame led straight back to Pat Stong, who tomorrow would push his ugly face once too often into other people's business.

XIV

When Goliad backed out of Vir McCady's room, Vir had stood by the brass bedstead for several moments, wondering if Tucky had made a bad mistake. The youngster had been scared to death. It seemed to Vir that weakness had twisted Goliad's face out of the Sartrain lines, thickening his lips and giving his features a loose look. You couldn't blame him for being some scared, considering what he had come to say, but still he hadn't struck Vir as much of a man. If Tucky had to have a Sartrain, she could have picked one of Haswell's kids. But this was the way it was, so Vir would back her up as he had promised, remembering all the time what had happened when he had been in love with a Sartrain girl. He had wanted to go straight to Bedford Sartrain and tell him he intended to marry Alice, but she had been aghast at the idea. So they had run away.

Vir could not remember that he had been as jumpy as Goliad, but he might have been. Goliad was Tucky's choice, whether she had made a good pick or not. Let Limba and the others sear themselves with memories of old grudges. Vir would fight, if it came to that, to see that Tucky had what she wanted. She must not have seen Goliad lately to tell him what Vir's attitude was, that he had offered her $5,000 as a wedding gift. Vir considered now going over to see her again and tell her that Goliad had misunderstood. For a sharp moment Vir knew it had been worse than that: Goliad had shown signs of cravenness. But Vir swung back to his dream for Tucky, which was in a way a dream for himself. He put her judgment above his own.

He started out to get a drink at the Otero, not even glancing toward his pistol when he left. Ranse Dayton, the clerk, was now behind his desk. He yawned. "What was all the screeching about a minute ago?"

"I heard it. I don't know what it was about."

Vir McCady and Bedford Sartrain met at the door. Bedford hesitated. His hawkish face lost much of its harshness. For a moment, he seemed to be looking through a filter that made clear and warm things of long ago. Vir stepped aside to let him pass. Bedford said: "Hello, Vir."

It was the first time he had spoken to Vir since they had stood together at a grave. Surprise held the younger man. When he returned the greeting belatedly, old Bedford was going toward the desk.

"When did Goliad go out, Ranse?"

Still slack-jawed from hearing Bedford speak to a McCady in a civil voice, the clerk stared at the old man. "I didn't even know he was here. I was having a little nap."

Vir went out. There were now no lights in Dr. Harlan's house. He went to the Otero, and, when he saw the quick, significant exchange of glances because he was not wearing a pistol, he decided that Tucky had better give him her decision about going away with Goliad no later than tomorrow. Limba and Ruthven McCady were not going to be in the dark forever.

Sitting on the wagon box on the dark side of Youngblood's stable, Pat Stong watched the movements and counter movements of men on the street. His father, the Jackson kids, and Busby Youngblood prowled around like watching wolves each time Goliad and Kinkaid moved together. Todd Brewslow was having another meeting in his store. Occasionally he or some other member of the council came out and eyed the street. They called the marshal in and he was there a half hour. Avlona held a conference with one of the Archuleta kids in front of the Shavano House, and she kept pointing toward Dr. Harlan's place.

When Marshal Doty came up the west side of the street and started to cross, Stong called his name softly. Doty swung around with a lurch, reaching toward his pistol. "Oh! Stong!" He stood beside the wagon box shifting his boots nervously. "I told Goliad. . . ."

"Tell Kinkaid. He's the one that Goliad figures to ride into trouble."

"I told them both."

"They may listen." Like hell they would, but there was no use in shattering Doty's character any more than it was already broken.

The marshal stayed, taking confidence from this man who sat so quietly in the darkness. After a time he sat down, but he rose with a jerk when Kinkaid Sartrain came from the Boston and kept walking up the street with no sign of stopping. "He's headed for your office! Goliad will be working up the alley. . . ."

"Sit tight," Stong said.

Kinkaid passed close to them, going on around to the end of the building. In a moment they heard him demanding his horse of Pete Snell, and shortly afterward he left town at a fast trot. Snell spoke from the inside of the barn, close to where Strong and Doty were. "Kinkaid left."

"Going after some more Sartrains," Stong said.

"I don't like it." The sounds of Doty scrubbing dryness

from his mouth with his tongue were loud. "What are we going to do, Sheriff?"

Stong grinned. "Sit tight. Let me know if you need any help."

"This is no time to be insulting! You know damned well. . . ."

"I didn't mean it that way, Marshal. We're both lawmen. We'll stick together, won't we?"

"Yeah, yeah, we are at that, Stong. I made a fool of myself when the council appointed me. I'm sorry about that. But if both sides show up here, what are we going to do?"

"We'll just have to wait and see."

Doty walked away. Stong watched him go down the east side of the street, cross, and then Stong waited for him to scuttle toward Lulu's. Doty went instead into the Boston.

After a while most of the lights along the street began to go out. Mormon Forge had keyed itself for trouble, for drinking and conversation afterward, and then nothing had happened. But of course there was tomorrow. Only Kinkaid Sartrain had left town, and anyone could guess as well as Pat Stong where he had gone and why.

XV

She was a tall, straight figure standing alone in the yard when Dr. Harlan came from the house with his bag. He looked up at the stars. "Dreaming, Tucky?"

She did not answer.

"Where's Goliad?"

"Gone . . . for good."

"Sure. It goes like that for ten or eleven times before things straighten out. I remember. . . ." He reflected on her tone. It hadn't been off-hand or melodramatic. It had been, come to think of it, as flat and cold as a knife. "No tears?"

"I don't cry."

"I never did think there was any value in tears." Harlan walked over to her. "It's really all done?"

"Yes."

"You're certain?"

"He's been running to Avlona Oleano and God knows how many others. Why wouldn't I be certain?"

"You're sure that's true?"

"It's been hinted to me. Tonight I smelled her perfume on him. We had an argument about Pat Stong, and finally Goliad knocked me down."

"The son-of-a-bitch," Harlan said.

"I deserved it."

She wasn't even angry, and she hadn't wept. She didn't

know it but she was in a state of shock, Harlan thought. The pain would hit her after a while. She would be better off talking, moving, doing anything, than waiting for the smash that was bound to come. He said: "Ride with me to the east end of the valley."

"All right," Tucky said dully. "But Amy. . . ."

"She'll understand."

Harlan put his bag down. He went to Tucky's room and grabbed the first jacket he saw. It was across his arm when he stood in the kitchen doorway where his wife was washing dishes. She looked at the jacket. "Are they . . . ?"

"No," Harlan said. "They broke up. Lona Oleano and a few other items, I suppose. I didn't tell her, but when I crossed the river tonight I saw Goliad and Lona in a clinch on Rubrio Archuleta's front porch. I've run into quite a few things about Goliad. I. . . ." His wife's quiet scrutiny stopped him for a moment. "I'll take her down to the farm country with me. The ride will wear her out." He paused. "Don't you think that's a good idea, Amy?"

Her level look was unchanged.

"Best thing in the world for her." Harlan turned away quickly. "We should be back no later than noon."

The sound of his footsteps carried a note of evasion, retreat, deception, all things foreign to Munro Harlan. Amy stood with words formed on her lips, the hollow sound of them echoing in her mind as if she had spoken them. *Why, yes, that sounds like a good idea.* She dropped the dishrag into the sink and stared at the strained, lost expression of her face reflected in the window.

While the sound of the gate was still in the air behind them, Harlan said: "This won't look so good, come to think of it. I could go get the horses and lead them around town. . . ."

Tucky walked straight on. It was not childish defiance, Harlan thought. She just didn't care now what the town thought. The street was almost deserted, but the few stragglers who saw them were enough.

At the corner of the livery Harlan heard Pete Snell talking with unaccustomed vigor about a pistol fight with Texans. He and Pat Stong were sitting on the step that led up to the oat bin. There was a bottle of whiskey between them, and they looked like men who were perfectly at ease.

When they saw Tucky, Snell's face went blank; Stong rose with a surprised expression that turned to bleak displeasure when he heard Harlan ask for two horses.

Harlan noticed color in Tucky's face. She appeared to be on the verge of explaining something to Stong, and then he spoke to her with cold civility. She returned the greeting, and walked away into the shadows beyond the lantern light.

"Baby due down at the Sanderson farm," Harlan said.

Stong nodded. He sat down by the bottle of whiskey. "Yeah. One of the Sanderson boys has been by here three times in the last half hour, asking if you'd left yet. You figuring to ride along with him?"

"Not necessarily," Harlan said, annoyed at the defensive edge to his tone. "Why?"

"Just wondered."

Neither Stong nor Snell spoke again until after the doctor and Tucky had ridden away.

"Another drink?" Snell's eyes were wise and hard.

"No, thanks. It's late enough to go to bed. Quiet enough, too." Stong walked into the darkness.

A woman, Snell thought. Pat Stong, even if he didn't know it, was far deeper into trouble than the affairs of law he had set out to maintain. In spite of his calmness just now he had been ready to knock Dr. Harlan end over tin cup.

Snell took another drink and went to bed.

Stong was sitting on his cot when his father came heavily into the room. Old Matthew Stong scowled. "It's quiet. Bedford's in his room, Kinkaid lit out for home to bring a bunch back, and Goliad's hiding out somewhere, most likely down at Lulu's. You didn't gain much by avoiding him, Pat."

"Who?"

"Who? Goliad Sartrain. What's the matter with you?"

"I've got to the point where I don't give a damn what happens."

Matt squeezed himself into a chair that creaked. His pistol rapped the side of it. He unbuckled his belt and laid the pistol on the table with a thump. "What brought that about?"

"Trying to keep my mouth shut about too many things, I guess."

Matt grunted. "Let's hear about a few of them."

"In the first place, that story about me and Tucky is a lie. She told it to protect Goliad Sartrain. Like every other idiot in the country, he believes it himself. That's partly what started the trouble between me and him."

Matt's eyes squinted down in his lumpy face. "I was one of those idiots that believed the story. Your mother raked me over the coals for saying so." He watched his son intently. "What can you expect a man to think? She just went up the street with Doc Harlan, and him. . . ."

"There's nothing wrong in that. She's probably going to ride with him to where she turns off to the M. There's nothing wrong in her walking or riding with Harlan."

Matt gave out a deep-chested sound that was surprise and understanding. "So that's the way the wind blows? In that case you'd better go after Goliad Sartrain right now."

"What do you mean?"

"What I said. You're soft on Tucky McCady. Why she ever had anything to do with Goliad is beyond me. I saw through him the first and only time he ever came to the ranch wanting to take Jennifer to a dance. I ran him off. All right, Tucky made her mistake, but, by Ned, if you want her. . . ."

"Who said I did?"

Matt hesitated. "I said *if* you do. I ain't going to ask you. You're old enough to know your own mind." He squinted at his son. "You've got to admit she used poor judgment, walking up the street after dark with Harlan, riding away with him in front of the whole town. She. . . ."

"It was poor judgment. Be damned sure that's all you say about it."

Matt grinned. "I don't have to ask you what you think about her." He put one huge hand on the table. "You hold onto that Stong temper, Son, or I'll bat you right out of your boots. I'll jaw with you about something that ain't important, but now I'm not arguing . . . I'm telling you a few things."

"So has every lousy mother's son in the county. I'm fed up with being told things."

"Shut up. You've got more friends than you deserve, considering your big blabber mouth whenever anyone tries to talk to you. You sit there jealous because Tucky is with Doc Harlan. You're thinking of her and Goliad. Do something about it, for Christ's sake!"

"Do what? Go kill Goliad?"

"That's right. That's what you've got to do."

"Why?"

"Say you and Tucky get married. . . ."

"You're 'way ahead of yourself," Stong said.

". . . Say you get married. Goliad will shoot off his mouth. You may as well kill him now." Matt was matter-of-fact.

He was also right, and Stong knew it, and that put a water-soaked knot in things. "I'm the sheriff," Stong said.

"You're a man, too, I hope. Settle one thing at a time."

"The last time you were in here you told me to keep my nose out of affairs between the Sartrains and the McCadys, and now you're telling me to start a feud with the Sartrains."

"Sure. This is different," Matt said. "You were blathering around before about law and order. Now it's a deal between a man and woman. That's worth starting trouble over. I'll back you all the way."

"You've already been backing me."

Matt moved his shoulders irritably. "We got to have a square deal and you're my son, but who the hell cares about law and order?"

"I do." Stong could understand his father's view. Matt's thinking on some matters still lay in the days when law came from a pistol, with right dependent on the outlook of the man who held the weapon, and justice, if it came about at all, only an accidental by-product. So old Matt was now both right and wrong.

"Settle with Goliad, then sort the other details out as they crop up," Matt said. "Can the Sartrains object to a fair fight between you and Goliad? Another thing . . . when the McCadys know why you killed him, they'll be on your side."

"I don't want sides. I want observance of the law."

Matt grunted in disgust. "You had a stab at keeping the two families apart. Maybe you did check the McCadys a little, but nobody's going to do it when they got real cause to fight. Wait till they find out about Tucky and Goliad. They won't have him married to her, so all they can do is kill him. Then I'd like to see you keep 'em apart. It's better if you kill Goliad yourself. You ought to anyway, since you're soft on Tucky."

"I didn't say so, did I?"

"Oh, hell." Matt rose. He buckled on his pistol belt. "I don't know how you got me into this. You won't listen to me. What's your idea?"

"I don't know."

"That's just what I thought. When you do get a big, fat idea about this peace that the Lord Himself couldn't keep in this county, let me know about it. You got me and the Young boys sucked into things. . . ."

"The Young boys? Oh! Youngblood and Snell."

"Yeah," Matt growled. "Youngblood told me what you did with that dodger. It showed that you got just a gleam of sense at least." He went thumping out of the room.

Half the problems of the world were settled by accident or simply by letting them wear away, Stong thought. But a hands-off policy in Antelope County would be disastrous. He wondered what Tucky and Harlan were doing. He kept telling himself that Amy Harlan knew them both better than he did, that if she could trust them, anyone could. He wondered then how Matt had been so sure he was in love with Tucky. It was a fact; it must have been so for a long time.

Do something about it. . . . Tomorrow the Sartrains would likely be in Mormon Forge in force. Do something about that, too. It did not occur to Stong at any point in his thinking that Goliad was afraid of him; Goliad was merely sneaky, cautious, waiting for a sure hand before he declared himself.

The front door opened quietly, and then someone rapped on the inside casing. "Come in," Stong said.

It was the first time he had ever seen Amy Harlan with all her calm containment gone. Her dark blue eyes widened slowly in the light. She was moving her mouth nervously. Stong got up quickly. "Is something wrong?"

His concern seemed to steady her. She smiled. "Nothing. I just wanted to talk to you. I wasn't sure you were still in town."

"Why wouldn't I be?"

"Of course, why wouldn't you?" Mrs. Harlan moved restlessly around the room. "What do you think of Tucky, Pat?"

"What do you mean?"

"I mean. . . ." She turned and faced him squarely. "I watched you while you danced with her the other night. You're not a calm man. I've suspected for a long time that you think a great deal more of Tucky than you care to admit, perhaps even to yourself."

"Have you?"

"Don't tell me it isn't any of my business, Pat, because it is."

She was afraid, Stong realized, and there could be only one reason. "Why did you let them go, Amy?"

"Let him go! You don't understand Munro. He does what he pleases when the mood strikes him. That's why he's out here instead of having a practice in a city. He knows he can't fit into a staid routine. Sometimes he's like a child, but that is only on the surface. Tonight, Pat, is the first time since our marriage that I've ever been genuinely afraid of anything he's done. Tucky broke up with Goliad tonight. She's hurt and she must be in a terrible mood, and it was no time for her and Munro to be riding away together."

"Maybe she went just as far as the turn-off to the M," Stong said.

"No. She wasn't going home."

"Shall I go after them?" Stong asked quietly.

"That would make it worse."

"Don't you trust Tucky?" It was a plea for reassurance.

Amy said: "As far as any woman who has quarreled with her lover. Tonight, it's my husband I don't trust."

"I'll go after them."

"No!" The woman watched him steadily. "You love Tucky, don't you, Pat?"

He nodded.

"What a hell of a mess," Amy murmured, and then all at once she was against Stong and she was crying.

Pat Stong was in a mood to kill both Goliad and Dr. Harlan, and here he was standing with his arms around Harlan's wife. He stared savagely at the wall. After a time he said: "Let me take you home."

"I'm not going home. I'll get my horse and ride toward the mountains." Amy began to dry her eyes. She tried to smile and it made her look like a lonely child.

"All right," Stong said. "I'll go along with you." He wasn't going to get any sleep anyway.

Roused from sleep, Pete Snell looked at the couple owlishly. He made no comment. When they rode away, he blew out the lantern and stood for a while, listening. They would, of course, ride east after Doc Harlan and Tucky McCady.

Instead, the hoof beats went south and kept going south until Snell couldn't hear them any longer. *I'll be damned,* Snell thought, and went to bed a second time.

XVI

It was only an hour after sunrise when Harlan helped Tucky down at his house in Mormon Forge. He had thought it would be about noon when they returned, but she had pushed her steeldust along like she was carrying a rescue message to a cavalry troop. It was he who was utterly tired out from the long trip.

There was a new boy at the Sanderson farm. Mrs. Sanderson was already worried about doing the week's washing; her husband was going to pay the bill by keeping Harlan in potatoes for five years, and by that time there would be three more young Sandersons—Harlan wondered how large a pile twenty years of potatoes would make. He laughed.

"What's the joke?" Tucky asked.

"A mountain of potatoes. I wonder if I could make whiskey out of them."

Tucky smiled. There was color in her face now and she would never be more beautiful, Harlan thought. She had taken a wallop but she was coming out of it.

He got back on his horse and reached out to take the steeldust's reins. Amy was not in the yard and there was no evidence that she had watered her flowers as she always did early in the morning. She was probably at the grocery store. It was a comforting thought, a secure thought. Harlan went down the street, towing Tucky's horse. This time he didn't care what was going on in the minds of those who saw him, and there were plenty who did see him.

He gave the horses over to Pete Snell, who looked like he had had a hard night. "There wasn't any trouble, was there, Pete?"

"No." Snell was looking past Harlan, looking south. "No trouble last night," he said, and led the horses inside.

It was then that Harlan, with his mind on a hearty breakfast and a talk with Amy that he should have faced sometime ago, turned and saw his wife riding in with Pat Stong. Amy was laughing. There was more animation in her face than Harlan had seen in a long time. He spoke sharply to Snell.

"When did those horses go out?"

"Don't remember," Snell said.

Harlan's face was set in hard lines, but by the time Amy and Stong reached him and were dismounting, his face was pleasantly composed, almost. He tried to summon up the humor that had always served him so well but there was none in him at the moment. "Out for an early ride, eh?" Now that was a weak line, he thought instantly, as spurious as his expression.

"Quite early," his wife said. "In fact, we left last night." She smiled. "It was a beautiful sunrise."

"No doubt." Harlan laid a challenge then on Stong, and he received in turn a steady, brooding look. *Why, he acts about half sore,* Harlan thought. *He's got his guts.*

"How's the patient?" Amy asked.

"All right. Where'd you two go last night?"

"Just riding," Amy said. "Of course, we didn't go as far as you."

"What do you mean by that?" Harlan's voice sounded churlish, guilty to his own ears.

"Oh, there was no hurry." Amy smiled again, and Harlan thought of the doctors with whom he had competed for this woman, and she had smiled like that in those days when he was not sure of her. Now he was afraid again. "We were merely out looking at the stars," Amy said. "It was rather warm last night, didn't you think?"

"Let's go home." Harlan stared again at Stong and the same cold look came back.

Mrs. Harlan said: "Of course, let's go home. Pat is going to have breakfast with us."

"No, he isn't."

"Oh, but he is." Amy's composure was unruffled. "He and I and you and Tucky. Was it a difficult delivery, Munro? You seem upset."

"What do you expect?"

"A bath, some hot coffee . . . you'll be all right." Amy took Stong's arm. They started away, and Harlan was left with the awkward choice of tagging them or hoping to catch up. He did neither.

"Just a minute!" he said. They waited. "Stong, I want to talk to Amy."

It had occurred to Harlan that they were putting on a small show to discipline him for taking Tucky with him last night, but there was no bluff in Stong and there was no acting ability in him, either.

"If you two are trying to teach me a lesson for what I did last night. . . ."

"What did you do?" Amy asked.

Harlan said: "You know what I mean!"

"You'll have to speak very clearly, Munro."

"Tucky needed the ride. It helped her to adjust her mind to a changed situation. We went to the Sanderson farm and back, and that's it."

184

Having told the truth, Harlan suffered a bad moment when he thought Amy would not believe him. She studied him calmly, and then said: "In that case my ride helped me to adjust myself to an unchanged situation. I don't know where we went, but that, too, was it."

Harlan grinned. "All right. I guess I've been handled."

Mormon Forge watched the three go down the street, Mrs. Harlan walking in the middle. The town commented in individual ways. Todd Brewslow, who thought he understood things much better than the average citizen, stood in front of his grocery store and decided that the pillars of decent society were crumbling. And then he wondered with a touch of envy how an ugly brute like Pat Stong could get into so many scrapes with good-looking women.

Outside, after breakfast, Tucky was saying: "I'm sorry for all the trouble I caused you."

"That's done." There were many things that were not over yet and they were a weight in the back of Stong's mind, but for a while he could almost forget them. He said: "There'll be another dance this week. Will you go with me?"

"Why?" Tucky's lips barely moved.

"Because I'm asking you."

"But why?"

"Because I want you to go with me, that's all."

She studied him a long time. She nodded.

"Why?" he asked.

"Because I want to."

Stong guessed she knew by now how he felt about her. There was no time to enlarge upon the subject but there would be opportunity later. They both knew what they would have to face. Stong was satisfied.

A few moments later he was staring at the Sartrains riding into Mormon Forge. He counted fourteen of them before he gave Tucky a long look, and then he went up the street.

There were no youngsters in the group, just the hard, older, dangerous members of the Sartrain tribe. Jefferson was leading them, with Kinkaid riding beside him. They came slowly down the street, filling it from walk to walk. They watched the buildings. They turned short of Stong, ignoring him, and dismounted in front of the Five Nations.

Willy Golden was standing on the walk, almost directly in their path. He did not move. He let the Sartrains break around him, and then he touched the pleats of his white shirt and walked idly down the street toward the Boston.

Bedford Sartrain strode across the street from the Shavano House. Pete Snell and Busby Youngblood came out of the livery stable and walked unhurriedly to meet Matthew Stong in front of Weldon's saddlery. And now both Snell and Youngblood were wearing two pistols. Vir McCady walked out of the Shavano House. He was unarmed. He glanced across the street at the Five Nations, and then he went to the Otero saloon.

Marshal Doty saw the last of the dispersals when he came out of the Boston. He hitched at his pistol belt nervously. He saw Stong and waited for him.

"What are we going to do, Stong?"

"There's no McCadys here."

"Vir."

"They won't jump one man."

Doty kept nodding. "I'll go talk to the Sartrains. You want to come with me?"

"If you think you need help."

Doty hesitated. "I don't yet, I guess, not for talking. Where's Goliad, Stong?"

Stong shook his head.

"His horse is still in the livery. Lulu swears she ain't seen him." Doty hitched at his pistol belt and walked away.

Stong turned to look at the Harlan house. Tucky was still in the yard, her hair shining like dark copper. He went to meet his father and the others.

Todd Brewslow had on brand-new sleeve protectors. His arms looked like black clubs as he gestured. "You got us into this, Stong. You'd better get us out."

"With your help."

"I'm no fighting man!"

"We'll make one of you," Stong said. "You can hold a shotgun. We'll see how much you think of this town."

Brewslow shot a baleful glance toward where Tucky was standing at the Harlan gate.

"Don't say it, Brewslow."

Matt and his two companions watched Stong approach and their expressions were grim and critical. Stong felt the inadequacy of his experience balanced against what these three must have seen before he was born, but he walked in boldly.

He said: "If the McCadys come to town, I'm going to stand between the two bunches."

"Easy to say," Matt growled.

"How much baled hay have you got, Busby?"

"A few tons."

"I'll tell you what I want. . . ."

XVII

In the Five Nations, Bedford Sartrain hauled Jefferson away from the bar. "What the hell is the idea, Jeff? Did you listen to Kinkaid when he was drunk?"

"He said the McCadys were figuring to corner Goliad. What did you expect me to do?"

"Vir is the only one in town and he's not wearing a pistol."

"I got eyes," Jefferson said. "Maybe Kinkaid was a little excited but there must be something to it just the same. We'll stick around and see."

"Suppose I tell you to go home?"

Jefferson would not take the challenge and shame his father before the Sartrains. They had come here in anger and the day was past when Bedford could send them away with a wave of his hand. Jefferson said: "I guess we'd go, but it won't hurt to stick around a while, now that we're here. Will it?"

"Where's Goliad?" Bedford demanded. "He rigged this whole deal."

"I don't know. I'll send Kinkaid. . . ."

"No, you won't send Kinkaid!" Bedford glared down the bar. "He's half drunk already. You find Goliad and bring him here. We're not backing away from the McCadys, but we're not starting a damn' fool fight over nothing, either, and the whole bunch of you had better understand that."

Jefferson dispatched two Sartrains to look for Goliad. "Try Lulu's place," he said.

Marshal Houston Doty came in. He cleared his throat and addressed himself to Bedford. "I don't want no trouble, Bedford."

Bedford merely glowered at him. The rest of the Sartrains grinned. Doty hurried away.

Spath and Tanner Sartrain were curt in their demand at Lulu's. "Where's Goliad?"

"I ain't seen him since yesterday." Lulu's face was blank but her thoughts were vicious. At dawn that little hellcat, Avlona Oleano, with a gun in her fist, had roused Lulu and forced her way inside, and she, too, had wanted Goliad. Lulu knew how to deal with a knife, but the pistol had chilled her, and so she had taken Avlona to Goliad's room. And then she had waited for shots but they hadn't come. Goliad had talked the girl out of it. Then there had been tears and, later, silence. Avlona was still there. My God, if the Sartrains found her. . . . As places of this kind went, Lulu's house had been fairly decent. Now it had a fine chance of getting a bad name. Lulu shook her head. "I don't know where he is."

Spath and Tanner walked down the hall and walked into the first room they came to. It happened to be Oklahoma Sal's. Her hair was in her eyes and her mouth was loose and twisted as she reared up in bed and cursed.

"Where's Goliad?" Spath demanded.

"I don't know and I don't care. Get to hell out of here!"

"Was he here last night?"

"He wasn't around at all."

They tried two more rooms and neither of the girls knew anything about Goliad. Tanner flung open the door to

Lulu's room. "You bastard, that's my room!" she cried.

Tanner gave her a brief look. "He sure wouldn't be in there."

"He ain't anywhere here," Spath said. "Them gals would have known. Let's go. At this time of day a place like this could turn a man's stomach."

"Nobody invited you in," Lulu said.

After they were gone, she went into her room, closed the door, and spoke softly through the connecting door. "Get out of here before you ruin my reputation."

Goliad laughed. He was standing on the other side of the door. Avlona was in bed. She peered at him fearfully.

"She'll be gone in a minute, Lulu," Goliad said.

"You, too. I'm fed up with you, Goliad Sartrain."

"Beat it. You've got nothing to worry about."

Lulu left. The doors had banged shut in the hall, and the disturbed girls were quiet once more.

"She's right," Goliad said. "You get out of here as fast as you can."

Avlona was sulky. "You liked it when I came."

"Sure, sure, but now you've got to beat it." Goliad began to roll a cigarette. The Sartrains were in town. One half of the plan was working. "Do you know if Vir McCady left last night right after I talked to him?"

Avlona began to dress. "He didn't leave. He was up this morning when I sneaked away from Callie."

"Didn't leave! You're lying!"

"Now you say I lie! I saw him. You and the McCadys, always something about that Tucky! I think. . . ."

"Keep still!" Things were in a pretty pickle now. It was incredible that Vir had not lit out for home to spill what he knew. Goliad had no wish to face his family now after tolling them in on a false alarm. It was better that he stay hidden. His horse was in the livery. If they got to thinking something had happened to him, they would stick around. "Sneak out the back door and send me that Archuleta boy."

"I am tired of sneaking. Everything we do is a sneak. When do we marry, Goliad?"

"As soon as we can. Now get me that kid. . . ."

"As soon as we can! I hear that always!" Avlona's eyes were narrowed. "I will tell Bedford that you made me lie about not wanting to marry you, and then. . . ."

"Get me that Archuleta kid, Lona!"

"No! First about the marriage."

"When this trouble is over. Next week."

"You promise."

"I promise," Goliad said. His eyes were clear and steady. "Now send me the Archuleta kid."

"Why do you want José Archuleta?"

"An errand."

"I will do it."

"You can't go into saloons, Lona."

When Avlona left, Goliad paced back and forth in the tiny room. Here he was trapped in a miserable dump with everything going wrong. No part of it was his fault. It seemed forever before José Archuleta came. Avlona was with him.

"Get out of here, Lona!" Goliad was furious.

"You said bring him back. I am worried, Goliad. What will I say to Callie when I go back?"

"Beat it! You've got nothing to worry about." Goliad pushed her through the doorway and closed the door. José was staring about him fearfully, as if he expected sin in some terrible form to grab him by the seat of the pants. Goliad took a $5 gold piece from his pocket. He flipped it and the boy watched it, fascinated. "Now here's what I want you to do for me, kid. . . ."

In the filthy alley outside, Avlona raised her foot to kick at the door, and then all the anger left her. She looked around her. The place was like her relationship with Goliad, drab and miserable in the clear light. She remembered the misery in her mother's face, and she could envision the fury that would run in the eyes of her tall brothers when they knew. She was Jim Oleano's daughter and there had always been great pride in that, but now she spat upon the memory of her father. She knew now that Goliad had never wanted to marry her, had never thought to do so. And she had loved him. His last words to her when he thrust her out had been the same words he had spoken to the evil woman who ran this place, and he had said them in the same tone of voice: *Beat it! You've got nothing to worry about.*

Avlona was sixteen years old. She had thought she was grown up, but now she knew she was a foolish child. She ran like a child. She ran toward the hotel to find Callie Sartrain, who would hold Avlona in her arms and let her cry.

XVIII

Stong and Marshal Doty were on the load of baled hay that Busby Youngblood stopped suddenly in the middle of the street. Doty did not look happy but he worked with the others when they began to kick the bales off.

The Sartrains crowded along the front windows of the Five Nations. "What do you make of that?" Tanner asked.

Old Bedford grinned mirthlessly. "You ain't been far from home, Tanner, have you?"

"Just at the fort," Jefferson murmured, "to keep order between the tribes."

"Them three out there? If the McCadys show up and start something. . . ." Tanner paused.

"Count again," Bedford said.

Matt Stong, Pete Snell, Andy Kopperwit, and Todd Brewslow came in sight in the middle of the street. They were carrying shotguns. They put them down and went to work with the others, and soon there was a broken circle of bales in the street, about three feet high.

"So the town's against us," Tanner said darkly. "That lousy Pat Stong. . . ."

"Be quiet," Jefferson said. "You and Spath are sure Goliad ain't around?"

"We looked everywhere he ought to be. Nobody seems

to know where he went after he came out of the hotel last night."

Kinkaid was mean drunk. "If you ask me, that Stong and Vir McCady got him in an alley somewhere."

"Oh, hell!" Bedford said, but he was worried. "Did you look in the jail?"

"Yeah," Tanner said. "Goliad ain't in town. His horse is here. Where would he be? Him and Stong had trouble, Vir McCady shows up for no good reason. There's your answer to where Goliad is."

There was a quick, tightening silence among the Sartrains when Vir McCady came out of the Shavano House wearing his pistol. He walked over to the hay barricade, put one foot on a bale, and began to talk to Pat Stong.

"What did I tell you?" Tanner said.

"Stay here, all of you." Bedford went across the walk and directly over to Stong and Vir. They paid no attention to him until he was very close.

"Where's Goliad?" Bedford asked.

Stong shook his head. "Did you try Lulu's place?"

"He ain't there." Bedford eyed them with heavy suspicion. "Where is he, Vir?"

Vir shook his head. "I haven't seen him since I talked to him in my room last night."

Now both Bedford and Stong were staring at Vir. Sitting on a bale nearby, his hands sweating on the shotgun he held, Todd Brewslow strained his ears.

"Why did he come to see you?" Bedford growled.

"Tucky." From under heavy brows Vir gave the old man back a steady look.

"That boy is my grandson, no matter what he's done. If I thought that either one of you had waylaid him. . . ."

"I should have killed him," Stong said. The yellow flecks

in his eyes glinted. "I may yet, but it happens I wasn't close to him after he rode in last night."

"He's your grandson," Vir said quietly. "The McCadys are my folks, too, but if a shooting fight starts here today, you know where I'm going to be? Right behind this hay with the rest to keep fools from carrying on something that's made this county a miserable place to live in. You can remember one big reason, Bedford, why I'll be here. I hope you remember the way I do."

Bedford went back to the Five Nations, walking tall and straight, but in spite of that the oldness in him was there to see.

"Have you seen Tucky today, Vir?" Stong asked.

"No."

"She and Goliad busted up."

"Probably just a spat," Vir said. "It happens."

Stong let it go at that. He looked at Brewslow, now moving toward the north end of the barricade where everyone else was gathered around Matt. He wondered how much Brewslow had heard of the tense conversation. He watched Avlona Oleano run across the street, coming from the west side of town. She did not come up the walk, but disappeared behind the line of buildings.

Marshal Doty was the most nervous man inside the circle. He was chewing an unlighted cigar and spitting. Stong called him over. "What do you think, Marshal?"

"I got it up in my neck. I wish I was out of this."

"Avlona Oleano just came from the west side. I'm just wondering if Goliad could be hiding out at the Archuleta place."

"What would she have to do with that?"

"Nothing much, I suppose, but it wouldn't hurt to look over the Archuleta place, would it? If we turn up Goliad, it will take some of the pressure off."

Doty looked northeast, in the direction of the M. "I'll go over there." He spat out his cigar and stepped through a space between the piled bales.

There was an even chance that he would come back, Stong thought. You could carry a man so far, but if there was no courage in him at all, he would drop out some place along the line.

Some of the Sartrains led the horses up the street. A heavy sun brought sweat and thirst to the men sitting on the hay. Kinkaid Sartrain came out on the shaded walk in front of the Five Nations, holding up a mug of foaming beer. "Anyone out there want this?" After a while he poured the beer slowly into the dust of the street and went back into the saloon laughing.

Shortly afterward there was a commotion at the side of the Five Nations. Willy Golden was rolling a keg of beer. He eased it across the walk and kicked it on over to the hay. He took a bung starter from his pocket, and went back after steins. When he returned, the spigot was in place.

"Mind if I stay?" the gambler asked.

Matt Stong blew foam off his beer. "Where's your pistol?"

"I've never owned one. I don't intend to use one now. I thought I'd stick around just to declare my principles. I have some, although I'll admit they disturb me when they crop up like this." The mockery in Golden's eyes was now aimed at himself.

"You've declared your principles," Stong said. "Leave the rest to us."

"I believe I'll stay. There might be somebody that needs to be dragged clear."

"Stay, then."

Marshal Doty came up the middle of the street.

"I've lost a bet with myself," Golden said, looking with a half smile at the paunchy, sweating lawman.

Doty drew Stong aside. "He ain't there. Mrs. Archuleta says her oldest boy lit out on his pony a while ago. He wouldn't say where he was going, but his sisters said. . . ." Doty pointed toward the M.

"Yeah," Stong said. "Have a beer, Marshal."

For a while the life of the town flowed on as usual. People went back and forth on the street. Mrs. Youngblood did her shopping. Farmers walked quickly past the hay fort, eyeing it curiously. Bartenders came out on the street and stood in their white aprons, sizing up the situation.

"What did you do with the Jacksons?" Stong asked his father.

Old Matt growled: "I kicked their tails and sent them home. I wish I was there myself."

Youngblood and Snell looked at each other and smiled. This could be deadly, Stong thought. It was peace predicated on violence, which was completely wrong even if it worked. But there was no other way.

Dr. Harlan had a long look inside the Five Nations before he came over to the hay. He was carrying a pistol under his belt. "The women want to know if you're hungry."

No one was hungry.

Harlan leaped the barricade and sat down with his feet inside. Cartridges rattled heavily in his pockets.

"No," Stong said. "Not you, Munro. You wouldn't be worth a damn to anybody, Sartrain or McCady, with a slug in your belly."

They combined against him and made him leave.

"Slug in the belly. That was a hell of a thing to say." Marshal Doty looked at his bulging stomach.

The street was hot. As time crept on, it became less noisy.

And then from the top of the Shavano House a man cried loudly: "Here they come! Here comes the McCadys!"

Matt Stong drew a stein of beer. He drank it slowly, grinning as he watched the front of the Five Nations. It was still a long wait before the McCadys came in sight at the north end of the street.

Tucky and Amy Harlan ran out to them. A cloud of dust rose as the horses stopped. Limba McCady shook his head to whatever the women said. The horses moved again. There were about twenty of them, Stong estimated. Twenty was right, for that was the number of heavily armed men who walked up the east side of the street a few minutes later. Limba waved his hand. The McCadys swung left and went behind the buildings, while he and Ruthven came on.

"You want to talk to them, Marshal?" Stong asked.

Doty was pale. "You talk."

Bedford and Jefferson Sartrain came out of the Five Nations while Stong was going to meet the two McCadys. Limba kept staring past Stong, looking at the barricade in the street. It was obvious that something besides the hay was claiming his attention.

"Anything you start won't be worth it, Limba."

There were only shotguns showing from behind the barricade now and they were pointed toward both sides of the street.

Limba ignored Stong. "Vir!"

"I'm here," Vir answered. "I'm staying here."

"It's him, all right," Ruthven said. "I thought it was."

"Come here, Vir!" Limba ordered.

Vir did not answer.

"Go take a look," Limba said to Ruthven. The old man

198

studied Stong then. "You're hard-headed enough to be a McCady." He glanced at the hay. "But it wouldn't have been enough if Vir had been hurt."

"So that's what the Archuleta boy told you? And you fell for it." Goliad's work.

"He left word with someone at Benoni's place, and then he ran before anybody could question him," Limba said.

There must have been steeldusts racing all over the Antelope Hills after that.

Ruthven returned. He said in a puzzled voice: "Vir's all right but he's standing against us, Limba."

"He's in the middle," Stong said. "He's got a belly full of the Sartrains and the McCadys fighting like feudal barons when they please. So have a lot of us."

"Is that a fact?" Limba said. He swung his heavily boned face in a slow look across the street. The Sartrains were no longer bunched in the Five Nations. Some of them had gone out the back door and were now stationed in open places between structures on both sides of the saloon. And on this side of the street the dark faces of McCadys were looking out from similar positions.

"Now that we've gone to the trouble of coming here, I guess we'll stay a while," Limba said. "Come on, Ruthven."

Both sides would stay, of course, like two great dogs sidling around each other, finding no reason for an immediate fight but willing to wait for one, and in the meantime making sure that their courage could not be doubted. One shot from an excitable McCady like Benoni, or one unthinking act from drunken Kinkaid—anything—would touch it all off. Making it worse, the men behind the hay were not bluffing. Stong watched Limba and Ruthven go into the Otero. He walked back to the barricade. A waiting silence lay upon the street as men on both sides watched each other quietly.

"Where's Brewslow?" Stong asked.

"He faded," Matt said. "What did you expect?"

Andy Kopperwit's face was gray. He kept staring at Stong and the sheriff knew what was on his mind. "Go ahead, Andy, if you want to. Nobody'll blame you."

Kopperwit looked at Marshal Doty. He could not take courage from the grimness of old Matt and Youngblood and Snell, but he could find help in knowing that another man was as afraid as he, and so he watched Doty for a moment and said: "I guess I'll stay. Do we really shoot to kill if they start something?"

"We do," Matt said flatly. "There ain't no other way."

"Stand up," Stong said. "I'll swear you all in as deputies." That was done. Now it was as legal as he could make it.

Willy Golden was holding a shotgun. He smiled faintly when he saw Stong's hard, questioning look. "A principle is not much, Sheriff, unless a man backs it up with more than words." He brushed dust from the stock of the shotgun. "Do these things kick much?"

Time and the obvious determination of his men might make the situation tail out to nothing, Stong thought, but every minute of waiting increased the chances of something priming an explosion. At the moment the match was lacking, but if the McCadys found out about Goliad and Tucky. . . .

Limba and Ruthven came out of the Otero. One glance at their faces was enough to make Stong's heart sink. Ruthven was in a dark-faced fury and old Limba was cold with rage. They came over to the barricade.

"Since you've set yourself up to run the affairs of everyone in this county, we'll concede you this much," Limba said to Stong. "Tell the Sartrains to give us Goliad in fifteen minutes or we'll go get him from them."

Now that the worst was here, Stong was no longer afraid. From the corner of his eye he saw Todd Brewslow come out of the Otero and trot across the street toward his store. Sure, Brewslow had overheard Stong and Vir and he had run to the McCadys, thinking perhaps to reduce the issue to Goliad and make it possible to settle. But all Brewslow had effected was creating an issue impossible to settle.

"Nobody knows where Goliad is," Stong said.

"The Sartrains know. Fifteen minutes," Limba said. He and Ruthven went back to the Otero.

"Goliad," Doty muttered. "You should have killed him, Stong. Look at the mess he's got us in now."

"Go bring Reverend Gilbert Pesman here," Stong said.

"Pesman." Doty gulped. "Even if you could find Goliad, the Sartrains ain't going to hold still over there for any shotgun marriage, and the McCadys. . . ."

"Get the preacher, damn you!" Stong leaped the barricade and went to the Five Nations. Bedford and Jefferson were just inside the doorway. "Limba wants Goliad in fifteen minutes, Bedford."

"I'll give Vir McCady the same fifteen minutes to explain where Goliad is," Bedford said.

"My God, man, you don't think Vir has anything to do with Goliad being missing, do you?"

Bedford hesitated. His face was bleakly stubborn. "No matter what I think, Limba McCady ain't dictating to us."

Stong went swiftly down the street, a worried man who still believed that law should be based on peace. Over his shoulder he saw Marshal Doty hurrying toward the preacher's house. Tucky and Amy Harlan were standing in the yard.

"Limba and your father know," Stong said. "They've given the Sartrains fifteen minutes to produce Goliad."

Tucky was frowning. "Is Vir behind that hay?"

"Yes. He thinks you're still in love with Goliad. Are you?"

Tucky gave him a level look. "I never was."

"Will you marry me right now?"

"Because I started this?" Tucky asked.

"It was started long before we had anything to do with it. Will you marry me?"

"Will that stop a slaughter?"

"I think so," Stong said. "I hope so. In time I would have asked you anyway."

Tucky studied his face. "In time I might have said yes. Since there is no time, I'll say yes now."

Amy Harlan trotted with them up the street. From the opposite side of the town Marshal Doty was ushering the Reverend Pesman, a slight, frail man who carried a Bible as he hurried. Standing at the window of Mrs. Fleetwood's millinery shop, with a prayer on her lips and remembrance of Texas searing her, Mrs. Youngblood caught on quickly. She half dragged Mrs. Fleetwood with her and ran down the street. Mrs. Pesman, who believed that marriage was a sacred rite, even under the most unusual circumstances, removed her apron and hoped her bread would not burn. From an upstairs window of the Shavano House, Bedford's wife had been watching everything. Avlona had gone through several stages, from tears to rage and back to tears again. Callie had been worried because of her quietness during the last hour.

"You'll be all right for a few minutes, Lona? I have something to do."

"I am all right."

Callie Sartrain put on her bonnet, and went out to add her weight to the protest of women against the idiocy of Sartrain and McCady males. Dr. Harlan was there when she arrived. He was grinning.

Vir McCady grabbed Stong by the arm. "If this is mockery, Stong, if you think you can serve. . . ."

"He asked me to marry him, Uncle Vir," Tucky said. "It is what I want and I will do it."

"But I thought it was. . . ." Vir looked across the street. "I thought. . . ." He was badly confused. "But here, here in the street! What kind of marriage . . . ?"

"The place does not matter," Callie Sartrain said. "It is the act, and it is better that it be here than never."

Vir looked at Callie Sartrain and saw that she was thinking of something very close to him. He turned again to Tucky. "You're sure of what you're doing?"

Tucky nodded and Vir was satisfied.

Benoni broke out from where he had been lurking between two buildings. The sling on his arm flapped as he ran. Limba and Ruthven joined him, and for a moment it appeared that the three might hurl their bodies instead of their voices into the situation.

"What do you think you're doing, Stong?" Limba bellowed. "If you think we'll let her marry. . . ." He stopped. He had almost said Goliad. Limba glared. Like Vir, he was confused.

"There'll be no wedding here!" Ruthven said.

"It's me she's marrying," Stong said.

"That's worse!" Ruthven yelled. "Who said she was marrying you?"

"I'll back her," Vir said. "I'll back both of them against the whole bunch of you."

"You've got nothing to do with it," Ruthven said.

Matthew Stong's voice cut through the tension like a cold, harsh wind. "Maybe we'd best let the people involved in the marrying say what they want." He was holding a pistol on the McCadys outside the barricade.

"She ain't going to do it!" Ruthven said. "It's a trick!"

Busby Youngblood swung his pistol toward Benoni when Benoni started to go over the hay. "Stay put," Youngblood said so casually that his deadliness could not be doubted. Benoni stopped with one foot astraddle a bale, and then he withdrew carefully. "I reckon you McCadys better listen a while," Youngblood said.

Reverend Pesman licked his lips. "Miss McCady, are you sure. . . ."

"I'm sure," Tucky said. "This is what I want to do." She held her head high and her McCady temper down as she looked at her father and Limba.

"He's tricked you," Ruthven growled. He looked across the street at the Sartrains who were enjoying the spectacle.

Stong looked at Tucky. "Are you ready?"

She nodded.

"There are certain regulations," the minister said. He cleared his throat. "Now the matter of a license. . . ."

"There will be one afterward," Stong said.

"The ceremony, of course, will be no less binding in the eyes of God." Pesman's voice was shrill. He kept watching Limba and Ruthven from the corner of his eye. "Is there a ring?"

Amy Harlan twisted a gold band from her finger. She put it in Vir's hand and he stood beside Stong.

"It is somewhat out of order in the ceremony but I will

ask now if anyone has reason why these two young people should not be united in holy matrimony." Pesman looked at Ruthven.

"You're damned right I object!" Ruthven said.

"What is the reason, Ruthven?" Pesman asked.

Ruthven looked at Limba. Suddenly there was no support there. He looked at Benoni, who had a hot temper but no words to offer in answer to the question.

"Are they unfit?" the minister asked gently.

"No, but. . . ." Ruthven did not finish.

"There being no objection, then, I will proceed."

The barricade bristled with weapons. The minister's eyes strayed to them as he spoke and now and then he stammered. Across the street the Sartrains strained to listen. The watchful, dark McCadys on their side of the street were quiet. Mrs. Pesman, who wept at all weddings, made no exception of the occasion. When Vir McCady gave the ring to Stong, he turned to look at Bedford Sartrain, standing tall beside Jefferson and other Sartrains in front of the Five Nations. There was a faraway look in Vir's eyes then. The corners of his mouth bent with a smile as if something at last was at rest in him.

The minister pronounced the final words. Munro Harlan said: "This must be the first marriage in the state of Colorado where the shotguns were directed against the spectators instead of the groom."

There was a murmur among the women. They carried on as if the ceremony had been performed in church. And then all of them but Callie Sartrain went down to Amy Harlan's house with the bride.

"You haven't settled anything, Stong," Ruthven said. "The fifteen minutes is still. . . ."

Stong said: "Shut up!" He stepped over the hay and

walked up the street several paces. "Ruthven, I want to say something to you and Limba." Benoni came with the other two. Stong looked them up and down. "You had a case a while ago. You haven't got it now. Tucky is my wife and Goliad is my problem and I want no McCady interference in my family affairs. She married me of her own free will. I would have asked her to later on anyway. I don't deny that I rushed to try to keep you and the Sartrains apart. I'm proud that she accepted me." The yellow in Stong's eyes glinted as he looked from one McCady to another. "When she needed your help and understanding, she didn't get it. Your only concern was pride. You wanted to kill somebody without even having the facts straight. Vir was the only one among you with the decency of reason in him. Tucky's my wife. She's suffered enough already. Her family isn't going to make it any worse."

Limba's tufted brows were drawn down fiercely. "That all you got to say?"

"That's it," Stong said.

"You're quite a speech maker," Limba growled, "but, if I hadn't known you're also a man, you wouldn't be married to my granddaughter."

That was good enough from Limba. Stong gave Ruthven a questioning look. "You're her father."

"Nobody would have known it, for all I was considered a while ago." Ruthven looked at the Sartrains in front of the Five Nations. "It could have been arranged different. Since you're handling all the chores now, Stong, what are you going to do about Goliad?"

Benoni said: "Yeah! What about him, Stong?"

"I guess we'll be around till that's settled," Limba said.

The McCadys walked away, and Stong went back to the

barricade. Marshal Doty asked hopefully: "Is everything all straightened out now?"

"Just beginning," Stong said. The Sartrains were all keyed up. He had married a McCady. When he went looking for Goliad, he might be setting himself against all Sartrains. He had hoped that his marriage to Tucky would jar the McCadys from their headlong determination, but now, he thought bitterly, he should have known better. The only chance for peace was based on the hope that the Sartrains would stand aside for a fair fight between two men. Stong looked at his father. "I want everyone to stay here." He started across the street.

Stong walked up to Bedford. "There's something between me and one member of your family. Just one." It was then he saw Goliad standing inside the Five Nations.

Bedford hesitated. Jefferson answered for him. "You can go in, Stong, but don't figure on coming out."

Matthew Stong, Youngblood, and Snell were coming across the street, spread out, moving slowly. The McCadys were still tense and watchful. Stong damned the fact that so much violence hung lightly because of one worthless excuse of a man like Goliad. "I'm going in," he said.

He was almost at the doorway when he heard Avlona's voice. "Goliad," she said. "Goliad!" Her voice sounded old, hollow and yet there was a childish tenseness in it.

"Watch her!" Kinkaid cried.

The two shots came close together. Facing the doorway with his hand on his pistol, Goliad had turned sidewise when Kinkaid shouted, and it was then Avlona put the two shots into him. He clamped his elbows against his sides and bent his shoulders, and then he spilled over.

Kinkaid tore the pistol from the girl's hand. He knocked her against the bar and was cursing her wildly when Bedford reached him. With his shoulder the old man sent Kinkaid reeling. He put his arm around Avlona and stood looking down as they turned Goliad over.

There were hard, bitter looks on the faces of Matthew Stong and Youngblood and Pete Snell. They watched him and they watched the Sartrains, and after a moment they grasped the truth. They put their pistols away.

Dr. Harlan came rushing in to kneel with Jefferson beside Goliad. It was only a moment before Harlan said: "He's dead."

Jefferson stood up slowly. His gaze faltered when he tried to meet Bedford's grim, accusing stare. He looked at Avlona. Her face was almost formless with shock and terror. One of her fists was pressed hard against her mouth.

Bedford said: "He had it coming." He led Avlona toward the doorway, pausing as he came to Stong. "You know what a jury would say, don't you?"

Stong knew well enough. "It's a Sartrain problem now, Bedford." He watched Bedford take the girl across the street. Callie Sartrain ran from the hotel and took charge of her.

Bedford stood uncertainly on the walk, with McCadys looking curiously at him. Vir walked over to him and began to talk. They were going toward the Otero when Limba stepped out to join them. There was no handshaking and there seemed to be no words. The three men walked along together and disappeared into the Otero. The feud might not be broken entirely, Stong thought, but there was an awful dent in it.

Marshal Doty nudged his arm. "What happened?"

"There was an accidental shooting."

Stong went out, turning to his left. He walked down the street to see his wife.

Four Graves West

I

No one in the Bondad country had the guts, or enough vanity, to be caught on a flashy pinto, except one man. So it had to be Asa Kirker who was riding up the sump trail toward the Wagon Wheel. A month ago none of the McCools would have cared who came toward their place, but things were different now.

Old Purs McCool twisted around from looking through the window. He glanced at his four sons. All but Ed, the oldest, were still eating. Purs pushed his chair back and rose. Ed and Lance and Steve got up, too. When Purs McCool finished a meal, so had everyone else. Art, the youngest, did not rise. He was fifteen. He went right on gulping, although a rebellious look about the eyes told that he knew he was violating one of his father's prime rules.

Ed took another glance at the pinto, stopped now while Kirker was opening the gate at Steam Springs. Then Ed looked around the kitchen. Lance and Steve were scared, but secretly delighted to see someone defy old Purs. Their father was standing stockstill, staring at Art from cold blue eyes, waiting. Ed knew he was also fighting down his anger.

Purs McCool was a big man, slightly stooped, with gray creeping upward from his temples into Indian-straight black hair. Life had slashed hard at his features, making them harsh, almost bitter. There was a hell of temper in him that

Ed had seen in flame only three times, but he had seen his father fight it down a hundred times.

"Art!" the father said.

The youngest son stuffed in another hasty bite. His words came thickly through the food. "It's just old Kirker, the old skunk. He's alone."

"*Mister* Kirker, Art," Purs said. "Don't get flip with your talk."

It was said in the Bondad country that the McCools were all alike, that when you had seen one, you had seen all five of them, that old Purs kept them under his thumb so tightly they never had a chance to think except as he thought. Ed McCool knew how wrong all that was, even if his father was worse than a mother hen about watching young ones.

"Art," Purs said softly. When his voice went down, that was the last warning. Only twice that Ed remembered had the sons pushed on past the warning.

The Brat—after all, he *was* the youngest—was enjoying the stage, but he knew when to quit. He rose, still chewing. "Yes, sir," he said. "*Mister* Kirker, Pa. Mister Skunk Kirker."

Purs hung fire for an instant. Steve and Lance lowered their heads to grin. It was not funny to Ed. He loved his father too much, and this sort of thing had gone on too long for it to be funny any longer. It was costing all of them too much.

McCool let it go. He glanced toward the window again. Kirker was trotting his horse into the yard. "Get around!" Purs growled.

Since Ed could remember, his father had used that expression when it was time to go to work. Some bosses said: "Let's go, boys!" On the railroad they blew a whistle. Old

Purs just said: "Get around!" They all knew what to do. The Wagon Wheel operated like an Army post, without the waste of effort.

In the corner of the lodgepole pine corral Ed piddled along with his saddling. Steve and Lance likewise. They should have been halfway to Boston Ridge to work on the new drift fence, Ed thought. Kirker came into the yard and stopped. Standing on the edge of the porch, Purs did not ask him to light. Purs waited, trimming his nails with a long-bladed knife.

Asa Kirker was a handsome man, no getting around it. His features were clean and sharp, lacking the slash lines of bitterness that lay on Purs's face. Kirker's dark brown hair was curly, and it stayed nicely in place, instead of slopping all over the way Ed's did, no matter how he tried to hold it. Kirker's skin was a clear bronze. Like all the McCools, Ed's skin had a tendency to be swarthy. Kirker's boots cost more than Ed's entire go-to-meeting outfit. Ed admitted it—he was thinking of Kirker and himself in relation to Marcia Townsend.

"Mind if I get a drink, Purs?" Kirker asked. His voice was easy, self-assured.

McCool inclined his head toward the water box in Bustos Creek. "There it is, Kirker."

Steve and Lance came up beside Ed. "*Mister* Kirker," Steve said. "Mister Skunk Kirker." He laughed quietly.

"Shut up," Ed said. "We got enough trouble."

"You ain't the boss . . . yet," Lance whispered.

Purs knew they were there, not going about their business. He shot them a hard glance, and they knew they would hear about it later—even if they figured on getting away before the talk with Kirker was completely over. They should be ranged on the porch beside their father. That's the way everything about the Wheel ought to be, Ed thought. But Purs wanted to do everything himself. It was not that he didn't trust his sons' competence. Ed did not know exactly what it was. Ever since the death of their mother, ten years before, Purs, who had never been soft to start, had been harsh and close-mouthed with his kids. Fair, yes, but riding herd like a man in rustler country.

"Nice day," Kirker said. He swung down and went toward the creek. Someone had told him that pistol experts wore their holsters tied low, so that was the way he wore his. He was no pistol man, Ed knew, but he grudgingly admitted that Kirker probably was tough enough. Kirker had built the Ladder into the biggest ranch in the country. He was not afraid of work, and he had done plenty of it. But it never seemed to show on him, Ed thought. Marcia Townsend had mentioned once, during a dance over at Dot, that Kirker always looked like he had just stepped out of a bandbox. Sweating, his shirt too tight across his shoulders, his hair beginning to slip over one ear, Ed had gone out for several drinks of whiskey right after that remark.

Kirker stood with a dipper in his hand. "You've sure got good water here, Purs."

They had a lot of it, too, Ed thought, and that was worrying hell out of Asa Kirker, whose Ladder ranch was suffering worse than any in the valley during this drought.

Purs McCool just stood. The sunlight caught gray streaks in his hair that Ed had not noticed before. The Brat came sneaking from the back door. There had been no dishes rattling for some time in the kitchen. When he crossed to the corral, Art was in view of Purs, and McCool turned his head for a quick look.

Art was swinging one arm, but the other, on the side away from his father, was stiff. Art was carrying a six-gun in that hand. The idiot, Ed thought. No McCool and no one who ever worked at Wheel had worn a pistol. Purs was violent about that. His own pistol was in a trunk in the harness room, and, as far as Ed knew, Purs had not worn it for twenty years. But still the four sons owned pistols. Ed had seen to that, and Purs had fretted for three weeks about the disappearance of six steers on Calumet Creek. Pistols came high. After the young McCools owned six-guns, it had been necessary to keep them hidden, and to practice with them only when clear behind the rim rock that circled the Wheel.

Perhaps Purs did not see the pistol, but he saw the stiff arm and knew Art was carrying something. He started to leave the porch, but just then Kirker came back from the water box. Art slipped through the corral bars and joined his brothers.

"What's the idea?" Ed whispered.

Art grinned. "Let that Kirker start something, and I'll get me a mister!"

Ed jerked the pistol away and put it in his chaps pocket, and then he took it out, kept his back to the house, and checked the loads. As usual, Art was carrying the thing cylinder-full. Ed removed one cartridge. "You never learn, do you?"

"There's six holes," Art said.

"Yeah." Ed let the hammer down on an empty well. "Someday you'll catch that hammer on your clothes or something, and you'll make a hole where it hurts."

Kirker glanced toward the corral. "Hi, boys," he said, and then he forgot them.

They were just the McCool kids, the rim rock cubs, Ed thought bitterly. Their old man did not let them carry guns; the old man gave the orders and made the decisions around here. The McCool kids did not count.

Kirker put one boot on the step and looked up at Purs. "Well, have you changed your mind?"

Purs shook his head.

Kirker was not used to curtness, but his voice showed no irritation when he said: "You don't care then . . . if the rest of us are ruined." It was not a question.

"I got all the cattle here I can handle. A thousand more in here and the Hummocks would look like sheep had been through my place."

Kirker looked around slowly. Wheel sat in the middle of a broken O of rim rock, the break opening toward the valley. Bustos Creek and Calumet Creek ran through the ranch, and a dozen other tiny streams oozed from the dark clefts of the rim rock. In wet years much of the land on both sides of the creeks was swamp, not deep but soggy, choked with willows and brush. Farther down, near the opening in the O, where the water began to sink again into the ground, the Hummocks formed bumpy stretches of rich grassland that always held good native hay.

Kirker smiled. It was the sly, patronizing grimace that always infuriated Ed when he and Kirker happened to meet at Dot, with Marcia present. "You were pretty foxy when you picked this place, Purs," the Ladder owner said. "I could have owned this myself . . . like that!" He snapped his fingers.

Yeah. Ed made a wolf-like grin there between the corral poles. Anybody could have owned the place, but back in those days the valley was a cinch for wintering choice cows and the range beyond the rim rock was good for more stuff than anyone had money to buy. Who cared then for bushy swamp ground under the rim rock, and stretches of hay land so bumpy they had to be harvested by hand?

"I picked this place," Purs said slowly, "not because I

was a smart man, looking years ahead, but be. . . ."

"You were foxy," Kirker said. He made it sound as if McCool had rigged some sly, underhand deal.

"I never thought of dry years burning up the valley." Purs shook his gray-streaked head. "I never once thought of the rim rock range getting grazed bare. I picked. . . ."

"You cinched the water, McCool." Kirker managed an air of sadness, as if an old friend had betrayed him. "You hogged the water and the Hummocks."

Ed saw the signs. His father's jaw muscles were working hard. If he turned white and stuttered a little, that meant his temper would explode. It seemed to be what Kirker wanted. Ed took Art's pistol from his chaps.

"See!" Art hissed. "See?"

"I never hogged water!" Purs said. His voice was loud. He was not really angry yet. "I never tried to hold a drop of it here, even when a little dam here and there would have meant a great deal to me. I can't help it if the creeks in the valley turn to scum and the grass dries out, like it has in the past two years."

"No," Kirker said, and he drawled it long, and his tone was still digging to rouse McCool's temper. "But you don't care a hang if we're ruined. You won't let us bring our fall shippers in here for the summer."

"*Your* fall shippers, Kirker. No one else has asked me."

"Dab Townsend has."

"He only mentioned it. He knew, like me, it wouldn't work. Sure, for one summer, and then next year I wouldn't have grass enough here for my five hundred head."

Kirker shook his head sadly. "We've always been good neighbors, Purs. I hate to think you had this in mind when you settled here."

Ed was gripping the pistol at his side so hard his fingers

ached. Deliberate unfairness always made him boil. His father was like that, too, and now Ed was surprised that Purs
had held to his temper so well, in spite of Kirker's efforts to
pick a fight. It was clear enough to Ed, and maybe it was
clear enough to Purs. If Kirker could start something, he
was armed and McCool was not. Afterward, it would be
Kirker's word against the version of the young McCools,
the word of the biggest rancher in the country, a well-liked
man, against the word of four rim rock cubs. Kirker must
have known, when he rode up, that McCool had not
changed his mind and that he never would. So the Ladder
owner must have come with the intention of removing the
big McCool. The sons did not matter too much. They had
been dependent on the old man all their lives, so they could
not offer much to stop Kirker after Purs was gone. It figured that way in Ed McCool's mind as he gripped the pistol
and looked through the corral bars.

"Shoot him, Ed," Art whispered tensely.

"Shut up," Ed said. "He's not going to get any fight out
of Pa." Ed was the oldest, and he had learned that force
does not settle everything.

Purs said: "You know, Kirker, that I had nothing of the
sort in mind when I took up this place. I picked it because I
wanted land that no one else wanted, so my kids would
never be in trouble over land."

Kirker smiled, nodding slowly. "I see. The Holt County
war was riding you, eh, McCool?"

Ed saw his father's face turn ashen. Purs brought his
right arm back, the muscles so tight his clenched hand
trembled. His face was like gray, water-carved stone. "I
think I heard you right, Kirker, b-but say it again." Purs's
voice was soft. He had stuttered. It was evident that he intended to knock Kirker clear under the belly of the ground-

hitched pinto if the man mentioned Holt County again.

Kirker took his boot from the stone step. He moved back a pace or two, standing straight. His right hand hung above his pistol. Purs came down the step, his cocked right hand still trembling. Kirker moved back, but it was not retreat.

"What'd I tell you, what'd I tell you?" Art muttered rapidly. "Shoot him, Ed!"

Slowly Kirker backed toward his horse. McCool paced after him, his body moving with terrible slowness. Kirker's back touched the saddle skirt. He went a step ahead then, and stood there with his left foot extended, his right hand ready.

"I said this, McCool. . . ."

"That's all, Kirker!" Ed yelled. The pistol was steadied across a corral pole. "Stop there, Pa!"

Purs stopped. He did not look toward the corral. Kirker did, just a quick glance to let him see he was flanked by iron. He laughed gently. "So the McCool cubs never carry guns. You've switched your ways, McCool. You saw it coming, eh? You should have. You started it."

"Get on your show horse," Ed ordered.

Kirker said: "Well, I guess you wanted it the rough way, McCool. That's the way you'll get it. Remember, you're the one that's starting it, and that's the way the valley will have to look at it."

Lance yelled: "You're a dirty, stinking liar . . . Mister Kirker!"

"Shut up," Ed said automatically.

Kirker rode out with no haste. He had left the wire gate at Steam Springs open on his way in, and now he did not close it. Purs stood in the yard until the pinto was out of sight, then slowly his arm came down, and his shoulders seemed more stooped than ever.

Ed looked at his brothers. To Steve and Lance he said: "Build your fence." To Art he said: "Get back to your pearl-diving, Brat."

"You ain't the boss . . . yet," Art said, but he left, and the others finished saddling quickly and rode away.

"Edward!" Purs called, not even looking. "Where'd that gun come from?"

Ed went through the poles and walked toward his father. "It's mine. I've had one since I was fourteen."

Purs's voice was like grating rock. "Your brothers, too?"

"They may have. It's time."

Purs started to grow pale. "You're talking to your father, Edward."

"We all should have been *standing* by our father when Kirker rode in here," Ed said. "Instead of being the McCool kids hiding in a corral, while their father tries to carry all the load."

The gray thatches of Purs's brows drew down hard. Color began to seep into the rough groovings of his face. He held out his hand.

Ed hesitated, and then he laid the .45 into his father's hand. Standing at the window with a dishrag in his hand, Art groaned silently and shook his head at Ed in disgust. Purs examined the pistol. He gave Ed a wicked look. "That cost a lot of money, Edward." He was not quite Purs McCool, for Purs McCool seldom commented when the facts were clear.

"Four guns . . . and a pile of ammunition . . . cost the price of six prime steers," Ed said. "From what happened today, I'd say the investment was worthwhile."

"I'll judge that," Purs said savagely.

Ed blinked in surprise and almost fumbled the pistol as Purs held it toward him, butt first.

"You have led the others into disobeying me, Edward. On your mother's deathbed I promised her that none of you would ever wear and use guns against his fellow man."

"We haven't." It was a poor argument, and Ed knew it, so he shifted to another subject. "You've held us too close, Pa. You've tried to do everything for us, including our thinking. People think we haven't got minds of our own. They. . . ."

"I've done what was best. I've brought you up as your mother would have."

The way he *thought* their mother would have, Ed reflected. "We're facing a fight, Pa. Why can't all of us have a hand in the planning? Why don't we . . . ?"

"I'll handle affairs at Wheel, Edward."

It always came to that. Purs ran the ranch, and he ran it well, but there never had been a time when the five McCools sat down together to discuss their problems. Four of them just sat to listen. The trouble was, old Purs had been dead right so much of the time, there never had been any large problems to argue and discuss. But it was different now.

"Get around," Purs said. He started toward the porch. "That is Arthur's pistol. I saw him carry it from the house. You lied to me, Edward. Now get around. I will speak about your lying later."

Never a word about the fact that Asa Kirker would have shot him dead after Purs made a wild swing here in the yard. Ed was nettled, or he would not have asked: "What was it about Holt County . . . ?"

Purs's boots scraped hard as he swung around. "Never ask that again," he said softly.

Ed set his lips. There it was. This family was just a working arrangement, because the father never took anyone

221

into his confidence, never put any of his fears or weaknesses out where talk would have made them understandable. Ed's thoughts went back to a summer years before, when Art was seven. The four brothers came down with slow fever, days and nights of it. Alone, Purs nursed them through it. The lines in his face had become cañons and his eyes had burned red from loss of sleep.

All the way through it he had been as gentle as a mother, and everything he thought about them was on his face during those bad days. When Ed was recovering and it seemed that Art was dying, Ed had wandered weakly from the bedroom one night when he heard his father talking. Haggard, with tears running in the deep lines of his cheeks, Purs McCool was standing before the picture of their mother, telling her that it was all in God's hands now, that he had done as she would have done, and then he had knelt on the floor and prayed for the life of Arthur, and everything that he thought of his sons was in his voice. Stumbling from his own weakness, and with tears on his own cheeks, Ed had gone back to bed.

II

Ed McCool was thinking of that old scene now, as he stared at his father's glowering face. "Yes, sir," he said, and turned away.

"Take that sack of staples up to the drift fence, Ed," Purs ordered. "I see Lance and Steve forgot again."

It was "Ed" once more. Relations at Wheel were right back in the groove. But maybe not, Ed thought, because, when he rode away, he saw his father standing at the water box, staring toward the valley. Ordinarily Purs was not one to waste time like that. Maybe the old man was considering some of the things Ed had said.

Steve and Lance stopped working when they saw their brother. They waited for him to ride up the ridge. This drift fence was the first defensive move against the squeeze already started. For several weeks cattle, mostly Ladder stuff, had been coming into the Wagon Wheel the hard way, through the narrow clefts in the rim rock. "They're just naturally looking for good water and grass. We can't keep 'em from floating that way," Asa Kirker had said.

The McCools kept pushing the stuff out of the open end of the O. They put aspen log barriers across clefts where no cow would go, unless driven, and still the cattle had kept coming in. "They'll smash through anything to get at good range," Kirker had said. "The poor critters. I feel sorry for them."

Ed had wanted to ask him about the horse tracks, but as usual Purs had done all the talking.

Ed swung down beside his brothers. He untied the sack of staples and tossed it on the ground near a post.

"Is there any use to go home tonight?" Lance asked, grinning. He was the lightest of all the McCools when it came to coloring. His hair was brown, with a little curl to it, instead of straight, lank black. When he was not working, he was drawing pictures of horses. Take him to a dance, take him anywhere, and he would likely wind up off in a corner drawing pictures of horses.

"He's cooled off," Ed said. "He even gave me back Art's gun."

Steve grunted. "Maybe he's scared of what's coming." He spoke with the contempt of a youth about twenty without sense enough to be afraid of anything. "Why don't we call Kirker's hand before things start? We know danged well he's going to try to get Wheel any way he can. He has to have the Hummocks and the water if he's going to be able to hang onto two thousand cattle through the summer."

"He can sell his cattle, like the small ranchers have been forced to," Lance said.

Lance would do all right when the chips were down, Ed thought, but still he was one who always hoped and looked for the easy way out of things.

"We know Kirker won't sell enough of his stuff to get by," Ed said. "Dab Townsend might, but. . . ."

"You got influence with old Dabney's daughter." Steve grinned. "Work on. . . ."

"Shut up," Ed said. "We got a big problem. Pa won't let us plan with him. He won't even tell us what he thinks about anything."

Steve slammed a pair of pliers at the fence. They caught and spun twice around the twanging wire before they fell. "Sometimes I think I'll just ride out of here. Twenty years old, and still stuck here in a hole under the rim rock!"

You had to handle Steve carefully. He went from one mood to another so fast even Purs sometimes was thrown off by the sudden changes. Their mother had always said that Steve was the one most like Purs when he had been young, but Ed had no way of judging that now.

"You wouldn't ride out on the old man now, would you?" Ed asked.

"You know I wouldn't!" Steve sat down beside Lance, and raked his heel across the sketch of a running horse that his younger brother was making in the dirt. "This ain't getting us anywhere. We got to go after Kirker." He glanced sharply at Ed. "What was that remark Kirker made about the Holt County war?"

"I don't know." Ed shook his head. "I know this, though . . . better not ask Pa about it. I did. He. . . ."

They heard the sound of a horse splashing across Bustos Creek, and then they heard it turn from the trail and start through the aspens toward them. Steve took his pistol from his chaps pocket.

Art came out of the trees on Bad-Eye, a steeldust hellion that he would not have saddled up if Purs had been home.

"Where'd Pa go?" Ed asked.

"Toward town. Gimme my gun."

"What for?"

"It's mine."

"You're careless with it," Ed said.

Art swung from the saddle. Bad-Eye tried to whirl and go down the hill. Art was alert. He jerked the steeldust's head around. The gelding snorted and tried to rear. Art threw weight into the reins and fought Bad-Eye all the way, leaping sidewise when shod hoofs crashed down at him. He got the animal under control, then led it to the fence and tied it.

"Gimme my gun."

Steve laughed. "Tough pearl diver!"

"Next week is your turn, Stephen." Art held out his hand toward Ed. "You ought to be glad I brought my pistol out to the corral, or else by now Pa might be dead."

"Promise to keep the hammer on an empty hole?"

"There's six holes. . . . All right. Gimme the gun."

The four young McCools tried to plan what to do about Kirker. It was not so easy to figure out. They lacked experience in any kind of planning. Steve considered the men Ladder employed, eight of them. Six were just ordinary hands. Largo Andrews and Río Keene, the ramrod, were quite a bit tougher than ordinary. Steve made it sound simple. Just eliminate Kirker, Andrews, and Keene, and that took care of things.

Lance was drawing another horse. He did not look up. "We just go out and shoot the three of them, huh?"

"Sure," Art said. He had pushed the cylinder of his .45 away from the frame and was spinning it.

"Shut up!" Ed said. "You're fifteen years old, and you're trying to sound tough."

"Shut up yourself! I was the only one that brought a gun out to the corral, wasn't I?"

Steve groaned. "We'll hear about that from now till whales start swimming up Calumet Creek."

They were not getting any place at all, Ed thought. Maybe Purs knew what he was doing when he never bothered to ask their opinions on any matter. Ed scowled at the thick stand of spruce trees clotted above the pale green of aspens at the base of the rim rock. Responsibility was lying heavily on him, and he did not have an idea of what to do.

Lance said: "Maybe old Dab Townsend. . . ."

They all heard it, the crashing in the timber below the rim rock.

"More Ladder stuff," Steve said. "Just wandering in. I feel sorry for the poor critters." He tried to imitate Kirker's voice.

"Wandering in, yeah," Art said, "after somebody beats dust off their rumps with a rope."

"I said that first . . . three weeks ago, Brat." Steve scowled at the timber.

"Oh, oh," Lance murmured. "I saw a hat, just the flash of a gray hat."

Art snapped the pistol cylinder into the frame and threw the lever down. "This is the showdown!" he said.

"Shut up," Ed said. "Just set. It sounds to me like they're swinging along the hill. If they do, they'll run into the fence when they turn, and then let's see what happens."

He was right. The crashing sounds stayed on the hillside, in the timber, until the cattle were on Bustos Ridge, and then they came straight at the fence. Four McCools rose up from behind a windfall of aspen trees when the first cattle began to bawl and spread along the wire. Largo Andrews and Río Keene were driving them. Keene, bulky, pale blond, and burned red by sun, was just loosening his rope.

"Figuring to rope a post?" Ed asked.

Andrews stabbed at his pistol, and then he relaxed. He was a stringy, big-nosed man, with eyes set so wide apart they seemed to be pushing at the temple bones for release. He put his hands on the apple, and looked at Andrews.

"Where's your old man, boys?" Andrews asked.

"In town," Steve said. "Why?"

The Ladder foreman laughed, but his pale eyes were tight and searching. "I thought you were the second oldest, Stevie. Do you always speak out in the lead?"

"It doesn't matter," Ed said. "We're all together. What do you want with Pa?"

Andrews's horse seemed nervous, but Ed observed that the blond man was clever with his knees. He was moving the claybank in and crowding cattle against the fence. Keene took the cue and began to crowd on his side of the animals. Some of them slipped along the fence and escaped, but others were being forced into the wire.

"Don't put 'em into that fence!" Steve said.

Andrews grinned. He tried to look apologetic and hurt. "Why, boys, we wouldn't do that. Dog-gone, they're sure spooky." He kneed his horse in harder. "We seen this bunch drifting over the rim rock, but we couldn't catch 'em, so we figured we'd best come on down and drive 'em through your place to the valley."

"That stinks!" Art cried. Like the other McCools, he now carried his pistol in his belt against the small of his back.

Andrews had looked them over, Ed thought, and now he was sure of himself. No gun belts, flat chaps pockets, and the fact that Purs had never let his kids wear guns. The Ladder foreman was damned sure of himself. Ed was mad enough to start it, but he knew this was no place for trouble, not with unpredictable Steve and the crazy Brat along. Good Lord! They were just kids.

"Wait a minute!" Ed said. "We'll let you through."

"Why, that's right neighborly, boys," Andrews said. He grinned like a lobo wolf looking down on straying calves, and he kept pushing his horse in. A wall-eyed steer, hemmed in, growing frantic, reared up and tried to turn to bolt from the fence. Andrews waved his rope. *"Hy-yuh! Hu-yuh!"* he yelled.

The steer twisted and slammed ahead into the fence. Posts cracked, wire creaked, and the whole mass of cattle started to jam the fence.

Steve reached behind him, pulled his pistol, and began to shoot into the herd. A steer went down. Another reared and bellowed in pain. Another got its front legs over the wire and tried to lunge. Steve shot it dead. The weight settled on the strands. Wire broke with a twanging protest. Art began to shoot into the herd.

Lance and Ed had no choice. They drew their pistols and put them on the two men across the wire, and they caught both the Ladder men sitting their saddles in slack surprise. Six animals were down. Art calmly shot a wounded steer that was bellowing. The rest of the herd broke along the fence and hightailed into the timber. Art started to finish another wounded steer, and his gun hammer clicked.

"Six holes, load five," he muttered.

Steve finished the steer. And then it was silent. Andrews and Keene got their horses under control.

Ed was in a savage mood. He was afraid, too. He had not figured on this at all. Maybe it would have been better to have let them smash through the fence. The hell! It had to start some time.

"You came down over the rim rock, Andrews," he said. "Go back that way. Better put up the log block you knocked down, too. Tell Kirker his game has run out. Tell him to try something else."

The scabby patches of sunburn on Andrews's wide face were dark red from his anger.

Río Keene tapped his fingers on his saddle horn and

looked sidewise at this boss. "The rim rock cubs got claws after all, Largo. What d'you know!"

"You crazy brats," Andrews said. "There was some Dot stuff in that bunch." He pointed at a dead steer with the DT-Inside-a-Circle brand of Dabney Townsend. He pointed to another steer that wore the Flying M brand.

The M was a two-bit spread that was almost out of business, Ed knew. Those two dead critters were probably the only two in the whole bunch that had not worn a Ladder.

"Nobody's going to like it when they hear that Purs McCool's kids went hog-wild and started blasting valuable beef for no reason." Andrews shook his head.

"You were jamming 'em into the fence on purpose!" Art yelled. He had reloaded his pistol.

Andrews made a *tch*ing sound with his tongue. "We was trying to clear 'em away from the fence, wasn't we, Río?"

Keene nodded. "That's exactly it."

Ed McCool had never learned how to combat outright lies told blandly. All he could do was point his pistol toward the rim rock and say in a choked voice: "Get out of here."

The McCools stood by a broken fence where flies were beginning to buzz. They listened to the sounds of the Ladder men riding back toward the rim rock. Art was the last to put his gun away.

"We sure handed it to them!" he said.

Lance stared at the dead cattle. "We played hell, you mean."

That was the way Ed was seeing things. They had caught the two men utterly by surprise. It would never happen again. Ladder would spread its version of the incident all over the valley, and down there, where people were already halfway set against the McCools simply because Wheel was secure while others were suffering, folks would readily accept Ladder's version. Then there was Purs. He was not going to like this at all. The brothers looked at Ed. "What do we do now?" Steve asked.

"You didn't ask that a minute ago," Ed said sourly. "Now you want me to straighten everything out."

"Sure." Steve grinned. "You're the oldest, ain't you, Eddie boy?" That was Marcia's name for him when she wanted to tease him.

"Get that mess of beef off the wire! Fix the lousy fence! Get around!" Ed yelled.

They laughed. After a while Ed grinned wryly. They repaired the fence.

Art was still laughing about the way they had put the run on Ladder when it was time to go home. Maybe that was why Art was careless when he went up on Bad-Eye. The steeldust never missed a chance. Bad-Eye exploded before the youth was fully in the saddle. Art grabbed the horn and tried for the other stirrup, but he did not make the riffle. He lasted until the second jump, and then he was thrown hard on the rocky hill. Lance rode like a madman to catch the steeldust.

Steve and Ed were still pouring water on Art at the creek when Lance came back, leading Bad-Eye. There was a little cut on the back of Art's head, and that was all. But he was as limp as a wet saddle blanket, and his face was gray.

"He ain't got a busted neck, has he?" Lance asked.

"No," Ed said. He did not know. He was afraid that that was just what was the matter. Unconsciousness stripped Art of everything he had been and done that day. He was just the baby brother now. His hair was flat from water, and it looked the way it had when their mother had bathed him as a baby in a wooden tub by the cook stove.

Ed said it out loud: "Oh, God, he's just a little kid. Let

him be all right, please!"

"What'll we do, Eddie?" Steve asked.

Art lay there on the moss, gray and motionless, with water still running from his face.

Ed leaped into his saddle. "Hand him up easy. One of you lead my horse."

On the way in, Steve said savagely: "If he dies, I'm shooting that steeldust dead!"

"You can't blame the horse," Lance said.

Purs was throwing a saddle on his big blue roan when he saw them coming. He dropped the rig in the dust and went over the corral fence like a huge cat.

"Where's he hit?"

"Back of the head. He won't come to," Ed said miserably.

Purs gestured toward the house. All the harshness was gone from his face, and the stark cast of grief on his features made his sons look away from him. They put Art on the same bed where he had been born. He lay without moving, and his breathing was barely evident. Purs's hard, scarred hands moved gently as they felt Art's neck and back. A big thumb pushed up an eyelid. Ed went sick when he saw the cold, unseeing stare of the exposed eye.

Purs turned the injured lad on his side, and looked at the back of his head. "That ain't no bullet mark."

"No. He got thrown from Bad-Eye," Ed said.

"I thought. . . ." Purs put Art on his back again. He removed his boots and loosened his clothes. "All we can do is wait. He ain't got a broken neck, I'm sure." Purs eased himself down on the bed, and he glanced over his shoulder at the oval picture of his wife on the wall. His lips moved, but he made no sound.

They waited for more than an hour. Purs never moved,

just sat there with his hands clasped. The bawl of a cow somewhere down by the Hummocks came to Ed as the most mournful sound he had ever heard.

Lance began to blink hard when Art's head started to roll weakly from side to side. Art's tongue moved aimlessly in his open mouth. He made little muttering sounds.

Steve ran his sleeve across his face and began to grin, and a little later Art opened his eyes, and after a while he saw them all. "That Bad-Eye horse," he murmured. "Oh, man. . . ."

"Look here, Art." Purs pointed down at his own knee. Art raised his head. "I don't see nothing," he said, and lay back again.

Purs McCool smiled at the picture of his wife. Ed walked out of the room quickly and stood on the porch. The sun was going down above the rim rock. He had never seen a prettier sunset, and the sounds of bawling cattle near the Hummocks were the most beautiful sounds he had ever heard.

III

Purs sat with his chin in his palm and looked across the supper table at three of his sons. "An ill-considered deed," he said. "You should have let them through."

"Ed said he would," Steve explained. "They didn't wait. They wanted trouble."

"All those cattle have been driven down off the rim rock," Ed said. "The evidence is clear enough."

The father's cold blue eyes went from one face to another. Long habit made them all feel uneasy. "I know that," Purs said. "Did you four help the situation any by your act today?"

"We couldn't help ourselves," Lance said.

"Who started the shooting?" Purs asked.

The brothers looked at each other. "Me," Ed said.

At the same time Lance said: "All of us."

"I did," Steve said. "I started it."

Purs stared at them. "I have raised a gang," he said, "and the truth is not in them."

"You've caused us to set ourselves apart from you." Ed knew it was a dangerous statement to make, and then he was surprised to see that it seemed to strike deeply into his father. Purs's steady stare gave way. He took his hand from his chin and rubbed it across his heavy mane, and stared at the table.

"You made a promise about guns," Ed said. "We don't understand why . . . but that's all right. Suppose we had brought Art in the way he was a while ago, not from being thrown, but from being shot down when he was unarmed? Suppose Lance . . . ?"

"That's enough." Purs's face was marked by an inward struggle. Ed had always known that Art and Lance were the favorites, and he had played on that. "Violence never settled anything," Purs said. "It only brings ruin to lives."

"Somebody ought to tell Kirker that." Steve's voice was flat. "He intended to kill you today, Pa."

"I know that! Are you trying to tell me what I learned when I was thirteen?" Purs flared, but the heat was not in his words or manner. He was unsure.

They had him hemmed in, Ed thought. They had caught him in a weak moment. In a way it was unfair to crowd him like that, but they had never had the chance before. They had to put their weight on him to make him admit there was only one way to defend Wheel. It might help, Ed thought, if they knew why he was so afraid of violence.

"I will talk to Townsend," Purs said. "He has some weight with Kirker."

"When Andrews tells his lies about what happened today, Townsend will have no use for us," Ed said.

"Maybe they learned their lesson today." Purs licked his lips, staring at the table. "They may leave us alone."

Steve's dark face turned toward Ed, and Steve shook his head gently. It left Ed uneasy, off balance, to see his father trying to twist away from facts.

"There are men in the valley who won't be fooled by Kirker's lies," Purs said. "Men like Chapo Brown . . . others. . . ."

Lance was moving his fingertip in deft drawing gestures

on the oilcloth. He looked at Ed quickly.

"Chapo Brown," Steve muttered.

Purs was not even talking sense now, Ed thought. Brown, a half-breed Apache, was respected in the Bondad country only for his ability to track and read sign. He owned nothing but a cabin, did little except hunt. If deer were ranging far, he took a slow-elk. Ranchers had always growled about that, but, as far as Ed knew, he himself was the only one who had ever caught Chapo Brown in the act. That was several years ago, beyond the rim rock. Ed rode up on Brown skinning out a Wagon Wheel calf. Brown just grunted hello, and went on with his work. First, Ed was in a rage, and then he was bewildered by Brown's casualness. The man looked tougher than week-old blood. He wore a pistol and a knife, and he was good with both.

After a few minutes of watching the flashing knife, Ed had said: "Uh . . . nice-looking meat." And then he beat it back to report to Purs.

Purs had listened without expression. Then he said: "Our stuff wouldn't be straying that high if you and the boys did your work right. Forget it. Chapo ain't no longrider. He's just hungry."

And now Purs was mentioning Chapo Brown, as if his opinion counted against Ladder's and Dot's—and all the rest of the valley. Ed's eyes narrowed. He stored two thoughts away.

"There's just one thing to do . . . fight," Lance said.

Purs's face was heavy and old. "You, too, Lance." He gave Ed a dark look. "You've poisoned them all, Edward."

Ed shook his head. "They know the truth when they see it, that's all."

"I'll judge what's the truth!" Purs got up. The others did not rise, and Purs did not seem to notice the fact. He stamped out of the house, without even saying: "Get around!"

Steve shrugged. He looked at Ed. "You and your big conferences with the old man! Where did we get? There's just one way. . . ."

"Sure!" Art called from Purs's bedroom. "Shoot Kirker, Keene, and Andrews."

Steve grinned. "Bloodthirsty Brat. Hit him on the head again, and he'll want to clean out the whole valley."

"Shoot old Dab Townsend, too!" Art called. "But save his daughter for Eddie boy."

They choused the stuff out of the brush and willows and the bog ground on the lower side of Calumet Creek. There were eighteen head, mostly Ladder and Dot, two Flying Ms, and one each from Duck Foot and Two Stars. Every brand had been worked over into Wagon Wheel, and some of the work was very crude. They held the bunch at the Hummocks and waited for Steve.

"We'll go straight to Townsend first, and show him," Purs said.

Townsend was being sucked into this thing against his will, Ed thought, and Townsend was sour because he was selling in a bad market, forced to by the drought, while the Wheel was sitting pretty. He knew it was no one's fault, but still he was leaning toward Kirker's lies.

When Ed went the last time to see Marcia, Townsend had met him at the gate. Kirker's pinto had been in the yard.

"I ain't sure just what did happen at the fence," Townsend had said. "But maybe you'd better not come over for a while."

"What's a while?" Ed had started to open the gate.

"No, don't do it. Maybe a while is for good, McCool."

"I'll ask Marcia about that!"

"She's my daughter. You better ride, McCool."

"To hell with you," Ed had said. "You won't keep us apart, unless she wants it that way." He had looked savagely at Kirker's pinto, and ridden away.

And now, waiting for Steve to return from the drift fence, Ed thought that nothing had been improved by hot words flung at old Dabney.

Slouched on his rusty bay, Lance shook his arm toward the cattle. "Would anybody believe something as crude as that!"

"I dunno," Purs said. "I dunno."

Steve came galloping down the creek. They crowded around him. Art was still pale, but he was all right now. Purs had not said a word when Art threw a rig on Bad-Eye.

"They didn't cut the fence," Steve said. "They took up four posts and laid it down . . . and then they put it back. They were mighty careful about dragging out tracks."

Purs turned his blue roan. "Let's get 'em out of here."

It was too late. Townsend and Kirker were riding up the sump trail. They crossed Calumet and rode over to the cattle. Townsend would not look at Ed. Kirker smiled and spoke as if greeting old friends.

He said: "I was a little hasty the other day, Purs. I've told Dab that, and now I've come. . . ."

Townsend grunted. He was looking at a changed brand, and it was his own steer. His sharp features seemed to grow sharper. He threw Kirker a quick look.

"Eighteen head, all changed to Wheel," Purs said. "We been gathering them up all morning on the creek. Somebody brought 'em over the rim rock and through our drift fence."

Even in his tension, Ed did not overlook the "our".

"Would you know anything about that, *Mister* Kirker?" Steve asked. He fingered the unbuttoned pocket of his chaps. His pistol was inside.

Kirker could look as innocent as a sheep-killing dog, Ed thought. The Ladder owner did not lose the expression as he rode around the bunched cattle. "Even some M stuff," he said. "Now that's mighty odd."

"Damned odd, the whole business," Townsend said darkly. He looked at Purs, and then he looked at Ed. "Cut your drift fence, eh?"

"Laid it down," Steve said. "You heard. Maybe you. . . ."

"Shut up," Ed said. "We were just going to bring the stuff over to Dot for you to see, Mister Townsend."

"I imagine," Townsend said dryly. "We can relieve you of the job, eh, Kirker?"

Kirker nodded.

"You both showed up just right," Steve said. "How come?" He looked at Kirker.

"That happened to be my idea," Townsend said. "Asa and me have been talking over a proposition we were going to make to Purs. I suggested coming over."

That meant nothing, Ed thought. Kirker was clever enough to handle the timing.

"G-get out with your s-s-stuff!" Purs said suddenly.

He whirled the blue roan and started up the valley.

"You heard him," Steve said.

"Don't crowd, button," Kirker said wickedly. "I ain't a helpless steer caught in a fence."

Ed moved his horse between the two. He gestured down valley. The McCools were silent as the cattle were driven away.

"One more big lie against us," Lance said.

Marcia Townsend was waiting in the dusty cottonwoods at the big bend of Valley Creek when Ed rode into the grove on sandy ground where even brush was withering. Mrs. Townsend, who ran her husband without his ever realizing it, had sent a rider to Wheel the night before to tell Ed about the meeting, and right there Ed knew at last that he had beaten Asa Kirker in one way. Dab Townsend, too.

Ed swung down and faced Marcia awkwardly. She was the prettiest girl in the world, sturdy slender, laughing brown eyes. Her features were clean brown, with none of her father's sharpness in the lines.

"It's been a long time, Eddie."

"Twelve days."

They started to sit down on the ground, but ants were swarming there. Marcia's horse stamped impatiently. The cottonwoods were pale with dust. From Valley Creek came the smell of scum and stagnant water.

This grove is the most wonderful place in the world, Ed thought. "I'm going to see Chapo Brown," he said to Marcia.

"Chapo Brown!"

"Your father knows he's the best tracker in the country, don't he?"

"Doesn't he? I suppose so, yes. What . . . ?"

"It's just an idea," Ed said. There was more that she did not need to know. "Your old . . . your father . . . wouldn't be so hard to get along with if Kirker was out of this, would he?"

She took a deep breath. "No. Asa Kirker prods him all the time. I know. Kirker tells him how wonderful it would be if they owned Wheel together. The drought won't last forever. Kirker says Dot and Ladder could use the Hummocks for choice cattle in ordinary years, and as a place to fall back on in bad years."

"It wouldn't quite come out that way. Kirker would have to have everything."

She nodded. "You think I don't know him? He's been trying to court me for two years. In the back of his mind, my father must realize how he is being used, but he's desperate, Eddie. He's selling cattle at a loss now. He's trying to hang on. Dot can make out, if we strip things pretty close. But all the time, there's the Hummocks and all that clean water at Wheel. My father's only human, Eddie, and Kirker keeps jabbing at him, and rigging those lies against Wheel."

"You don't believe we rustled, do you?"

"Of course not! My mother doesn't, either, and I don't believe my father really believes it, either . . . but it's a good excuse to move against Wheel." She bit her lip. "My father, Eddie, is not as strong-minded and hard as yours."

She did not know that Purs had not been very strong-minded about anything lately. Purs had been fighting himself, and he could not seem to get organized.

"I must go," Eddie said. "I'll meet you at the Devil's Bridge on the rim rock, three days from now . . . at noon." He added: "If I can."

She walked to his horse with him. "Kirker is *buying* cattle, instead of selling them," she said.

They looked bleakly at each other, because of her words, and because their love was tangled in the net of events that were moving toward violence.

"Work on your old man," Ed said. "Put your mother on him. He's going against trouble if he rides with Kirker."

"We've tried. We're still trying." She smiled. "It will

241

come out all right, Eddie."

Sure it would. Sure it would. He was like Lance, hoping. Her last words were bright for a while, but then he was gone from her and the words were nothing, and he knew that it was going to take plenty to make things come out all right.

Chapo Brown, a spring-steel blade of a little man, with eyes like a beaver's and Apache on him everywhere, except for close-cropped gray hair, drank strong tea from a coffee pot, and heard Ed out.

"I can look at the tracks. I can say what is truth afterward."

"The sign is two days old."

Chapo spat through the open doorway of his cabin. "It is dry. I can tell."

He had not said that he would. Ed waited. Chapo put sugar on the tea leaves and ate them. It was enough to kill a man, but he had been doing it for years. He was an old man now, in years, but he looked as if he never would die.

He finished the tea leaves. "I will do it," he said. He grinned. "Uh . . . nice-looking meat."

"Then tell Dab Townsend the truth of those tracks, but don't tell him I sent you."

"He will know, but I will tell him."

Ed wanted him to leap up and get going, but that was not Brown's way. And so they sat, with Chapo belching contentedly now and then.

"You used to come to Wheel pretty often," Ed said. "When I was a kid."

"I am your father's friend, but I learned at last that my face reminded him of things he did not want to remember. So I do not go to Wheel any more."

Ed put stored facts together.

"You and Purs were in the Holt County war together."

Chapo's black eyes were like chips. He gave a little nod.

"He didn't tell me all about it," Ed said. "What it was that made it so awful for him."

Chapo stared at a weedy hillside, but his eyes, glittering fiercely, were looking down the years. "It was just a fight, over grass, over water. But it was bad for Purs."

"Why?"

"He killed his brother in it. Your mother's brothers were on the other side, too, and they were killed." Chapo stood up. "That was a long time ago, Ed."

It was only yesterday to Purs, Ed knew. This present struggle had brought it all back.

Chapo picked up a heavy Sharps rifle. Suddenly he put a hard stare on Ed. "You knew nothing about Holt County. You guessed, and you tricked me into telling you what I thought you already knew."

Ed nodded. "How is it that Kirker knows?"

"A weasel knows many things. I will look at those tracks under the rim rock right now."

IV

The McCools sat at their big table in the living room. It was growing dark outside. There was no fire or light in the room.

"No," Purs said. "No, I can't run away."

"You've got to," Ed said. "They're coming tomorrow morning . . . Ladder, Dot, the whole valley. Chapo Brown told me. They'll hang you for rustling."

"They don't want us," Steve said. " 'Get the old he-lion, the cubs will be helpless then.' That's what Kirker has been telling them."

"How do you know that?" Purs asked.

Ed said: "We have friends in the valley."

"Not enough of them . . . ," Purs muttered.

"Go to the brush cave in the rim rock," Ed said. "They'll look around. They'll threaten. They'll leave. In a while they'll calm down when they realize how Kirker has used them."

"No. I won't do it," Purs said.

"Then you'll cause a fight," Lance said softly. "Do you think we'll stand by an' watch them hang you?"

"Violence never . . . ," Purs began.

"It has to be in some things," Ed said. He took a deep breath for what he had to say next. "The Holt County war has ridden on your shoulders. . . ."

Purs lurched up. His chair fell over. "I told you. . . ."

"Sit down!" Ed's tone was brutal. The brothers had planned this in advance, and now they all echoed his words: "Sit down!" It was like the tone of judgment in the dark room.

Purs McCool fumbled for his chair. He righted it with a little clatter. His body went into it heavily.

"You've carried that old fight long enough. You're not passing the results on to us," Ed said. "Your brother was killed, our mother's brothers were killed in a fight we know nothing of. It's done. Where right was . . . it doesn't matter now. It's done. Our mother forgave you before she married you, or else she wouldn't have married you. You let it ride you, in spite of what she said. When I was little, she told me all about it, and she said she hoped you wouldn't hold a feeling of guilt forever." Ed cast around for his next words.

"She never told you!" Purs said. "You found out from Chapo Brown!"

"She told me," Ed said. Probably only Lance, of the other brothers, knew that he was lying. "She said . . . 'Your father knows that I have forgiven him for any part he had in that fight, but sometimes my forgiveness does not seem enough for him.' " She could have said it. She might have said it. The words did not seem like a lie to Ed McCool. "That was your fight, Purs," he said gently. "Tomorrow, whatever happens, is ours."

The father did not hear. "She said that? She told that to a little boy . . . ?" he mused. "But she promised never. . . ."

"Eddie told me about it long ago."

Coming from Lance, the words took the father's last doubts away. He was merely musing when he said: "She promised we would never speak of it to anyone."

"Time changes the meaning of a promise," Ed said.

"Our mother knew that. You should learn it, Purs."

The last light died above the sharp line of encircling rim rock. A coyote threw its mournful plaint into the dark. The McCools sat in a silent room.

After a while, Ed said: "Saddle the blue roan for Pa, Steve. Put some grub in a sack, Art."

Purs roused up as if coming back from far away. "I'll keep Art with me at the cave," he said.

Ed reached across the table and gripped the youngest brother's arm when a quick intake of breath foretold a protest.

The oldest brother said: "That's best, Pa."

When the sounds of two horses died away on the Bustos Creek trail, Lance turned to his brothers in the dark. He asked: "Who is actually coming . . . do you know, Ed?"

"Some of Ladder, maybe some of Dot . . . if Chapo Brown's word didn't go down with Townsend . . . and probably a few coyotes that would be afraid to speak up to Art . . . alone."

The open end of the O was an ideal place for ambush. Ledges of broken rock looked down on a narrow passage. Since one mind could think of that, another surely could, also, and so Ed forgot the place. He and Steve and Lance left their horses in the brush, and picked the roughest spot they could find close to the sump trail.

There was still dead grass from last year lying under new growth. It was open ground, if a man had to rise and run, but the sump trail, fifty yards from willows on the other side, was even more open. And that's where Kirker would be. No man could ride a horse full tilt across this section of the Hummocks.

The morning sun came down heavily on the three

brothers lying behind the bumps. Wetness began to seep up against their legs. Something scared three cows from the willows across the sump trail, and for a while Ed feared that Kirker was trying to bring his force in under cover. But there were no more noises. The cows began to drift toward the Hummocks.

They looked like a hundred when they rode up the trail; there were thirteen of them, Kirker and Townsend in the lead. Keene and Largo Andrews, two other Ladder riders, the Dot foreman, Provo from the Flying M, and five who were coyotes with little personal interests involved.

Ed let them come almost abreast.

"If they was figuring anything, it would have been back there," Andrews said.

"Just the same, we'll go in careful on the house," Kirker said.

Ed called out: "Never mind! You're close enough now!"

"Where the hell . . . ?" Andrews drew his gun and whirled his horse the wrong way, toward the willows.

"The Hummocks, you fool!" Kirker cried.

Townsend waved his arms at those behind him. The horses jostled to a stop. "Now let's not be hasty, boys!" Townsend cried nervously. "We got to consider both sides."

"You got religion a little late, didn't you?" Steve yelled.

Kirker said something in a low voice to Keene and Andrews. They began to turn their horses.

"Now, Ed, we don't want no shooting trouble!" Kirker called. He spoke to the two other Ladder riders behind Keene and Andrews.

"Then beat it fast!" Steve yelled at him.

Ladder was the hard core. The others were just the husk now, but still they were here. Two of the coyotes began to ease back down the trail. Kirker, Keene, and Andrews fired at the same time. Their bullets chunked into the Hummocks around the McCools. Kirker's men moved as they fired. Keene and Andrews lunged their horses down the trail. Kirker and the other two rowelled ahead.

"Flank 'em! Crawl in!" Kirker yelled.

Those left in the main body were slow to act. They tried to spread out. Their horses bumped each other. Men fired wildly toward the Hummocks. The two coyotes who had started to retreat kept right on going, and two more joined them.

Townsend was yelling: "Stop it! Stop it!"

Flat between grassy mounds, the McCools concentrated on Kirker and the two going ahead. Steve got a horse. It went down hard and the rider pinwheeled after he struck ground. He rose. His leg gave way and he fell, and then he crawled behind his dead horse.

Kirker and the second man got past. They veered into the creek and flung themselves from their mounts. The second man staggered and grabbed at his arm when Lance and Ed fired together, but a moment later the fellow had flung himself flat and was using the cover of bumpy ground, too.

Andrews and Keene had gone down the trail, crossed the creek, and now they, too, were working in through the mounds. They covered each other expertly with their firing. Kirker and the other man were getting closer.

Lance was white and scared, but he kept firing carefully, whenever there was a movement at which to shoot.

"Hey," Steve muttered. "This ain't so good."

Another man had left the group still in the trail. He went down and joined the four who had pulled out previously. They waited a few hundred yards away. They were coyotes, all right.

Townsend, Provo, and the Dot foreman were left in the open. "Hold it! Hold it!" Townsend cried.

Then suddenly he slumped from his plunging horse and struck the ground. Provo and the Dot foreman leaped down and began to carry him toward the willows. The shot had not come from the McCools, and that was all Ed knew about it.

"It's getting tight!" Steve said. The coyote riders waiting down the trail saw it, too. They moved up a little.

Lead churned the mounds above the McCools. Kirker had picked his men well. They knew how to fire and move in, covering each other. Lance turned on his side to reload. White as he was, he spoke calmly. "We can rush Kirker and the other, and get clear."

One or more of them would go down, Ed knew. He remembered Art's face when Art was lying unconscious. "No. Let them come in to us. Make it cost them!"

The heavy boom of a rifle from the willows startled Ed. He saw a gout of mud and grass erupt from a mound somewhere close to Kirker. There was one rifle in the country with a bellow like that—Chapo Brown's old Sharps. It spoke again. Largo Andrews let out a howl. Then, from somewhere a little farther to the left in the willows, Purs McCool's voice roared: "Give it to 'em!"

A pistol barked four times from close to his voice. The waiting coyotes fled. Provo yelled: "We're not in this!" He and the Dot ramrod were kneeling beside Dab Townsend.

The man with Kirker rose and ran. "Let him go!" Ed yelled, but Steve had already knocked the legs from under him. Chapo's heavy rifle bellowed again. Río Keene leaped up, his hands held high. Steve started to rise. "Shut up! . . . I mean, stay down!" Ed ordered.

Asa Kirker's contorted face suddenly was only a few

yards away. He had worked in closer than they realized, leaped up, and made his play. Ed missed him with a snap shot from a cramped position. Lance made a little groaning sound as his pistol hammer came down on an expended case. Steve turned too late from looking down the Hummocks, where Keene was helping Andrews to his feet.

Kirker went sidewise all at once. He fell, still trying to get on top of the three McCools with his pistol fully loaded. An instant later they heard the sullen, churning boom of Chapo's rifle. That was the last shot of the fight, and the one that counted most.

The Ladder boss was dead. Andrews was shot through both thighs. He had kept on firing to the last in spite of his wounds. The other two Ladder men had broken legs.

Ed ran over to Townsend. "In the shoulder," the Dot foreman beside him said. "Kirker done it. I saw the shot."

Kirker had played it to win everything, and he damned nearly had.

"I guess I saw the light a little late," Townsend said.

It was not late at all, Ed thought, but let Dab Townsend suffer.

Chapo Brown came from the willows and started toward Keene and Andrews.

"You were there all the time!" Ed accused.

"Sure." Chapo's face was Indian-blank. "You didn't need no help . . . for most of it."

Purs and Art came out of the willows farther down.

"We were a little late," Purs said, "but we *did* get here!" He was the old, rough McCool again—but with something new in his voice.

"He made me tell the truth about what you planned, Ed," Art said. "He took my pistol away."

"You can have it." Purs spun the weapon and gave it

back to his youngest son. "It shoots high, anyway."

Art put the gun in his pocket. He looked at Townsend's gray face, at Largo Andrews being half dragged toward them by Keene, with Chapo walking behind. Art looked at the man who lay with a broken leg beside his dead horse, and he listened to the other Ladder rider groaning near the creek. He glanced at the crumpled form of Kirker out in the Hummocks.

It would be a long time before Art McCool talked so loosely about shooting people, Ed thought.

In a conversational tone Purs said to Chapo: "You ain't been around enough lately, Apache."

"Maybe." Chapo glanced at Ed, and almost smiled.

Ed started across the creek to get his horse out of the brush.

"Give her my love, Eddie boy!" Steve yelled. "And don't make a big hero out of yourself when you tell it."

"Shut up," Ed said.

About the Author

Steve Frazee was born in Salida, Colorado, and in the decade 1926–1936 he worked in heavy construction and mining in his native state. He also managed to pay his way through Western State College in Gunnison, Colorado, from which in 1937 he graduated with a Bachelor's degree in journalism. The same year he also married. He began making major contributions to the Western pulp magazines with stories set in the American West as well as a number of North-Western tales published in *Adventure*. Few can match his Western novels that are notable for their evocative, lyrical descriptions of the open range and the awesome power of natural forces and their effects on human efforts. *Cry Coyote* (1955) is memorable for its strong female protagonists who actually influence most of the major events and bring about the resolution of the central conflict in this story of wheat growers and expansionist cattlemen. *High Cage* (1957) concerns five miners and a woman snowbound at an isolated gold mine on top of Bulmer Peak in which the twin themes of the lust for gold and the struggle against the savagery of both the elements and human nature interplay with increasing, almost tormented intensity. *Bragg's Fancy Woman* (1966) concerns a free-spirited woman who is able to tame a family of thieves. *Rendezvous* (1958) ranks as one of the finest mountain man books, and *The Way Through the*

Mountains (1972) is a major historical novel. Not surprisingly, many of Frazee's novels have become major motion pictures. According to the second edition of *Twentieth Century Western Writers* (1991), a Frazee story is possessed of "flawless characterization, particularly when it involves the clash of human passions, believable dialogue, and the ability to create and sustain damp-palmed suspense." *Look Behind Every Hill* will be his next **Five Star Western**.